THE KINGDOM OF ROSES AND THORNS

Debra Liebenow Daly

authorHOUSE®

AuthorHouse™
1663 Liberty Drive, Suite 200
Bloomington, IN 47403
www.authorhouse.com
Phone: 1-800-839-8640

First published by AuthorHouse   3/19/2009

ISBN: 978-1-4389-5488-2 (sc)

Printed in the United States of America
Bloomington, Indiana

This book is printed on acid-free paper.

You will travel to Africa somehow
believing that you will change it,
But Africa will change you.
It will capture your heart and keep a piece of your soul.
You will always be drawn back to the
beauty and mystique that is Africa.

Contents

Introduction

The women portrayed in this book are considered to be ordinary in their culture. In fact, they lead extraordinary lives.

These stories represent the inner beauty and perseverance of the women of Swaziland. It is with love and the deepest respect that I share their stories.

Name Glossary

Bawinde	(ba-win-day)	To be a winner
Busisiwe	(boo-see-see-way)	The blessed one
Duduzile	(doo-doo-zee-lay)	We have been consoled
Dumisa	(doo-mee-sa)	Glorify
Dumisani	(doo-mee-sa-nee)	Herald of the future
Inhlahla	(in-shla-shla)	The lucky one
Jabulani	(ja-boo-la-nee)	Be happy
Lindi	(lin-dee)	The one we have patiently waited for
Lindiwe	(lin-dee-way)	We have waited for joy
Makabongwe	(ma-ka-bong-way)	God's gift
Mashama	(ma-sha-ma)	The surprise
Mbulelo	(mboo-lay-low)	Give thanks
Mduduzi	(mdoo-doo-zee)	Comfort
Musa	(moo-sa)	Grace
Nathi	(not-hee)	With us
Ndumiso	(ndoo-mee-so)	Praise follows him

Nobantu	(no-bon-too)	Will be loved by people
Nomalanga	(no-ma-lan-ga)	Girl born on a sunny day
Rolilahla	(row-li-la-shla)	Troublemaker
Sibongile	(see-bone-ghee-lay)	Thanks
Sifiso	(see-fee-so)	A wish has been granted
Siphokazi	(see-foe-ka-zee)	A great gift
Themba	(tem-ba)	The one I have hope in
Thembekile	(tem-ba-kee-lay)	The faithful one
Zanele	(zan-ay-lay)	This is enough

Main Glossary

Afrikaans	South African dialect derived from the Dutch language
Afrikaners	White South African of Dutch descent
Apartheid	The former policy of segregation and political and economic discrimination against non-European groups in the Republic of South Africa.
assegai	Small lightweight Zulu spear
belumbi	Swazi slang term for white woman
beehive hut	Bantu style round hut that is thatched from top to the ground
boerewors	South African farm sausage
braai	South African bar-b-que
dagga	marijuana
emalangeni	Swazi currency – tied to the value of the South African rand
emasi milk	Swazi sour milk
gogo	siSwati 'grandmother'
kagogo	shrine to the ancestral spirits
kraal	wall enclosing a village or home; pen for animals

kraal mat	woven mat used for sleeping or sitting
lobola	bride wealth; cows given to the bride's family by the groom
marula	tropical orange type of fruit from the marula tree
mealy meal	corn that is mashed into a grits type of paste; staple of Swaziland
mkhulu	siSwati for 'grandfather'
muti	herbs, animal or human parts that are made into traditional medicines or potions
nginga	siSwati for 'problem'
unjani	siSwati for 'how are you?'
pap	mealy meal that is served thick and eaten as a savory with meat
rondavel	cylindrical one room house with a thatched roof
rand	South African currency
Rooibos tea	South African herbal red tea as known as 'bush tea'
sangoma	traditional healer; spiritualist witch doctor
sawubona	siSwati for 'hello'
siSwati	the language of the Swazi nation
sisi	term of friendship that women use for each other

siyabonga   siSwati for 'we thank you'

tshweshwe   print cotton dress that is gathered at the waist and has
               round neck and short sleeves

Umhlanga

Reed Dance   spring celebration by the maidens in Swaziland to
               honor the Queen Mother

yebo   siSwati for 'yes'

Chapter 1 – Anna

She came into the world with a wail. Later that would be a testament to her perseverance and strength. Her mother was lying on a woven mat in the grass beehive hut. She was weak and tired. The other women in the kraal soon ducked their heads into the hut to see the new baby girl. The hut was small with a low entry that forced visitors to bend over as a sign of respect. The kraal was a meager one that sat pitifully against the dramatic landscape of the Kingdom of Swaziland. Surrounding the huts were lush green mountains. The jacarandas were in bloom, and the hills were dotted with lavender and topped with a soft fog. A jagged stick fence surrounded the vegetable garden, the house and the animal pens. Dumisa, the baby's father, entered the hut. He was bitter of this new life. He already had one daughter, and he knew that neither of these girls would be worth much to him. His relationship with this sickly wife was strained, and he feared that he would never have a son. It was certainly bad luck to be cursed with two daughters and no heirs.

In keeping with tradition the new baby could not be removed from the hut until the last remnants of the umbilical cord had dried up. On that day the elderly women in the village took the dried bits and buried them near the ancestral home. This insured that no evil spirits could harm the baby. It also connected the child's spirit to the ancestral spirits that would guide her throughout her life.

The next week Dumisa held the tiny infant during the naming ceremony. As the father, it was his right to name the new baby. When a baby is a week old the father gives the infant a name that signifies some event, emotion, or feeling in the family. This innocent baby was named "fights a lot." Many years later she said that her parents must have argued terribly.

When she was three years old little "fights a lot" was given the Christian name of Anna. Her mother never lived to see that day. This weak and tired woman died shortly after Anna was born, and Anna has no memories of her.

Of course, Anna's father remarried quickly. He needed a wife to help raise these girls and take care of the kraal. Anna and her sister, Mary, were malnourished and thin. Their ribs protruded, and their arms and legs resembled stick figures. They had only scraps of clothes to wear, and the stepmother was cruel. Their father was still lamenting his plight as they grew. So what was the value of little girls? He put them to work around the house and in the field. They were not allowed to have friends. Laughing and playing were signs of idleness that were accompanied with a sound beating. Dumisa believed that if they were strong and hardworking maybe someday some perspective husband might give a small lobola, a bride wealth, for one of them. That seemed to be the only advantage of having two daughters. Once they reached puberty they could be worth some return on his investment. If they were only better looking they might bring in 10 to 15 cows each.

One day as he was sitting smoking outside his hut he had a surprise visitor. His brother arrived with his wife. Dumisa's brother had a better fortune than he, and this made him jealous. His sister in law was also healthy and strong. She was plump with broad arms and a wide smile. He hated that, too. It looked like pride to him. Why should his brother have more than he had? Why did his brother have to come by now and flaunt this over him?

"Anna and Mary need an education." His brother announced. He approached the kraal and pulled a cigarette out of his pocket. He lit the cigarette and waved the flame from the match.

"They must come home with me so that I can give them a better future. I can afford to send them to the mission school." He drew in a puff and calmly let the smoke pass through his mouth and nose. It was a tense moment that he tried to subdue.

His brother appeared authoritative and calm when he said those blasphemous words. He looked straight at Dumisa.

"Look at them." He pointed with his ash filled cigarette to Anna and Mary who stood near them. Both girls were dirty and shoeless. "They are too thin and stupid. Who will ever want them like that? Since you are not doing your duty, it is my obligation to look after these girls."

This enraged Anna's father. He had been avoiding his brother for years. Certainly, this was not a welcome reunion.

"Absolutely NOT." Dumisa screamed at his brother. He pulled his carving knife out of his pants pocket and swung it at his brother.

"Get off of my land and take that woman with you. You will never take these girls. They are my property. I suppose you think that you will turn them into young maidens desirable to men. Then you will take the cows when they marry. Is that what you expect?"

"Believe me, my brother, my friend. That has not entered my mind." He put out his cigarette under his shoe and squashed the butt into the dirt.

"I know your greed, and these girls will not see you again. Now get out and never come back." Dumisa kicked the dirt filled butt at his brother.

Interestingly, Anna and Mary never saw their uncle again. But it was not because their father willed it.

After their uncle left Anna and Mary were beaten severely by Dumisa. This was a lesson they would never forget. He let them know that he was the boss. The land was his...the hut was his....the kraal was his...they were nothing, nothing to anybody and they would never get any clever ideas about trying to be better than he was.

Later that night in their hut Anna wept quietly. Her thin body was bleeding, swollen, and she felt that her hip had been broken. Mary's condition wasn't much better, but she was older and had learned how to take the blows. There would never be anyone to comfort them. Somehow they had to take their lives into their own hands.

A few nights later Anna was lying on her mat. She was still in terrible pain, and the bruises were raised on her back and legs. Mary hugged her and leaned towards her ear. "We have to get out of here, Anna. It's our only chance for any life. I'm afraid if we stay he will kill us someday."

Anna lay quietly and listened to her sister's advice. Mary was the only person in the world she knew she could trust.

Mary went on and told her the plan she had been dreaming about for a long time.

In the dark of the night the two girls crept quietly out of the kraal. Mary had collected bits of food over the past several days, but that was all they took with them.

They walked into the pitch-black African night being careful not to step on sticks that would sound an alert. Dodging rats and snakes and terrified of the night sounds, they kept running. Anna limped after her sister. She would limp from a beaten and broken hip for the rest of her life.

They never looked back. They never saw their cruel father again.

≡ ≡

It took them two days to arrive at the industrial city of Manzini. It was a noisy and bustling place. Neither of the girls, now six and nine years old had ever been to a real city. "Don't look suspicious, Anna." Mary advised. "What if someone catches us and sends us back to our village? We will be doomed forever."

The girls walked slowly around the city all during the day. There were smells and sights they had never imagined. There were clothes of bright colors and shoes. Yes, shoes that even little girls could wear. The tshweshwe in the window of the dress store was blue print with puffed sleeves and a full skirt. Anna closed her eyes and wondered what it would be like to twirl around wearing something that cheerful. She opened her eyes noticed her own reflection in the window, and was startled. They walked on and saw women selling the most perfect and fragrant roses and other flowers in baskets on the street corners. The pedestrians fascinated them. Everyone was walking quickly, crossing the streets and having business to do. It was an amazing and unbelievable city. No one had ever told them about all the incredible things in the world beyond their village. They smelled the rich aroma of curry coming from a cafe. They were drawn to it, and along the way they spied a woman selling roasted corn and fried biscuits at a stand on the sidewalk. They were desperately hungry, and the bits of mealy meal that Mary had brought were gone by now.

That night they scavenged for food in a dumpster behind the local grocery. In the morning they were curled up together sleeping behind the dumpster when they heard a car horn honking by them. Mary was frightened. She jumped to her feet, but she was still weak, and fell back to the ground.

Anna heard the sound behind her and hid behind the dumpster. A large car approached and a white woman emerged from the driver's seat.

"Don't say anything, Anna." Mary whispered. "It could be a trick, and she will send us home."

They didn't need to worry about saying anything. The woman was an Afrikaner, a white South African, and couldn't speak a word of siSwati. Both of the girls cowered in front of her. The sun shone behind the white woman, and she looked like an angel in the haze of the light. The lady's hair was yellow....such an unnatural color for hair. She was wearing a flowing pink dress and had shoes to match. Most of all she smelled like the fragrant roses they had just admired in front of the store.

The woman kneeled down to the girls and spoke gently.

"What are you two doing living like this?" She stroked Anna's face and couldn't miss the bruises. "Are you hungry?"

Neither girl would respond. They just stared at her.

"Why don't you come home with me?" The woman stood up and took both girls by the hand. They couldn't resist and looked sheepishly at each other.

Now they would begin their adventures. Maybe their uncle would not be able to give them an education. Father would never get any cows for marrying them to some village boy. But who would have thought they would ever ride in a car?

$$\Longrightarrow \Longleftarrow$$

The car sped down the road, and even the potholes didn't faze the two girls. Anna loved looking out the window. She could feel the rush of warm air on her face as they drove through the streets. The rose stand flew past. The market rushed by, and the car was moving faster than all the pedestrians. Mary leaned back against the leather seat and fell into a restless sleep. She had visions of Dumisa coming after them with a stick and punishing them for running away. If he ever caught them…. the thought made her shiver and she trembled. She was awakened by the car horn honking for the guard to open the large wooden gates. Immediately, a slight built young Swazi man rushed out and pushed the massive gates away. Inside was a magnificent garden of flowers and the greenest grass. The house on the property was indescribably well kept and beautiful. He nodded at the white woman, but he kept his head down and glanced away in respect. The white lady navigated the car into the driveway and honked again. This time a heavy Swazi woman in a light blue uniform came out to the car. She lifted the groceries out of the trunk and quietly listened for her next directions.

Anna wasn't sure what the white lady was saying. She only understood that the maid's name was Sibongile. She talked and pointed to the girls in the back seat who were huddled together. They were frightened by now and wondered why they had accepted a ride with a belumbi (a white woman). Why did they trust someone like that, and what had possessed them to get into her car to be taken to a place they had never seen?

"Don't be afraid, little ones." Sibongile spoke softly to the wide-eyed girls. They were pressed up to the back of the seat and wouldn't speak or move.

"You can stay with us here." Finally, Sibongile could see that her gentleness wasn't budging them. She knew that it was her responsibility to take these girls under her wing, and she wasn't going to let them embarrass her in front of Madam.

"Get out of this car." She said firmly in siSwati. "You must get out right now if you know what is good for you. Do you want the belumbi to send you back to Manzini?"

This was all the encouragement the young girls needed. Mary gave Anna a nudge and pushed herself away from the security of the backseat. The girls emerged, and they looked worse than Sibongile had expected. She shook her head and folded her heavy arms in front of her.

"First, we will bathe you. Next we will feed you and find suitable clothes. No one in this house will accept you looking like this." Sibongile looked sternly at both girls. "Then you will tell me where you have come from. What in God's name has happened to you?"

She led them around the outside of the white woman's big house. The girls had never seen a house that looked like that. It was beautiful and sprawling. They would not be allowed in there until they were bathed and redressed.

Sibongile led them to her rondavel in the back of the garden. Even this amazed Anna and Mary. The rondavel was made of mud that had been whitewashed to match the master's house. It had a real floor and a well manicured thatched roof. Inside there were two rooms. Anna didn't know that anyone lived in buildings with walls on the inside.

Down a short pathway was a toilet. There was water that came from a faucet and a modern tub and flushing toilet inside. Sibongile ordered the girls to bathe while she looked for something they could wear.

Anna sat in the warm water and sighed. She had never used a tub. Her family had always bathed in the river near their hut. Everybody bathed together in the muddy river, and nobody ever thought the worst of it. All of the village children played while their mothers washed the clothes in the same dirty water. It was a great social event with laughing and splashing. This new small confined space was strange, but wonderful and comforting. Soon Sibongile appeared with two large dresses.

"You two will have to wear these until we can find something that fits." She tucked in the extra material and pinned up the hem. They were tshweshwes like the ones she had seen in the shop window. These were faded and much too big, but Anna could hardly hide her excitement.

"Now go sit down outside and eat your dinner." Anna and Mary felt confused, as if they had been transported in some kind of bewitching dream. The table was laden with chicken and gravy, pumpkin greens and mealy meal. That night they slept on woven kraal mats on the floor in Sibongile's rondavel. Mary dreamed again of Dumisa's beatings and brutal punishment. Anna couldn't sleep at all. She was sure that the morning would bring her father to the door, and the magic would end.

The morning did come, but there was no menacing father at the door. Sibongile awakened them at dawn. She gave each of them a scrambled egg on a piece of bread with a cup of sweetened tea. She ushered the frightened girls into the Master's house and through to the kitchen.

"We must make the breakfast every morning before Madam awakens. Mary, it will be your job this morning to set the table, and Anna, you must set out the jellies from the icebox. Whatever you do, move quietly. You must not disturb Madam."

Anna and Mary stood dumbfounded. They had no idea what she was talking about. No one had ever told them about table settings and silverware. They had never seen a refrigerator or electric stove.

Sibongile was disgusted. "It is clear that my job is going to be much harder than I thought. Don't you think I have more important jobs here than to educate you two? You must learn fast and don't complain about anything."

The girls nodded and said nothing. They certainly did not want to awaken Madam.

That morning they learned a lot about the world where the white people live. There were soft cloth napkins and breakable china dishes edged in gold with roses in the middle. The glasses were cut crystal that reflected the light around the sunny dining room.

Later in the afternoon Sibongile laid out the tea with delicate little cakes and more amazing dishes. Anna noticed that the Madam was having a long conversation with Sibongile. She knew that they were discussing her, because they would glance her way every now and then. Anna finally looked away out of fear. Actually, Sibongile was telling Madam the incredible story of Mary and Anna's escape from their abusive father.

"Anna, you must come here to Madam. Be respectful, but step up right now. Madam has a job for you and you must be grateful. Smile and don't answer 'yebo.' Say 'yes' in English so she knows you will cooperate."

"What is the job?" Anna asked. She knew she was not in any position to refuse, but she was confused about all of these new surroundings. Certainly there must be a heavy price to pay in return for food, clothes and a dry sleeping place.

Sibongile continued. "Madam has a very old gogo. White people call her a grandma, and she cannot see. She cannot walk and she is very ill. You must take care of the gogo and be kind to her."

That didn't seem like a terrible job. Anna had been taught to respect and admire elderly people, so she thought that this job might actually be fun. After all, in her village the gogo was very wise, told wonderful stories and hugged little children.

Sibongile led her down the long tiled hallway. At the end of the hallway was a darkened room. Thick drapes covered the windows leaving just a hint of sunlight across a narrow line to the center of the room. As her eyes adjusted to the dim light Anna could see a white woman sitting quietly in a wicker wheelchair. She didn't look anything like the gogos in the village. This woman was much older and wrinkled like a dead leaf. Her long straight pure white hair frightened Anna and she drew in a sudden breath. Her skin and hair gave the appearance that she was already dead. What if she was a zombie sent here to trick Anna into returning home? Everyone knew that witchdoctors could put terrible muti on people and turn the dead into zombies. Anna trembled uncontrollably.

Sibongile took her hand firmly and whispered, "Do not behave badly. This is how you will earn your keep here, and you should be proud. Madam and Master are very important people in the sugar industry. You are so lucky to have clothes and food. You must never ever forget that. Get past your fears and be strong. There is no place here for that nonsense." As she spoke her hand gripped Anna's arm tighter, but Anna knew better than to pull away from her.

Anna spent the next year caring for the old gogo. They never understood each other's language, but that was not important. Every morning after Anna set up the breakfast she retired to the darkened room at the end of the hallway. There the old gogo sat like a stone waiting for her. Anna had a routine of combing the woman's long hair and braiding it into a bun. The act of doing that fascinated her. The texture of her hair was so different from any hair she had ever touched. Finally one day Anna asked Sibongile how the gogo had such soft and long hair. "It is a different culture hair." Sibongile replied. And that was the end of her explanation.

After the woman's hair was in place Anna brought in a large basin of warm water and a soft towel to bathe the wrinkled white woman. This was a slow process that required considerable adjustment. The old lady sat in the chair and barely uttered a sound while Anna scrubbed her loose and wrinkled skin. It was so white, so pale and as thin as paper. She was afraid she would break the surface if she rubbed too hard. Once she thought she was washing away a dirt spot, but it was a raised mole on the woman's spindly leg. The old woman screeched, and Anna bolted from the room out of terror. White people had a lot of culture things about their bodies.

Mary worked harder than Anna. Her jobs included all the things that Sibongile didn't want to do anymore. She had to haul firewood, lift large pails of wash water, and carry heavy laundry on her head out to the clothesline. Once at the clothesline Sibongile ceremoniously tacked the clothing onto the line while she complained of her bad back.

The two girls reconciled that this was still a good place to be. Madam and Master paid them for their work. They were fed, clothed and had a dry sleeping place. So how could they be unhappy? At night Jabulani, the family guard, told them great stories of leopard hunts and historic battles of the proud Swazi people. They were sure that some of his stories were exaggerations, but they made a great audience, so he made the stories greater, too.

After a year the girls were feeling comfortable in this surrounding. Then the unthinkable happened. Sibongile came crying into the kitchen where the girls were laying out the breakfast.

"The gogo is late. Oh, what will happen now?"

Anna and Mary knew that it meant she was dead, but they couldn't believe it. Now seven years old Anna never dreamed that the gogo she had cared for over a year could ever go away from them.

Sibongile slumped into a kitchen chair and used her sleeve to wipe away the tears. "She has died. She is really dead." Of course, this could hardly have been a surprise to anyone. The woman was visibly aged and infirmed, but they all knew that their lives were about to change. There was much talk and grumbling between Sibongile and Jabulani about their fate. Mary was alert to all of this. She had much more exposure to the family than did Anna. Mary always thought it was amusing that white people imagined they were in the house alone. They expected servants to do all the dreadful things they didn't want to do, but they discounted that these servants had ears and eyes and knew exactly what was happening in the house. At times Master and Madam would argue. Other times they would have long conversations about the country and the local government. They failed to appreciate that the household help overheard everything they said.

So the servants knew before they were discharged that the white people were going back to South Africa. They had only stayed this long because the gogo couldn't travel. Now they were unfettered from that burden and planned to return to Cape Town. Madam was thrilled. She didn't like Swaziland, a tiny landlocked country with great variations in the climate. She longed for the seaside, the wine country and the continental feeling of the Cape. She had sacrificed enough for her husband's business, and with that she ordered Sibongile and Mary to pack up the house. Anna washed and folded the dead gogo's clothes.

She packed up everything in the depressing room, but before she did that, she thrust open the long drapes and let in the sunshine.

$$\Longrightarrow \Longleftarrow$$

There was hardly time to grieve for the South African family. Housing in Swaziland was always at a premium and no one doubted this was one of the most beautiful houses in the area. In keeping with tradition, the household help was passed on with the house. So the day the Portuguese family arrived they were able to settle in with ease.

The family quickly relaxed in their new environs, but Sibongile, Jabulani, Mary and Anna weren't sure what to expect. The girls had never learned English, and now these people spoke Portuguese. That didn't bother Sibongile since they also spoke English, but she had to adjust to a new palate. She had never cooked peri peri chicken. These people ate so much more food than the last family. They liked food spicy, heavy and rich. They seemed more demanding, but perhaps that was because they had new expectations.

Mary advised Anna to do whatever these new people wanted. It had only been a year since they had fled their home, and she was still nervous about the consequences that awaited them if their father ever found them. Indeed, the new family had very different interests and demands. They also had a young daughter, Isabel, who was Anna's age.

Anna and Mary grew to love this new family. Anna learned to sew, and Mary took over some of Sibongile's domestic chores. Sibongile was not in the mood, at her age, to learn a whole new way of cooking. She was getting tired earlier in the day and started thinking about retiring to her ancestral homeland.

There was much more time to play which was a new concept for Anna. In the heat of the afternoon she and little Isabel played in the garden. Anna learned English from her. Isabel spoke very broken English with a Portuguese accent, but this was a critical turning point for Anna. Having knowledge of this language was essential. It mattered little that Anna would speak broken English with a Portuguese accent for the rest of her life.

The Portuguese madam owned a hair salon in Manzini. The master owned a business in the city. They fled Mozambique just as the civil war began. The civil war would rage on for many years while the Portuguese family thrived in Swaziland.

Every Sunday Sibongile and Jabulani attended the mission church in the area. Anna and Mary were expected to attend, and they enjoyed the time away from the house. They learned Christian songs in English, but they weren't really sure what the words meant. Neither of them would ever receive the formal education the uncle promised for them. They could not even write their own names. Church on Sunday gave them a chance to meet other Swazis in town. In the beginning they were afraid of being discovered, but finally they became comfortable with their new life and stopped fearing the wrath of their father. Years passed, and the girls grew into women. Dumisa had been right about one thing. No one would offer lobola to marry these girls. Mary, in particular, looked older than her years. Any man watching her would be wary of her early signs of aging. Anna loved her sister and vowed that she would always take care of Mary.

The Portuguese family was happy and prosperous in Manzini. Anna and Mary earned very little money, but they had very few needs. Over time Anna managed to hide bits of money in a little wooden box Isabel had given her for Christmas. At the end of every month the master paid all of the household help and gave them the same advice and warning. They were to be careful of their money, don't squander it on foolish things like beer and cigarettes. They must manage it wisely and make it last for 30 days when they would get paid again.

≡ ≡

Anna had her eye on the tall young Swazi man in church. Surely he had noticed her, too. She had never trusted men, but this man looked so strong and after all, she was fifteen, a perfect age for marriage. They started meeting after worship service and often had lunch together under a tree in the mission yard.

He professed his love to her and made her feel beautiful. No one in her life had ever made her feel like that. "I don't have many cows to give to your father," he apologized.

"That's okay," she replied sweetly. "It doesn't matter, because I love you, and I promise I will make a good home for you."

Sibongile was horrified when she heard this response. How would that man ever respect Anna if he thought she had no background and no pride? She argued with Anna to demand more from a man if she wanted him to stand by her.

In the end Anna married the tall young Swazi. It was a tribal ceremony without much fanfare. They could only be together on the weekends, because she was devoted to her Portuguese family who had looked after her for the last several years. Her new husband understood this perfectly. It was a common type of living arrangement. It also gave the husband a lot of freedom.

Within a year Anna delivered her only child. It was a baby girl. Sibongile and Mary were by her side when Lindi came into the world.

"Oh, Anna, don't feel bad, because you have delivered a daughter. Next time you will have a son." Mary thought she was comforting her sister.

"Why would I feel regret?" Anna stroked her baby's face while the tiny child suckled. "I will never let anyone hurt her."

They both knew that having a daughter was probably a sign of bad luck, but the infant was so delicate and innocent. Anna kept working for the Portuguese family. Many times she cleaned the house with Lindi strapped to her back with long cloths tied in front of Anna's waist. The emalangeni in her little wooden box accumulated, but she kept it a secret from everyone. Life was turning out better than Anna could have dreamed it would for her and Mary. They were healthy, well fed and happy with the Portuguese family that employed them.

One weekend she and Lindi took the bus to the village where her husband stayed in their cinder block house tucked away in the hills. It was a very modest dwelling, but it was better than the beehive hut of her childhood. She held little Lindi by the hand as she walked up the red clay path to the house. There was smoke coming from the roof, and she sang gospel hymns as she walked.

She prepared Saturday night dinner for her husband. He sat staring at the fire with a cigarette and was quiet. "I'm so lucky." She thought. "I have food to give my family, and tonight when it rains we will all be warm and dry together."

She put the dinner on the table. It was a hearty meal of beef stew with mealy meal, corn mash, and bread. For a treat she had bought him a Castle beer at the petrol station near the bus stop. She moved close to him, stroked his face and kissed his warm cheek. He was generally a quiet man, but tonight he was more pensive than usual.

The three of them ate dinner, and then the tall Swazi husband spoke without looking up at her.

"Anna, you know how hard it is to make money in Swaziland."

"That's okay" she replied. "I make a good living with the Portuguese. You don't have to worry. What do we need anyway?"

Her husband picked at the scraps of mealy meal on his plate and continued as if he hadn't heard a thing she had just said.

"The other men in town have been talking. There are jobs in the mines in South Africa." He took his fingers and pushed the last scraps of food around the wooden bowl.

Anna sat shocked and couldn't even speak. She would not listen to this conversation anymore. She stood up and took the dinner bits away.

He grasped her hand as she approached him at the table.

"Anna, I love you, but what can I do? There is nothing for me here. That means there is nothing for us. I have to go. The other men are going in the morning, and I will be with them."

"How can you go there?" She cried. "Everybody knows how terrible the white people treat the blacks in that country. You are not even one of them. You are a Swazi. Do you hear me...you are a Swazi. They will never give you anything. You can't leave us. You can't go to that place. The mines are dangerous. People die there." She dropped to the floor and sobbed her heart out while little Lindi stroked her hair comforting her.

In the morning the tall young Swazi tied his few belongings in a cloth and kissed her good bye. He promised he would write. They both laughed since neither of them could read anyway. He promised to send her money. He promised to come back soon. He broke all of his promises, and she never saw her handsome husband again.

≒ ≒

The months fell into years, and little Lindi grew into a young woman. Anna made sure that Lindi had an education. Since education came at a price she saved until she could afford a good mission school near

Manzini. No one in Swaziland has the right to a free education so everything from tuition, books and uniforms came from the money saved in the wooden box by Anna's bed.

When Lindi passed her standard exams and graduated from high school Anna wore a new floral dress that she had sewn. It was rare for Anna to indulge herself that way, but she wanted everyone to believe that Lindi came from a good family. She sat with pride at the ceremony so that everyone could see that she was the mother of this fine tall woman. She even wore a hat to the event. Usually Anna wrapped a scarf around her head and covered her short hair with a turban. There was never very much time to play with her hair.

After the graduation ceremony Madam invited Lindi into the den. She explained to Lindi that she could train her in the beauty salon. That way she could make a good living, and people in the community would know her. Since Lindi could read and write and calculate money she would be an asset. Besides, she was attractive and spoke both English and siSwati with ease. The prospect of this excited Lindi. She couldn't wait to get to Manzini and make some new friends. She was tired of being outside of town in that sprawling house where she and mother and aunt had lived in a rondavel in the back yard. Maybe her mother had a hard life, but she didn't intend to follow in those footsteps. She looked down at the floor while Madam laid out the plan. Lindi quietly looked away and thanked her for her most generous spirit. She held out both hands to Madam in gratitude for her kindnesses to all of them over the years. Once she was outside she threw back her head and laughed. She didn't feel grateful at all. Certainly this opportunity was the least they could do for her. All those years her mother washed their floor on her hands and knees. She would never bow to that humiliation.

Mary was not thriving at all. She never found a man to love her. She had pain in her joints and couldn't get up at dawn anymore to prepare the breakfast. Ever since Sibongile had retired it had fallen to Mary to be the senior maid. Anna tried to finish Mary's chores so that she could set up the dinner for the family. At night they all slept in the same rondavel that had been their home for so many years.

Little Isabel grew into a charming woman who was educated in Lisbon and stayed in Europe. Once she came to Swaziland with her new husband, but he never saw the beauty in the country that Isabel loved. Instead of seeing green mountains dotted with lavender jacaranda trees, flame trees and, lush valleys he saw cold and dampness and fog. Isabel laughed and waved as they drove down the dirt roads, because she knew all the people that they passed along the way. Her European husband was annoyed with pedestrians, cows and goats littering the shoulders of the road. The Portuguese family also had a son who was older than Isabel. He had left for Europe many years ago and had children of his own.

The time came when the elderly couple realized what they wanted to do with the rests of their lives. They planned to sell the businesses in Manzini and go home to Portugal. It was clear that they would never go back to Mozambique with the war continuing to rage there. That had been their original intention, but now, as they aged, they feared the war would outlast their lives. They also surmised that the war would leave behind unbearable devastation. Already Maputo had gained a reputation as the city of one-legged people. So many people had been maimed by land mines. While serving dinner Anna overheard them grieving that they would never again have tea at the posh Polana Hotel. They lamented never seeing Xai Xai again with its magnificent beaches along the Indian Ocean.

Anna grew worried. She had lived with them for most of her life. Her husband had left her, and now this last bit of security was leaving, too.

Late at night she counted her money. She made plans for the future…not her future, but for the future of the people she loved. She felt that she was strong and could work forever if she had to, but poor Mary was declining in health.

In the morning she asked Madam if they could have a talk. She told Madam her plan, and with a calm smile, Madam agreed. Anna was thrilled and nervous and waited until the weekend to surprise her daughter.

The three of them took the crowded bus home to the countryside for the weekend. Here in the same little house where her husband said he loved her, and then left her, she laid out her plans to Mary and Lindi.

"Lindi, I have talked with Madam. She says that you are doing very well at the beauty salon. She thinks that you are smart enough to stay there after she leaves. Madam said that she wants to make you the manager, but I told her that I have saved much money over time, and you won't do that anymore."

Lindi jumped up and scolded her mother. "How could you tell her those things? I love working there. I have friends in the city, and they all come to that place because of me. What do you mean I shouldn't manage the salon? I won't live like you have all these years. I can do better!"

Anna smiled and calmly rose from her chair. Her feet were calloused and swollen. She ignored the stinging insult that her daughter had thrown at her. "And you are right, my dear. So I bought the beauty salon for you to own." She presented the deed from the deep pocket of her tshweshwe. "Now you never have to work for anybody else in your life."

Mary shrieked with joy for Lindi's good fortune. Tears streamed down Anna's face as she watched her daughter dancing around the room holding the deed to the shop. For a moment there was joy like Anna had never known. This made her happier than anything she had ever done in her lifetime. Lindi ran over and hugged her mother.

"Oh Mama, I am sorry to talk so bad to you. I know you love me, and I will make you proud. I can't believe I am a shop owner in Manzini. I have prayed for so long that I would have a good life, and now I can make all my dreams come true." Anna should have been listening more carefully to what Lindi was saying. She didn't hear how many times Lindi referred to herself in her praise. Perhaps Anna knew that she would lose her and decided it was fate.

When the excitement calmed down Anna continued with her plans for the future.

"Mary, my dear sisi, you have taken care of me your whole life." She sat down next to her older sister and took her hand.

"I would be dead surely if you hadn't had the courage to escape when we were children. We have had good lives, because you have guided our way."

Mary looked down at the floor. Then she looked up at the shelf where there was an old photo of the two of them. The South African madam had taken a picture of them when they lived with her. The little girls were wearing matching dresses and holding hands. She remembered their early years and thought they had done very well for themselves. She was proud, but she was not a person to insult God's good favor by boasting. So she sat quietly listening to her sister.

"Mary, when the Portuguese family leaves we will have no home and no job. What security do we have for all our years of working? You cannot keep working so hard. Look at the way it is hurting your body." It was true that the years had taken a great toll on Mary. She had already developed diabetes and a weak heart. Her vision was failing, and she was not able to afford any optometric care. Some days her legs were so swollen and red she couldn't put on her shoes.

Anna went on with her idea. She was so happy that she could feel her voice rising as she spoke.

"There is a small house in the village that I have purchased for you." Mary looked like she would faint. She put her hand over her mouth and was afraid to breathe.

"Also, you must not work anymore. I bought the little house next door as well. With this you can get a tenant who will pay you rent. Then you can stay home and rest and be a madam of leisure."

This was more than Mary could believe. For so many years Anna had stuffed bits of money into the wooden box, and now the wooden box had rewarded them.

All evening the three women laughed and cried with delight. They made plans and vowed to look after each other forever. Before they went to sleep, Lindi promised her mother that she wanted Anna to work at the beauty salon. There was a small flat upstairs from the salon where they could stay during the week.

The plans were so perfect. What could possibly go wrong?

$$\Longrightarrow \Longleftarrow$$

It was a sad day when they moved out of the rondavel behind the big whitewashed sprawling home. They had lived there for over thirty years. This place had provided sanctuary, income, and love. Now they would embark on a new future without being dependent on any white person.

Mary set up her little house in a style that reminded her of the white lady's house. The Portuguese family had given them many household items when they left for Europe. She put a tablecloth on the supper table and placed a vase of wildflowers in the middle of it. They had given her some old lace curtains, and these she hung gracefully on the windows of her living room. She had pillows now and a soft duvet for her bed. It wasn't long before the extra house was rented, and Mary was a real landlady.

Lindi changed the name of her salon to "Lindi's Locks," and the business went well. She was right that everybody in Manzini knew her. There was never any concern that the business wouldn't succeed. Clients filled the chairs, and Lindi developed a reputation of being an excellent businesswoman. In the back of the salon Anna washed the customers' hair. She swept up the floor after each trim and kept the washtubs clean. It was also her job to wash the towels and have everything in the salon organized and straightened. Lindi was so busy with her new social life that she often forgot that her mother was in the back of the shop. She wanted to forget. Anna was becoming an embarrassment.

Anna saw it coming the day the young man tapped on the window of the salon. This young man was dressed like a white man. He wore a suit. He had on a striped tie and crisp ironed white shirt. He wore black shoes of real leather. When Lindi saw him she smiled and waved. She did not pretend to be coy or disinterested. This was the man she was waiting for all her life. Joseph Dlamini worked for the royal government. He wasn't really a royal, but he bore the surname of Dlamini, and it meant that somewhere in his lineage there was royal blood. Certainly he acted like a royal. He stood up very straight and didn't look away when he spoke. There was confidence in his face and manners and walk. That he had a minor government job was unimportant to Lindi. To her he looked like a prime minister.

He walked into the salon and gave her a quick kiss on the cheek. It bothered Anna to see a public display of affection from a man her daughter barely knew. And how could Lindi act so pleased? She actually made little giggling sounds around him. Anna came from the back of the salon to see what the fuss was about and to greet him.

Before she could get to the front desk Lindi had taken off her apron and had dashed out the door holding Joseph's hand. Yes, Lindi was impatient to be alone with him, but she was also in a hurry to leave before she had to introduce her ignorant mother.

That night over dinner Lindi and Anna never discussed the incident. They ate as they always did discussing the clients and the work for the next day. Lindi spoke rapidly and nervously hoping the conversation would never come up, and Anna avoided it, too. She hoped that her instincts were wrong.

Joseph Dlamini became a fixture around the salon. He arrived every day at 1pm for lunch, and together, he and Lindi would often stay out for hours at a time. Anna wondered how he got any work done in his government job. She knew that the salon would not survive if Lindi continued acting so childishly.

One night over dinner she approached Lindi with this problem. Lindi retorted in an angry voice. "Mama, this man is going to be my husband. You will have to understand that. I know you don't like him, but it's just because you have had bad luck with men, and you don't trust them. This is a good man who earns good money and has prestige in the community. We are getting married and moving into his house, so you had better learn to get along with him."

Anna was used to Lindi's defiance, but marriage comes with lobola and permission. "So when is your young man going to come and talk to me about this marriage?"

"Joseph says that he will give you 20 cows, and that's more than you deserve. Look at you. You have no land. You cannot even read."

Lindi regretted this last statement, because it was always a hurtful subject. It brought back memories of Anna's uncle trying to help her, and the beating she took for it. In Swazi culture it is tradition for a relative, especially a brother or uncle, to help another less fortunate member of his family. Her uncle believed he was doing the right thing, but his rebuke led to an entirely different future for Anna.

"I'm sorry, Mama." Lindi sat at her mother's feet and tried to console her. "Let's plan a beautiful wedding and not talk of bad things and the past anymore."

It was strange, but Anna rarely talked of her past. She had a tenacity, strength, and Christian faith that moved her forward in life. No matter how hard the days were, she could pray and give her problems to God. Looking backward was a waste of energy for her.

One day Anna was sweeping up the trimmed hair on the floor when an old friend came into the salon. She didn't have very many friends. There was never much time to develop those relationships, but this woman was a member of her church.

"Anna, Anna, I have news for you." She began. "Make us tea, and we will talk. We must talk. It is very important news that I'm bringing to you."

"We can sit in the back room for tea, Togo." Anna pointed the way to a small curtained area.

Once in the back room Togo relaxed in a chair while Anna put the kettle on a hot plate.

"The weather has been unusually warm." Togo said as she leaned back. "In Mbabane they have such cold damp weather. I'm glad to be in Manzini where we have sun and no fog. How do people live up in that mountain area?"

"Well, they may have colder weather, Togo, but they boast that they have no malaria up there. I guess it is something about the height of the city."

She finished steeping the tea and set out two cups and saucers for them.

"So what is so important, Togo, that you must come here today? You only come here one Wednesday in a month to get your hair fixed. What is your news?"

Togo enjoyed the suspense that she had created and played this scene with a long and dramatic pause. The news she had to tell was big and she knew it.

"A man came to town and was telling the men in my village about working in the mines in South Africa. At first I didn't listen. What do I care for those things?"

She glanced up from her teacup to check the expression on Anna's face. She was not disappointed. Anna was visibly shaken.

"So, my brother asked this man if he knew your husband." Togo dragged out every word as if she was a diva on a stage.

"Oh, Anna, I have news to tell."

"Then say it!" Anna rose to her feet. All these years she had heard nothing from him. Finally, she had given up and assumed that her tall Swazi husband, the man she adored, had died in a mining accident. Those things happened all the time. The mines were deadly, but that meant nothing to the white people. Workers could be buried alive in the pits. They could fall into bottomless holes. Many bad things happened in South Africa. Sometimes people had unfortunate encounters with white people, and then the accidents were of another kind. Apartheid was still the law of the country, and a black Swazi had to be very careful what he said, what he did, and where he walked.

"Anna," Togo took her hand and motioned for Anna to sit back down in her chair. "your husband is still alive."

Anna felt herself reeling. Alive. He's alive. She never had hoped for such news. She sat and gazed out the window. In her heart they were together again. He would come home and envelope her in his arms. They would tell each other wonderful private things late into the night, and she would convince him to stay with her forever. She couldn't wait to tell him all the news of their little Lindi, and how she was an educated shop owner with prestige in the city. She wanted to share everything with him, but mostly she wanted to love him and hold him. She put her hands on her hair and felt her face.

"I must make myself look young again so he will know me when he comes home." She said breathlessly. "Oh, I have aged so, he must see me as a desirable woman so he will stay home now."

As she was daydreaming of her past and her future she felt Togo tugging on her arm. "Anna, Anna, wake up. What's the matter with you? Haven't you heard anything I'm saying?"

"I am listening to you." Anna replied, "but I have much to do now. What if he is coming to the house, and I'm not there."

"You are not listening." Togo's voice became soft, and she released her hold on Anna's arm. "Your husband is alive, it's true, but he has a new life in South Africa. He married a woman there many years ago, and they have five children. Anna, I am sorry to be the one to tell you that he is never coming back."

Anna had so many blows over the years she thought that nothing could faze her anymore. It wasn't true. This news hurt as much as the day he left her. It hurt as much as her father's beatings. It was more painful than she ever believed any disease or pain could be. Why couldn't she die right there and end all the disappointments once and for all? She covered her humiliation by remarking to Togo that she hadn't seen her husband in so many years she probably wouldn't recognize him anyway. Togo comforted her by saying that the new wife was apparently ugly and cruel. None of this was true, but Anna appreciated the lie.

She continued to sweep the trimmed hair, and this time she also swept up her broken heart.

The work at the salon kept Anna busy, and she put her husband out of her mind. At first it was difficult to sleep at night imagining him in the arms of another woman who had given him five children. She shivered at the thought and pushed it aside. "It's in the past." She decided. "It must stay in the past." She said her prayers to God that he would heal her pain and went to bed.

⇒ ⇐

Lindi was the happiest woman in Manzini. She loved owning a business and bought lavish clothes to match her new affluence. Any spare time she had went to preparing for her wedding. She purchased a wedding dress from a shop that white people frequented. She had a florist design a special bouquet to match the lace covered white dress. After an elaborate ceremony in a Catholic church she and Joseph went on their honeymoon to the northern mountains of Piggs Peak. Anna was given 20 cows as lobola from the new husband. Anna felt pleased since she never had any cows of her own, and cows were an important status symbol in Swaziland. Of course, rich families normally gave many more cows for lobola, but Joseph had still given more than the minimum acceptable of 15 cows. He insisted that Lindi was so valuable to him that he wanted to give a proper lobola, but Anna suspected that it was for his own ego to appear substantial in the community. Anna remembered a story in a village south of Manzini. A young man had given the girl's family goats instead of cows. He felt that if he gave them 25 goats they would accept that in lieu of 15 cows. The groom was beaten and stoned by the angry father in law and the other people in the village. How could he be so insulting? Did he think they were so stupid that they couldn't tell the difference between a goat and a cow? Finally, the chief intervened and banished the young man from the village. He was never allowed to marry the girl.

A young boy delivered the cows to Anna by herding them with a stick for several miles along the local road. Anna kept the cows in a pen, or kraal, that was encircled with a fence made of large sticks and logs. Some people let their cows roam all over the place, but she wouldn't take the chance of losing any of them.

Joseph Dlamini still preyed on Anna's mind. She knew that he looked down on her, and he paid his respects to her only as an obligation. She convinced herself that Lindi was happy, so that was the only thing that mattered.

After the honeymoon Lindi and Joseph moved into a government house in Manzini. Anna thought that life would return to normal now that the wedding was behind them. After a long hot day in the salon Lindi approached her mother with a new problem.

"Mama, I want you to know that you have always been good to me. I do appreciate that." Lindi choked on the next words she was about to say. Anna sat quietly, and somehow she thought she knew what those next words were going to be. She had guessed for some time that this moment was coming. She could tell by the way Lindi insisted that Anna stay in the back of the shop. It was obvious that Joseph didn't know what to do with her. It had gotten to be so blatant that she could feel the patrons' eyes watching her as she worked.

" I am asking you now to please leave my shop." Lindi finished her sentence quickly. It was better to get it out than stumble over the words and delay the truth.

"It's just that...well, that Joseph thinks that having you work here is not appropriate for our social standing in the community."

Anna did not explode in anger. She could hardly pretend to be surprised. She really couldn't think of anything to say at all. What good would it do to remind her daughter of all the sacrifices she had made for her? Why should she lower herself anymore than she was already by begging Lindi to let her stay? No, that was one thing she would never do. Many years ago she begged her husband to stay, and it only brought her more pain.

Anna leaned her hand against the table and pushed her heavy body out of the chair. She said nothing. She simply picked up her few belongings that she kept in the flat and walked out.

"Mama" Lindi called after her. "I do love you, but you have to understand that I am trying to improve my life. Isn't that what you always wanted for me? "

Anna never turned around to look at her daughter. She was afraid she would lose her courage and pride if she backed out now. Lindi decided not to follow her into the street. After all, how would that look to the other proprietors in the area? Anna would live out her life never seeing her three grandchildren.

Anna took the bus as far as it went to her home. Then she walked the rest of the way. She found herself walking to Mary's pretty little house with the lace curtains in the window. Mary was always happy to see Anna and welcomed her into the living room.

"Oh my poor sisi." Mary looked worried when she saw Anna enter the house. Anna was slumped over in despair and sadness. She told Mary what had just happened.

"You will stay with me. Yes, that is what you must do. Together we can tend to the cows and the house."

"No" Anna replied. "I have always worked, and I don't know how to do anything else. I suppose I will work until I die. So I must think about what to do."

The two sisters ate supper together. Afterwards, Anna headed off on foot in the darkness to her own lonely house. When she arrived she lit some candles, and the house took on a warm glow. She washed her face and feet and lay down on her bed for the night. Somehow, she would move on with her life.

She was working in her garden a few days later when Togo came around to see how she was getting along in the house. Anna always had rose bushes under her window. It was a reminder of the fragrance of the flower stands in Manzini. Roses were a symbol of beauty and freedom. Somehow, roses grew strong and gracefully out of the dry red clay soil. In fact, Swazi roses were so amazing, that European florists imported them in the winter. On the side of the house was her vegetable garden. It was full of spinach, beets, sweet potatoes and pumpkins.

Anna looked up from her pumpkin patch and greeted Togo. "My dear Togo" she smiled. "What brings you by on this sunny day?"

"You know, Anna, I have heard that a new family from South Africa has arrived and needs good household help. I know that you may not want to do that, but maybe it is an idea, if you are interested."

Anna held her hand over her forehead to shield her eyes from the sun. "You must tell me more about this family. Maybe they will provide a job for me." She laughed as she wiped the sweat from her brow with her hand. "After all, I know how to run a white man's house. I can do that again easily."

"There is one problem, though, Anna. They have three children, and I have heard that these children are not well mannered."

"I know all about children." Anna shook her head and laughed. "Tell me more, and I will put on my flowered dress and show them how a strong Swazi woman can run their house for them."

She left her pumpkin field and hurried into the house. She would go to see the new family in the morning. But first she would bathe, wash her hair and iron her best tshweshwe.

Early the next morning she caught a bus for Mbabane. The trip took about 45 minutes though it was actually only about 20 miles away. The road to Mbabane had a reputation in the <u>Guinness Book of World Records</u> as having the greatest number of fatalities of any stretch of road in the world. Malagwane Hill was a treacherous mountain road full of curves and lacking any guardrails. Cars would whiz down one side at high speeds and miss the turns. Cars heading up the steep mountain often had trouble gaining enough speed to make a comfortable and safe climb to the top. In the rainy season the edges of the road floated down the sides of the mountain leaving only a portion of asphalt.

The dusty bus was packed with people. There was a strong pungent odor of chickens and hot sweaty bodies. Anna was too nervous to notice. She was confident of her domestic abilities and walked two miles from the bus stop, which was in the center of town, to the home of the South African family.

They hired her immediately, and the white madam seemed relieved to have help with the house, the laundry, the cooking and the children.

The job, which seemed to be the answer for her, didn't last long. The children were spoiled and unruly. They had been raised to feel superior to black people and felt they had the right to treat Anna as a subordinate. She had been through a lot in her life, but she didn't feel that at this age she should have to look up to children. The work was unusually difficult, too. No one had ever demanded so much from her. She was ordered to polish the silver every week. She had to take the pictures down from the wall almost every day and dust behind them. Finally, after a month Anna decided that this job was not what she wanted to do with the rest of her life. She had never quit any job before, but she was resolved to find new employment. Madam didn't seem too shocked by the news. She had heard before that her home was a challenging place to work, and she seemed proud of that. She paid Anna the amount they had agreed. That was the end of her work for the family with three spoiled children. As she was walking out the door Madam made an offer that surprised Anna.

"Anna, you look tired, and it is starting to rain. I will call a taxi to take you to the bus stop." Anna didn't object or refuse.

When Anna got into the taxi she had no idea that it would create another turning point for her. The next two years would be some of the happiest years of her life.

Dumisani ran the Dumi Dumi taxi company. He sat in the driver's seat of the red Opal and asked Anna where she wanted to go. For a minute she was silent. She just realized that she lost her job, or rather, that she left her job and didn't know what she was going to do.

"Are you going to the bus?" Dumisani asked. Dumisani was a healthy young man of about 30 years old. He had a medium build, but his best feature was his broad smile that looked so trusting and kind. He was a gentle and hardworking man and now he turned around to the backseat to look at Anna. She said under her breath "I have no job now, so I guess I should go to the bus stop and go home. What else can I do?"

Dumisani felt sorry for this woman. It was obvious that she was aging. She appeared worn and sad. Would you be willing to work for another white family?" He asked in a cheerful voice as he drove to the bus stop. "If you are interested, I know a very good couple who are new to Swaziland."

Anna didn't want to look too interested, so she replied in a low voice. "They are probably like all the rest of the white people here. I think I am finished working for other people."

Dumisani laughed and threw back his head. He had such a healthy laugh and looked so comfortable and confident weaving the taxi through heavy traffic. He dodged people and buses as he wheeled the car into

Mbabane. "This couple is older. They are kind and gentle and have no children with them. I know them, because they have asked me to drive Madam around to do her errands. I have an arrangement with her husband that whenever she needs to go to town to shop she calls me. Then at the end of the month her husband pays for the time I spend looking after her. Believe me, these are people you will like and trust."

Anna's optimism took hold of her again. She smiled and became animated. "So, okay, Mr. Taxi man. How can I meet these people?"

"We shall go to their house now." Dumisani turned the taxi around in the middle of the crowded street and headed up the hill south of town. The houses in the area were well kept and affluent. Ten-foot high walls finished on top with razor wire encompassed all of the properties. The scarlet bougainvillea grew up over the walls and draped down the other side. They arrived at a mammoth wooden gate that had the face of a Cape buffalo carved into the center of it. Dumisani honked the horn and a guard appeared. Anna was reminded of her first car ride to the South African woman's house years ago. Maybe that was a good omen for her. The gates opened electronically and inside the walls the gardens looked like Eden. In the backseat she whispered a prayer to God that this would be a good place for her.

Dumisani left her in the car while he went to the door and talked to the madam. Anna peeked through the front window of the taxi to see what was happening. The madam was a petite attractive Belgian woman. She seemed happy to see Dumisani and nodded for Anna to get out of the car. Once inside Anna kept her eyes low and sat quietly in the living room while the madam interviewed her for the position.

"We will be here for two years while my husband works with the Swazi government and the European Union." She went on with the questions. She wasn't sure of her English, and Anna's Portuguese English was difficult to understand.

"Can you cook? There isn't a lot of housework here. It is just the two of us, and we live a quiet life. The house is big, but it doesn't get very messy. You will have your own quarters by the kitchen. The room is very nice."

She rose and Anna could see that she was very thin and delicate. She was dressed differently from the other white people Anna had worked for over the years. This new madam dressed in a white blouse with a lace collar. She had on a simple black skirt that covered her knees. Everything about her was lovely and soft and understated. She showed Anna the room she would occupy during the week. There was a bed, a dresser and a television. Anna couldn't believe her good fortune, and the new Belgian madam could not believe how lucky she was either.

Dumisani drove out of the driveway alone. He felt great satisfaction in his act. He cared about these two women and was pleased that he could help them.

$$\Rightarrow \Leftarrow$$

The next two years went by much too fast. Anna found her sense of humor again. Laughter came easy in the house. The Belgian couple loved her and treated her like family. They had lived in many parts of the world so they understood her hard stories and appreciated her endurance. When the husband was out of town Anna would stay with Madam, even if it meant missing her weekend home to stay with Mary. There were times when Madam was tired and ill. Anna took pleasure in caring for her as a close friend. In return, the couple paid Anna better than she had ever been paid. They took her to the optician, because her eyesight was failing. They made sure she had better medical care.

Anna needed blood pressure medication and was developing diabetes like her sister, Mary. There were days of Anna singing gospel hymns in the kitchen while she prepared their dinner. Anna insisted that all the clothes were ironed even when they didn't need it. She wouldn't have anyone think that she didn't take excellent care of her new family. When Madam went to town with Dumisani Anna would run outside and greet him.

In the back of her mind she knew the day would come when they would leave. All the white people eventually left. It was natural to the culture...the coming and going of people. There was always an adjustment to a new family, and there was a grieving when they left Swaziland.

The gentle Belgian couple insisted that she was taken care of after they left, but Anna told them it was time for her to retire. She needed to go home to her sister who was so ill. She wanted to spend more time in her garden and nurture her special roses. They bought her several new bushes to cultivate as a farewell gift.

The day came, and they packed up everything they brought and everything they accumulated for the last two years. What they didn't take home they gave to Anna, bed linens, pans, dishes and other household effects.

Dumisani drove Anna to her home. There was too much to carry, including the television, to take a bus. It was the longest ride home, but she and Dumisani talked about the Belgian couple that had helped them both over the last two years. Dumisani helped Anna carry her precious belongings into her house.

After he left she unpacked and put things around the house. She placed more photos on the shelf in the living room. Next to the picture of her as a little girl with Mary she put a photo of the Belgian couple. She kept the photo of her daughter's wedding on the shelf. All of these things had shaped who she was as a woman. Life was hard, everyone would agree with that, but God knew her heart. He knew that she was a woman who tried her best to make the most out of the gifts and opportunities He gave her. She could laugh in the face of tragedy. She could lift herself up from the depths of sadness. Now in her 50s she was a whole and contented person. She sat back in her chair and looked out at her garden that was full of ripening vegetables and flowers.

"Tomorrow I will spend the day tending to my roses."

≡ ≡

That year Anna's beloved sister Mary died peacefully from heart failure. Anna was by her side throughout the last night. Anna wept over Mary's body until her own body shook with grief. There was no one now who understood her past or shared her life. She put her sister's belongings in a basket and cleaned Mary's little house. Mary willed her house and the rental house to Anna. Even in death the sisters cared for and protected each other.

≡ ≡

It was a horrible shock for Anna to learn just a year after Mary's death that her daughter, Lindi and her husband Joseph were dead. The news came to her as she was weeding her rose garden. They had been ill for some time, but no one had thought they were sick enough to die. How did they succumb to AIDS at such a young age and with so much promise for their future? There was speculation that Joseph had not been as faithful as he professed, and that he had brought the disease home to Lindi. She had struggled under the weight of TB, an AIDS related illness, until she didn't even have the strength to operate her beloved hair salon.

Sobbing and grieving, Anna dressed up and took the bus to Manzini. She was in despair, defeated, but she had to keep a level head. There were the three grandchildren to consider. They would need her now, though they didn't know her, and she had to be strong for them. The idea that any of the children might also be infected was something she certainly could not face.

When she arrived at the hair salon looking for the children Joseph's brother greeted her.

"Anna, it is such a terrible and sad day for all of us." He spoke quietly and sadly.

"Where are the children?" She asked in a matter of fact voice. She never liked Joseph or his family.

"Oh, my brother, why does God send down this plague to the poorest people of the world?" He sat in a chair and buried his head in his hands.

Anna couldn't help breaking down, too. She put her hand on his head and cried with him.

"This is not from God. But it doesn't matter now. We need to take care of these children and give them a home. I am going to pack up their things and bring them to my house in the country."

Joseph's brother looked up at her and cleared his expression.

"Anna, I have custody of the children." He stood now and voiced his authority. "As Joseph's brother I have guardianship over everything you see here. The children will be raised by me, and this hair salon is also mine."

"But they are my grandchildren. They are the only family I have in the world." Anna was angry now. "I can take care of them, love them, and share my life with them. Please, you can't be serious that anyone could cherish them as much as I can. I beg you. Don't do this to me. Take the salon. I don't want this memory, but leave the children to me."

Joseph's brother spoke in a quiet but firm voice. "Anna, this is not negotiable. When a man dies, his brother takes over the property and family. That is the way it is, that is the way it will always be, and that is the way it shall be here. I suggest that you should be relieved not to have the burden, financially, to raise these children. They will need schooling and shoes and clothes. What could you do for them anyway?"

What could she do for them? He didn't know about the wooden box, and its treasure. Even now she still kept the wooden box under her bed, and it could be filled again. What could she do for them? She remembered saving for Lindi's education. She smiled to herself when she thought about the night they had celebrated buying the hair salon and Mary's houses.

"Believe me, Anna, it is better this way."

She knew that could not be true, but how could she fight the law and the culture of her country? Even the wooden box could never support that legal battle.

Anna's perseverance never let her down. She took another bus, but she didn't go home. She rode the bus up Malagwane Hill to Mbabane, and she found Dumisani, her faithful taxi man, at the bus stop.

"Dumisani!" she called and waved to him. He was always happy to see her. He rushed across the dirt road and held her hands in his.

"Anna, what brings you to Mbabane today?"

"Is there another family living in the Belgian house on the hill?"

"There is always a family in that house." He laughed. "It is a house that is never empty."

"Take me there now, please. I need to work."

"But Anna, aren't you happily retired? I have heard news that you have the most beautiful rose garden in your village."

"Yes, but roses can wait. Some day my little grandchildren may still need me, and I will be ready to help them."

Chapter 2 – Sarie

There are many reasons people emigrate, leave their homelands and loved ones. Sometimes they leave in such a hurry they run for their lives and leave everything behind them. More often, though, emigration takes thought and time. The decision is one that nags at the individual and haunts his waking and sleeping hours.

This was the case with the Van Duffelen family. Helmut Van Duffelen was a strong Boer, a white Dutch South African, who raised sheep in the rural area surrounding Port Elizabeth. He owned a modest farm that had been in his family for generations. The sheep in Port Elizabeth produced some of the finest wool in Southern Africa. The farmers sold wool to the textile mills in Durban and exported virgin wool to the weavers in several nearby countries. The Van Duffelen family had fought for their land and nurtured it for over a hundred years.

Helmut had a hearty wife, Ingrid and five growing and strong children. He loved to have Ingrid working in the barn next to him. She could handle the shears and hold down the sheep. It didn't bother her to put in a full day right along with her husband. Her blonde hair was pulled back into a tight bun, but the curly tendrils that fell away from the bun framed her round face and rosy cheeks. This was the woman he loved since they were children and met at the Dutch Reformed Church in their village. Now years later, they still went to church there every Sunday with their two sons and three daughters.

What a handsome family they were in church all lined up in one pew. Helmut was over 6 feet tall with a robust stature and a large beard. Ingrid was a stately woman. She had put on some weight over the years, but her 5' 7" figure carried it well giving her a healthy appearance. Their sons were the older of the children. Hans and Andres were strong boys who would inherit the farm and continue their family duties. The daughters were equally handsome, resembling their mother. The oldest daughter was Sarie. She was two years older than her sister, Katie. Dinusha was the youngest. A tiny tot with curly blond hair, she would never remember the farm the rest of the family had loved for so long.

After church the family celebrated with a huge braai, or barbeque. Neighboring friends and relatives were invited to share the feast of the Sabbath. The garden overflowed with hydrangeas, and bougainvilleas grew wild up the trees. Several flame trees skirted the perimeter. Ingrid prepared large bowls of potato salad, beetroot salad and vegetables. Helmut barbequed steaks and boerwors sausages on their handmade brick grill at the back of the house. For dessert Ingrid brought out plates full of special puddings and koeksisters. That was her specialty, and she never divulged her secret recipe. Koeksisters were pastries, braided, baked and soaked in golden sugar syrup. Ingrid carried out the dessert on an elaborate hand painted platter that had been her mother's. The guests gave their approval, and Ingrid beamed. It was another successful Sunday afternoon.

=⟩ ⟨=

That night when the festivities had ended and the children were in bed, Helmut and Ingrid retired to their room. They lived in a Dutch style farmhouse that Helmut's father had built with his own hands. The house was set so far back onto the property that most motorists passing on the road would never know it was there. Their bedroom was upstairs, and sometimes Helmut had to duck his head because of the slant of the ceiling.

"Ingrid, dear one, you know what I think of my farm, my house and my family. This is everything I love and everything I have ever known. But I have serious concerns for the future."

He spoke in their native tongue of Afrikaans. It was the language of his Dutch ancestors, and it was the only language he knew for most of his life. He understood some words in English, but business was conducted in Afrikaans, and it was the language of the church. He couldn't understand people who said it was a language of prejudice and oppression. There were always troublemakers in the world. After all, he never felt that he had hurt anyone. He was a simple farmer.

"Oh, Helmut. Why must you ruin the Sabbath ending it with this discussion? We are fine. The business is fine. Yes, it has been better in the past, but you know that is the way with farming. Some years are better than others. You are just tired. You do this every night. You get too tired, and then your imagination runs wild with fear. This is our land and our home. Nothing can happen to us here."

"Can't you see Ingrid, that the wind of time is changing? We have a majority of people in this country who feel oppressed. That is a dangerous situation. We Dutch are the minority, and some day we will have to fight for our land again. I have no problem or issue with the black men, but they have issue with us. What is apartheid to me? It doesn't concern the way I run my farm. What do I have, four farmhands to do the work with me? I repeat, with me. Hans and Andres and I work along side of these men, and we get along with them fine. I pay them a good wage, and they are healthy. You have our maid, Rose in the house, and she is as a friend to you. These people are part of our family, but the rest of the country especially the city people are not of our mind. Some day, believe me Ingrid; some day life here will turn against us. It is better to leave now while our land still has value and we can make a profit." Helmut undressed while he spoke and he pulled the duvet back to get into bed. Ingrid finished brushing out her long hair and rose from her dressing table to join him in their demure bed.

"Helmut, what are we to do; move to Australia the way the Van Heradens did? They will never return, and it is too far for any of their family to visit. What kind of answer is that? We would leave everyone and everything we know and trust. Think again Helmut. This is too big a decision for my tired mind."

Ingrid kissed Helmut's dry lips deep within his beard. She loved this old man so much. He was the only man she had ever given herself to, and there were no regrets about that, but he could never get her to leave her home. Helmut returned her kiss and affection, but he continued to plan for a way to give his family a more secure future. That night he forged an idea in his mind that he felt would satisfy Ingrid and the children, and it would still serve his purpose.

≡ ≡

Another month of torturous discussion went by. Sometimes Ingrid and Helmut raised their voices so loudly at each other that the children were awakened. One night Sarie crept near her parents' closed bedroom door and listened by the keyhole. She had suspected that something big, really big, was going to happen. She had thought that maybe they were discussing adding to the family. That was a horrible thought in Sarie's mind. Just what she didn't need....more little Katies and Dinushas running under foot. What if she had to put up with more wild brothers like Hans and Andres. Of course they would defend Sarie against any outsider, but at home they would just as soon harass her themselves. What Sarie heard that night amazed her more than anything she could have imagined.

"We are going to move?" She whispered to herself. "Where would we possibly go?" She pressed her ear against the door and continued in awe. "Swaziland? Why would anyone on God's earth go there?"

She was so mesmerized by the conversation she didn't hear her father's footsteps. Suddenly the door swung open, and she fell flat into her parent's bedroom. She had a difficult time standing up with her nightgown tucked around her. She was pulled straight up by her father's massive arm.

"What are you doing here young lady? Is this what you do with your late hours? So, you want to know everything, do you? " Helmut's voice boomed, and Sarie, still held up by his arm, trembled.

"Father, I'm sorry, but is it true?"

Helmut glared at her, and he glared back at Ingrid who was sitting up on their bed.

"We'll talk in the morning. The way a family should talk.….. as a family, not as an eavesdropper at someone's door. Do you understand?"

Sarie cowered and turned to go.

"Now, give your papa a hug and run over there and kiss your mother. Say your prayers twice, and get you to bed."

They held the family discussion the next day. Helmut would have preferred to have the details worked out completely before sharing the news with his children. After all, children were to be told plans. They were not to be part of the process.

"So, family, this is the way it will be. Life here is going to change. To protect all of you and your future we are moving to Swaziland. Even now I have the farm up for sale, and there is a strong prospect of a buyer. There is opportunity in Swaziland for a man like me, and you will all be safe there."

The family sat in silence. The decision had been made. To the children it seemed like such a sudden move. Hans and Andres were angry.

"What about us, Papa? We should inherit this land and the farm. What will we have to our credit as men?"

"You will have your brains and your strength to serve you. God will not let us down on this venture. I have prayed much about this decision, and I know it is the right thing to do."

Ingrid sat silently. She was exhausted from the fight, and she acquiesced that her heart would follow her husband anywhere he eventually took them.

"But why Swaziland?" Sarie spoke up. She knew not to question Papa, but Swaziland. Who could live in that primitive country?

"Swaziland is close to our homeland and friends and family. We will be out of South Africa, but we will still be within a day's drive to our loved ones. It is a safe country, and there are still many ways to make a good honest living."

So there it was. The agonizing decision had been made, and the dye was cast. The farm was sold, and indeed, Helmut made a good profit. Years later he would still congratulate himself that he had sold his farm when the land had value and so did the Rand.

He moved the family and all their belongings, including the demure bed they had slept on since the day they had married. Their dogs went with them. The two German shepherds were the best and cheapest loyal security a man could have. As he was leaving the farm he took down the wooden plaque that his father had carved. It bore their family name and had hung over the front door. "I'm sorry, my father." He thought to himself. "I know you would not approve, but these are different times. I will take care of my family, as you took care of us. I have prayed hard for the answers, and God has shown me the way."

The trip to Big Bend took most of the day. It was a much longer ride than Sarie had expected. She hated long car rides and was impatient to arrive at their new home. Big Bend was the heart of the sugar industry in the Kingdom of Swaziland. The weather was warm, and the sugar plants grew tall in thick rows for miles. Helmut had no trouble getting a job as a supervisor in the sugar refinery. He could work tirelessly. He certainly knew how to organize men and was an intimidating figure. The few words he knew in English were invaluable to him, and he soon became very comfortable with the language.

"We must all speak English now." He proclaimed over dinner one night. The family sat around a large wooden table while Ingrid served a meal of mutton stew and bread with fruit and custard for dessert.

"In this country no one speaks Afrikaans, and we must be part of this country." Helmut served himself first and spooned a large portion of mutton stew into his bowl.

Looking at every member of his family he took the opportunity to exert his authority. He leaned his imposing figure into the table and spoke. "So that's the way it shall be. At school you will all speak English now. Anywhere you go away from this house you must speak English." He broke his bread and dipped it into the gravy of the stew and continued. "At home you speak Afrikaans. We must not lose our heritage just because we have left our country."

The sugar industry provided them with a comfortable complimentary cottage, and Ingrid resolved herself to make a home out of this new dwelling. It was reminiscent of her old farmhouse, but this new house was actually larger. The sprawling house provided plenty of room for the family. The boys shared one room upstairs, and the girls shared another large room on the other side upstairs. While they missed having their own home, the Van Duffelens were pleased to be able to bank their profit so the boys could attend college.

The question of education was on everyone's mind. The boys would soon be off to the university in Durban. Sarie and Katie were in the lower grades, and they would attend school locally. Sarie was now 10 years old, and Katie was 8 years.

"Why can't I go to the plantation school?" Sarie knew better than to be defiant, but she wanted to go to the school on the premises. All the workers' children went there, and they were her friends.

"Absolutely not!" Helmut held his ground on this, and Ingrid agreed. "You must have an education fitting of your culture and your background. This school is for common people who work in the fields. Don't you think you deserve better?"

The plantation owner was generous to his employees. In return for their work they received wages, but they also received housing and an on-premises school. They even had access to a small company store where they could shop for the essentials they needed making trips to town less necessary. With this plan the owner could limit the amount he paid his people, and the workers' families were never homeless or uneducated. It was a benevolent way of accommodating cheap labor. The Van Duffelen family lived in a comfortable home, but the black Swazi field workers lived in small cinder block square houses barely large enough for a family and hardly comfortable against the elements. Their tiny dwellings were lined up in dull rows of unpainted drab gray. Sugar plants looked impressive in rows, but their houses were a bleak reminder of their lot in life.

"You will go to the Dutch mission school, and I will not discuss it further with you. We have to have order here, and we must not forget who we are."

He stormed out of the living room and left Sarie in tears.

When the school year began she and Katie went off to the mission school as promised. They wore proper uniforms and dared not complain. Their shoes were uncomfortable but sensible oxfords. They learned English quickly. In fact, their English was better than their father's. They kept that fact to themselves.

The climate in the low veldt of southern Swaziland was warm and humid. Every day after school Sarie and Katie shed their uniforms and uncomfortable shoes and ran outside and swam in the lake behind their house. It was a relief after spending hours in a hot boring classroom. In the evening they helped Ingrid and their Swazi maid, Sibona, put on the dinner for the family. Sibona cleaned up the dishes at night so that Ingrid could have some quiet time to read her Bible before bed. The girls were ordered to sit in the dining room around the large table after dinner and study their lessons. Sarie hated that part of the day. She never thought that reading about dead people, heroes or otherwise, had any relevance to her. All those mathematics and numbers and science equations were good for the boys in the class, but to her it seemed like a language harder to learn than English had ever been.

On Saturdays she and Katie played with the local children. They spent hours swimming in the lake and lying around on the grass by the water planning their futures.

Katie was the studious of the two girls. She mastered the math and science quickly, and she teased Sarie about her lack of interest in history and literature.

"You think you don't care about the lives of the people we read about? Well, who will ever read anything about you? These people are immortal, because they did something important in life. What will you ever do?" Katie inquired.

"Oh, you are a silly goose!" Sarie laughed and rolled over on her back on the grass. "You think school is easy, but that's because you are in the easier grades. You wait until you are in my class. Just wait until you're 12 years old like me, and you'll see. That's when the real work begins." She crossed her thin legs in the air and ran her fingers through her light red hair. "Do you think that just because you like school that anybody would remember your life? I don't need to be remembered in a dusty book. I am going to live my life happily in this world." She jumped to her feet and twirled around in a wide circle waving her arms. The sun was radiant and she squinted looking up to the sky.

"You'll see. I am going to make friends, dance, sing, and meet BOYS!"

=≡ ≡=

One night during dinner Katie sat quietly and picked at the food on her plate. "I think I'm just too tired to eat tonight." She muttered. Without asking permission she rose from the table and headed for the stairs to her room. While the family watched in bewilderment Katie took two steps up and fell backwards to the floor.

"Quick, Hans, fetch a doctor." Ingrid screamed. "Helmut, carry her upstairs!"

Helmut carried his lifeless daughter to her bed. Ingrid pulled back the covers, and he laid her down. Her eyes were shut. Her breathing was slow. She moaned and drew up her legs to her chest, but she still didn't open her eyes.

"My God, Helmut, what is this?" Ingrid felt panic. She was accustomed to injuries on a farm, and she could stitch a wound herself. This was something she had never seen. She stroked Katie's hair and ordered Sarie to bring a cool cloth for her forehead.

"The doctor is delivering a baby away from here, and he won't get back until morning." Hans yelled as he threw open the door and dashed up the stairs taking the steps two at a time. Katie looked so helpless and small lying pale in her bed. Sarie was silent and stood away from her sister. Ingrid pulled Katie's clothes off gently and noticed red sores all over her arms and stomach. "What's this?" She murmured under her breath. "Oh please God don't let it be some kind of pox."

Sarie walked slowly over to her mother and put her hand on Ingrid's shoulder. "Mama, I have them, too." She raised her sleeve and the red welts appeared on her arms.

≡ ≡

All night Ingrid sat by Katie's bedside and kept cool cloths on her forehead. Sarie was in the bed beside her and lay terrified. If Katie were to die, then was this a death sentence for her, too? She started to weep quietly, and Ingrid was immediately at her side comforting her. "Are you all right, dear?" Ingrid swept her hand over Sarie's forehead.

She dipped another cloth in a bowl of water and wrung it out. Placing it on Sarie's warm forehead she comforted her daughter. "Don't worry, my darling. Papa and I will make sure that you and Katie are safe. We won't let anything harm you."

"Oh Mama, will we die? And if we die will you bury us back at the farm?"

Ingrid laid her head down beside Sarie on the bed. She was so frightened of this mysterious disease, but she would not allow Sarie to bring a spirit of doom into their house. She recovered her energy and sat upright. "I'll have no talk like this. Say a prayer and ask God for forgiveness of thoughts like that. You will be fine. Katie will be fine. Now sleep and don't talk anymore."

Little Dinusha was moved to another room. Sibona made up a bed on a sofa for her. They could not be sure if this illness was contagious.

Helmut and the boys couldn't sleep. Helmut was furious. He was angry that the doctor hadn't arrived, and he blamed himself for bringing his family to this dangerous and primitive country. He spent the night pacing the floor in the living room while his sons tried to calm his fears. The boys were planning to start college in another month, and they were frightened to leave their father in this state. They had never seen this great imposing man look so scared.

In the morning the doctor came to the door. "Where have you been, man?" Helmut demanded. Helmut's face was scarlet from anxiety and anger. Andres took him by the arm before he had a chance to strike the doctor.

"Now, Mr. Van Duffelen, you know I was away delivering a baby to a woman on another plantation. What a healthy little girl they have now, too."

"You insensitive maniac. I am the one with the little girl. And now she's sick, and her sister, too. Move sir, up the stairs. Faster, faster!"

He practically shoved the doctor up the stairs, and wouldn't allow any more explanations.

When the doctor came into the girls' room and saw their spots he shook his head and bent over them. Ingrid was ordered to leave the room a task she performed unwillingly. Outside the door she whispered to Helmut.

"How do we know this man can help? We don't have experience with doctors. The girls are so sick, and they aren't any better this morning. I think, in fact, that Katie may be worse. I suppose we have no choice."

She buried her head into Helmut's chest and wept. "Oh, my love, I'm so scared. I'm just so scared of this. I've never seen anything like this. I don't know what is happening to them."

Her husband held her in his arms and hugged her worn out body.

"There, there, now. Buck up, Dearie. This is a good doctor. I had a great feeling of confidence in him when I met him downstairs. You're tired and need rest, too. This doctor and I had a good talk and his credentials are excellent."

Helmut had never felt the need in his life to lie as he did now. He wasn't sure about doctors, either, but as the man of the house it was his position to appear confident. Ingrid didn't need to know that he almost wrestled the man in the downstairs hall.

The doctor stayed in the room with the girls for an endless amount of time, and when he came out he looked very grave.

"Mr. and Mrs. Van Duffelen I think I know what is wrong with both of your daughters. First, though, could you tell me if they have been swimming in fresh water lately?"

Ingrid looked confused and she looked up at Helmut to try to see what he was thinking. Helmut stood motionless. He gave no expression while he waited to hear what else the doctor had to say.

"Doctor, the girls swim in the lake near our house almost every day. But they've been doing that for more than a year now. What could this have to do with their illness?"

"I have to run tests, but I believe that they are suffering from a parasite known as shistosomiasis. It is better known as Bilharziasis."

"A parasite? My daughters have a parasite? How can that be possible? Isn't that something that, well, I hate to use the words, but, well you know…like farm hands and field hands. Well, don't they get dreadful things like that?"

She started pacing nervously around the hallway outside the bedroom.

" I may seem like a simple farm woman to you, Doctor, but aren't parasites bugs or worms that live in and feed off of the body? What could swimming have to do with that? I know that bad water to drink will make people sick. Do you think they drank the water? No, they would know better than to drink lake water."

"Mrs. Van Duffelen, no, they don't have to drink the water to contract this terrible disease. Let me try to explain. Shisto is a disease that is bred in the snails in the water. Birds fly over the water and contaminate it with droppings. In fact, any animal droppings can infect water. Then the snail becomes the host of the worm from the dropping."

Ingrid looked like she was going to be ill. She felt dizzy and queasy. The doctor kept talking of worms and feces. It was too much for her. She had helped deliver the lambs in her barn, but she could not face the idea of worms in her daughters. She could clean chicken cages without thinking twice about the odor, but this was too much for her.

"You see." The doctor continued. "These are not your garden variety of worms. These microscopic parasites burrow into the human body and eat it from the inside out. They penetrate the body through the skin. Sometimes water can be so infected with the parasite that a person can contract the disease within 20 seconds of skin contact in the water. Even clean healthy skin can become a host for the parasite."

Ingrid thought she would faint. She leaned against Helmut who pretended to be knowledgeable and strong.

"So, Doctor, sir. What do we do now?" Helmut was feeling a little embarrassed about his initial treatment of the doctor. "What can be done to help our beautiful little girls?"

"They need to be in a hospital and the sooner the better." The doctor spoke professionally, then he added, "Please, this is nothing you could have prevented." He placed his hand on Ingrid's shoulder and tried to comfort her.

"How have we not known about this disease before, Doctor?" Helmut asked. "We know so many diseases are here in Africa. We are aware of malaria and typhoid and so many illnesses. But this, this is devastating, and we never knew. Is it rare? Is it contagious? Do we quarantine our other children? What are the answers?" He felt his voice rising again, and he stopped himself so he wouldn't frighten Ingrid any more than she was already.

"This is not a new disease." The doctor replied in a matter of fact medical way. "Would you believe that 250 million people in the world suffer from Bilharziasis, but most of the people in the world have never heard of it? We have antibiotics for it now, and we can help the girls. Your other children are fine. It's not like malaria where the infected mosquitoes are all around and fly from one sick person to infect another one. Keep everyone out of bodies of fresh water, lakes and ponds.

That is my best advice for prevention. I know with children that job is difficult, but they cannot get this disease if they stay on dry land."

It was all so confusing to poor tired Ingrid. She shook her head and walked to the girls' room. There she and Sibona dressed the weak children and wrapped them in blankets for the ride to the hospital. Even Ingrid had never been in a hospital before. She had delivered all of her children in their farmhouse back in Port Elizabeth. She remembered the time Helmut had broken his leg years ago when a branch fell on him while he was clearing some land. Even then, he didn't go to a hospital. The doctor had set the leg and Helmut rested at home. Within a few days he was outside again hobbling around while doing the chores. Taking the girls to a hospital was a leap of faith for them, but they could tell by looking at the children that they had no choice.

Within a few days of being in the private hospital Sarie was feeling much better. She was taking antibiotics and had an IV in her arm. Although, she was weak, she felt that she was getting stronger.

"Well, now, this isn't that bad. Is it?" She remarked to Katie after about a week of resting in the hospital. "Look at all the school we're missing. I haven't been told to read or decipher anything in days. If I didn't feel like I had a bad case of the flu, it could almost seem like a holiday."

She looked over at Katie who was not faring as well. Katie attempted a weak smile and turned her head to look at her older sister. "We aren't going to die, are we, Sarie? I feel so weak and sick, and I'm in awful pain."

"Now, you don't worry, sis. Those doctors are pretty smart, and they're cute, too. We'll be out of here in no time, and then we'll have to go back to school and wear those ugly shoes again."

Sarie would go back to school long before Katie would be able to walk again. Later that day the doctors gave Ingrid and Helmut news that they had dreaded to hear. "We have run more tests, and we have news for you. Sarie is doing much better. She is strong, and her case has always been milder than Katie's. The sores on her arms where the parasite entered the skin are almost healed. They will probably leave a dull scar for a while, but they will fade in time. Katie, well that's another matter." The two doctors looked very serious knowing they must give news that no one wants to hear.

Ingrid gripped Helmut's arm and bit her lip.

"Katie's appendix is very inflamed. I'm afraid if we don't remove it we will have a rupture on our hands that could be fatal."

"Well then, do that." Ingrid let go of her husband's arm and sighed. Many people have appendectomies and they survive without complications. "Go ahead with the surgery. We are okay with that decision." Ingrid felt relieved. This wasn't so bad. She knew about that kind of surgery, and it wasn't that frightening to her. Of course, she wished Katie could just recuperate like Sarie seemed to be doing, but an appendix? That was like tonsils, wasn't it?

"There's more." The first doctor said in his professional manner. "Your daughter, Katie, well, her left kidney has been destroyed by the disease." He looked at them almost apologetically and continued in a compassionate tone. "We have to remove the kidney. It is already poisoning her body. She may not survive unless we perform the surgery immediately. I'm sorry to tell you this, but it's the best we can do for her now."

He stood looking at his notepad. He didn't know where else to fix his eyes.

Ingrid buried her head in her hands, and Helmut took her in his arms. "So that's what we will do." He replied to the doctor. "We will consent to the operation. She'll be okay. Of course, she's good stock, and she'll be strong again. I know this. I know this." His voice trailed off and he repeated himself again. "I know this. She'll be fine." He couldn't look at Ingrid as he spoke. He was used to being in control. He was the man of the house, the leader of the family. He had to be strong for everyone. He would pray to God to protect her, and he would will his strength into Katie's fragile body.

They operated on Katie that day, and the doctors seemed relieved when they came out of surgery and faced her parents.

"The surgery went well. Your daughter has a lot of spirit. We checked her other organs, and they are undamaged." The doctor took off his surgical cap and smiled at the weary family. "Katie will be fine. It will take time and patience, but we think she has a very good chance of having no weaknesses from the disease or its complications. Whatever you do, be sure she doesn't overdo or try to keep up with her feisty sister for a while."

"Yes, Doctor. You mentioned our daughter, Sarie. Is she doing better?"

The doctor couldn't suppress his laughter. "Sarie, now there's a girl with spirit. She has a will to live that is outstanding in one so young. You don't have to worry about Sarie. She could take care of all of you."

Helmut wasn't sure he liked that kind of comment about his daughter. Men should take care of the women. He would have to remember to have a talk with Sarie in the future about her role as a female.

The night after the surgery Sarie slipped out of her hospital bed and crept into her sister's bed with her. "Don't worry, Katie." Sarie whispered as she stroked Katie's matted hair. "We're going to be fine you and me. I have too much to do to sit here and be sick all the time. When we get better we will picnic and play again." She took her sister's limp hand in hers. "We are survivors, you know. No one can keep us down."

⇒ ⇐

The girls were indeed survivors. Sarie regained her strength quickly and was sent directly back to her studies. Katie took longer to become strong again. Ingrid prepared food that she believed would build up their constitution, and she made both of the girls drink Rooibos tea to strengthen their blood. Rooibos tea was an herbal red tea and most people called it 'bush tea.' Sarie hated the pungent taste of it, but she and Katie drank it obligingly. After all, Mama had almost died with them from anxiety and worry so they would not argue with her now.

Andres and Hans started college and left home. It was a strange adjustment having them out of the house. At first Sarie was sure she would enjoy getting rid of the rambunctious brothers, but she soon discovered how quiet the house was without them.

⇒ ⇐

Sarie decided that her 18th birthday was the perfect time to reveal her plans to her parents. Wasn't 18 years a good time to demonstrate her independence and adulthood? Ingrid had prepared a wonderful birthday feast for Sarie. Andres and Hans were coming home for the celebration, too. Hans was in medical school in Johannesburg now and rarely had time to make the trip back to Swaziland. Andres had finished his degree and was working in management with an industrial manufacturing company in Durban. Katie knew what Sarie had proposed, but she kept her sister's secret. Little Dinusha was the darling of the family. She loved entertaining the family by singing songs she heard on the radio.

She was singing one of these songs and dancing about the living room when Helmut came home from work at the sugar refinery.

"Turn down that noise." He complained. "Doesn't a man have a right to come home to a tranquil house after a long day at work? And what kind of music is that you're playing? I don't hear God fearing sounds coming out of the radio anymore. I think the world must be going mad." He stopped his tirade long enough to kiss Sarie on her cheek. "Happy birthday, daughter." He picked up the newspaper and sat down in his favorite overstuffed chair. "Ingrid!" He called out to the kitchen. "Have you seen this newspaper? I'm telling you. The world is turning upside down. Look at what is happening in South Africa. Didn't I tell you years ago things would change?"

Ingrid wiped her hands on a towel and stood behind his chair. "Well, dear, I have heard some things, and friends in Port Elizabeth have written to me about some problems."

"Problems? These are more than problems. There are demonstrations, fires; people are arrested all the time. Blacks are arrested for being in the wrong place, and whites are arrested for befriending them. I knew it. I was right to leave that country. Have you heard about the women, too? They are getting all these ideas about running things themselves. Now where did that come from?"

Sarie wondered if this was the right time after all to talk to Papa, but she had rehearsed it so many times in her mind she didn't think she could wait any longer.

It was a perfect celebration of Sarie's adulthood. Her brothers seemed so much nicer now that they were grown up. The dinner went so well that she took in a deep breath and stood up to address them.

"Papa, Mama and everyone. I have made a big decision about my life."

The whole family sat quietly. Only Katie had anticipated this speech. She could have said it right along with Sarie since she had been Sarie's practice audience for weeks.

"I know what I want to do with my life now. I've given this a lot of thought, and I feel very confident that I'm making the right decision."

Helmut smiled and lifted his glass of wine. "Wonderful, daughter. Tell us that you've decided to go to college in South Africa. I know you never enjoyed studies like your brothers or sister, but if you would concentrate you could probably pass the test to get into a really nice university."

Sarie knew this wasn't going to be easy. She would have to speak very quickly to get it out without interruption.

"Papa, I've decided that I don't want to go to university. I want to become a hairdresser."

Helmut froze, and Ingrid smiled. She had been concerned about Sarie's grades and ambition for a long time. She was actually relieved that Sarie had come to some conclusion about her future. There weren't any men in the area that appealed to Sarie, so a young marriage was out of the question. These days girls weren't marrying as young anyway, so at least Sarie would have a career...of sorts.

"A hairdresser?" Helmut rose to his feet and glared at her over the remnants of the dinner. "You want to be a hairdresser?" He emphasized the word hairdresser until Sarie felt it ringing in her ears. "What kind of profession is that for a nice Dutch girl raised in a good family?"

"Well, Papa. I've given this much more thought than you think I have."

"Thought?" He boomed. "Since when did you give anything in your life much thought?" He pointed his fork around the table at the family. Here is your brother studying medicine. Here is your other brother with a responsible management position. Here is your sister getting good marks, excellent marks every term. Now, where is Sarie? She is daydreaming...and if you aren't careful, young lady," He pointed his fork in Dinusha's direction "You will be following her to nowhere."

"If you would only listen to me, Papa. There is a Portuguese woman in Manzini who is a wonderful hairdresser. She has offered to teach me the trade."

"Manzini? Now there's a laugh. Why would you want to live in that city? It has no culture. Is there even a decent church in that city? There isn't anybody for you to meet and marry in that place. No matter what you want to do with your life, Sarie, you will eventually want a husband and children."

"Let me finish, Papa." Sarie glanced at Katie to see what she was thinking. Katie looked back at her encouragingly. That gave Sarie the fortitude to plead her case.

"I want to be trained in Manzini by this Portuguese woman, but after that I want to live in Mbabane. Now, how can you argue with that? It's the capital city. I have already thought through this. I could style the hair of the businessmen's wives, and there are a lot of diplomats from several countries who live there. It is a good opportunity for me to meet more interesting people...and their sons."

The last remark was one that Helmut and Ingrid couldn't argue. They knew that living in the middle of a sugar plantation didn't offer their daughters many choices of husband material. This was something they had talked about over the years. The boys could meet girls at the university, but where would their daughters meet anyone as long as they lived in such a rural area?

In Helmut's mind he was a modern man. He believed that girls should be smart and educated. They should also marry and have a family. That was the way life should be. He was sure it was written in the Bible.

≡ ≡

Sarie packed up everything she needed and a lot of things she felt she couldn't live without. She took her clothes and her special blanket that she had slept with since she was a baby. There were keepsakes and photos that went with her, too. Papa had bought her a little used Nissan as a birthday present. She loaded the car until she could barely see out of the back window. Everybody hugged and kissed, and she was off on her new adventure.

The drive to Manzini took at least three hours, but the roads were paved and easy to navigate. She listened to the radio and sang as she drove. Homesickness wouldn't set in for several days.

Papa wouldn't let her stay at a guesthouse or hotel. He thought those places were for women of less reputation than his daughter. He spoke with the pastor of their church who mentioned that he knew of an expatriate South African family who lived on the outskirts of Manzini. The pastor and Helmut made arrangements for Sarie to stay there. She paid the family a small amount for her accommodations and their extra expenses for having her in the house. It was a comfortable home, and they reminded her of her own family.

After she was settled and unpacked she drove into Manzini to the hairdressing salon.

"Sarie, how good to see you and welcome to Manzini." The Portuguese woman embraced her and led her into the shop. "I want you to meet everyone here so you will feel at home. You know, learning this business…it is rewarding, but it takes time. You will probably stay with us for maybe even a year, you know?"

Sarie was so excited. This was exactly what she wanted. No books, just practical life and fun on the weekends.

"This is our receptionist, Lindi. She has been with me for quite some time now, you know? And this is our master hairstylist, Janet. She is my right hand person, as you would say."

Sarie and Lindi became fast friends. They both loved to relax and party. Sarie had many black friends back at the sugar plantation, so it wasn't unusual for her to befriend another black woman here. Lindi didn't talk much about her family, and that surprised Sarie, because she always told stories about her own. She didn't even know where Lindi lived. It didn't matter, because they spent their friendship going out to lunch and occasionally going to the disco down in the valley.

Sarie turned out to be a talented hairdresser. She was so happy, because it was the most successful studying she had ever accomplished. Whenever she was finished styling someone's hair she had a feeling of accomplishment that school books had never offered her.

She heard people talk about the Portuguese woman leaving the area. She couldn't, wouldn't believe this. What would she do if her teacher, her mentor left?

Finally she faced reality. The Portuguese woman was leaving after all. She and her husband were going back to Portugal. Then she learned that Lindi was to take over the shop. What a lucky woman she was.

"Your family must be so proud of you, Lindi." Sarie said over lunch one day. "What a great opportunity for you."

"Well, yes, it is." Lindi pushed her food around on her plate. She wasn't sure how to respond to this remark.

"Wow! If I could only have some place like this to call my own. Well, I guess that's how it is when your family has money. You are one lucky girl, Lindi." Sarie's deep blue eyes flashed at Lindi, and she patted her on the back.

Lindi smiled and said nothing. She could never tell Sarie where the money came from; her mother was a maid for the Portuguese woman, and the money had come from years of savings in a wooden box.

When the Portuguese woman left, Sarie knew it was time for her to move on as well. She had learned all she could, and the rest was up to her own imagination and talent. She found a flat in Mbabane for rent, and she moved into it immediately.

She dialed up her family as soon as she had a job and a place to live.

"Mama, this is Sarie. You aren't going to believe my good fortune. I have a wonderful flat. Yes, it's safe. There are bars on the windows and two locks on the door. Of course I can park my car close to the building. Is Katie there? Can I speak to her?

Katie, you just have to come visit me in Mbabane. There are more restaurants here, and you would enjoy the shopping."

"Sarie, dear." Katie responded. "Mama and I want to see you soon. You know that I'm thinking of going to Stellenbosch to study in the new term. So we are going down to the Cape. Would you like to come along with us?"

Suddenly Sarie felt homesick. She couldn't take off that kind of time from work. She was an independent woman now and had bills to pay. Katie would have the luxury of idle studying near Cape Town, while Sarie would have to stay behind and work. Suddenly, studying seemed easier than being responsible for herself and her life.

"No, no, little sis. I have work to do here. You should see some of the women who come into the salon. I mean, the jewelry on these Europeans. You wouldn't believe it." Her voiced started to crack, but she spoke slowly so her sister wouldn't hear. "This is such an interesting place." Tears streamed down her cheeks. "Really, Katie, you must come for a visit."

After she hung up the phone Sarie sat on her sofa and sobbed. She hadn't cried like that in years. She was always so optimistic and cheerful. Maybe this wasn't such a grand place after all. She missed her family and the security they offered. She spent the whole night looking at their pictures and reminiscing over a bottle of wine.

The next morning she pulled herself together. She had slept on the sofa, and that wasn't the best night's sleep for someone who spent the entire day on her feet.

"I'm not going to cry anymore." She proclaimed to herself in the mirror as she dressed for work.

"This was my decision, and I love what I do. I know I'm doing the right thing for me, and Katie is doing the right thing for her." She combed her wavy red hair and put on her makeup. "Andres is doing what's best for him, and Hans is happy with his choice. I mean, look at the choices Papa made. He sold the whole farm, for God's sake, and no one could tell him anything."

She took a job in the best salon in Mbabane. Just as she predicted, the clients were very upscale. The salon offered a wide range of services from manicures and pedicures to massages and other beauty treatments. It was the kind of place where women could go and know they were treated in the manner they were accustomed. They were more pampered than they would have been in their own countries.

"Would you like a cup of tea while you're under the dryer?" Sarie asked the British diplomat's wife. The woman smiled, and Sarie ordered her black assistant, Ruth, to serve Madam a cup of tea, milk and sugar, please.

Yes, this was a pretty nice place. She rarely heard from Lindi anymore. Lindi was very busy running her salon and had acquired a boyfriend. That was something that Sarie wouldn't mind having for herself.

One Saturday night she and her best friend, Tess, drove down into the valley for a drink at the Royal Swazi Sun hotel. It was a four star hotel and a perfect place to meet European businessmen. All she seemed to meet were the same expatriate guy friends from Mbabane.

"Hey, girls, come over to our table." Mark called her from across the room. "We have brought someone you just have to meet."

Tess and Sarie thought they looked pretty good that night. Tess was a white Swazi. Her family had lived in Mbabane her entire life. Her mother had only left the country to deliver her children at the hospital in Nelspritt, South Africa. Her father was a supervisor with the forestry and pulp industry. The girls had a lot in common. Both came from families that lived on plantations. Both were hairdressers, and they were the same age. Sarie was clearly the better looking of the two of them. Tess had inherited too much of her father's body design without her mother's high cheekbones to compensate. Still, she was a good friend, easy listener and before long they shared the flat together. Sarie, on the other hand, had grown to be a tall slender woman with striking blue eyes and wavy strawberry blond hair.

"Oh, that Mark. He loves attention. He just wants us to come over there so he can impress everybody." Sarie remarked. She waved to him but didn't move.

Then she looked more carefully. Sitting at the table with the regular five guys she knew was an entirely different looking person. Who was this new guy and where did they find him? She had to know. She swallowed her pride and dragged Tess to the other table.

"Sarie, I want you to meet our American friend here."

So that's what it was. She should have guessed. Everything about him looked different from his dark brown eyes and long hair to his smile and his denim jeans. She should have realized it already. An American, now that's exciting.

"So, you're an American." Sarie thought that sounded dumb even as it was coming out of her mouth. "What are you doing over here?"

"Hi, Sarie, if I can call you that. My name is Brian. I'm here with the Peace Corps. Or rather, I should say, I'm with the Peace Corps in South Africa."

"We decided we should bring him over to the kingdom and show him a good time at the casino." Mark kept talking.

"Yeah" replied Tom at the table. "We were picking up supplies down in Durban and met him. So we offered for him to come for a weekend, and he took us up on it."

Brian looked at Sarie, and she returned the look. This must have been the most beautiful man in the world. She was completely entranced by his unusual accent.

"Actually, I have a meeting with someone at the embassy on Monday. Since I was coming to Swaziland anyway I thought I would look them up and see what the fuss is about going to the casino."

The evening went so well. Sarie held her cigarette away from the table. "Should I even smoke this at all?" She wondered. She had heard that Americans didn't smoke as much as South Africans. She was coy and flashed her eyes at him. The other young men saw this and knew they had made a match.

On Monday the wife of one of the American diplomats called Sarie to have her come to her house. She didn't like having her hair done in town where people might see her. Sarie was happy to oblige her in this request. Most women didn't mind coming in to the shop, because they enjoyed the comradery of the salon. The European wives enjoyed the time away from their fortresses and often went to lunch together after their hair was done. It was a regular social hour. This particular American, though, was not as social, and she seemed to have her own personal problems. Sarie wasn't one to divulge a confidence. That made her a valuable asset as well as an excellent stylist.

She gathered her styling tools and headed out the door. When she pulled up to the house the guard let her through the electronic gates. The maid answered the door and announced her arrival.

Sarie walked into the kitchen and spread out her designing tools. The American diplomat's wife walked in wearing her robe and carrying a drink. Sarie knew that it was probably alcoholic.

"Sarie, dear, thank you for coming over. It is just so hard for me to get to the salon these days."

She sat down in a chair and let Sarie put the towel around her neck.

"God, how I hate my life. I hate my husband. I hate this whole crappy little country. How do you do it, Sarie? You're such a young thing with your whole life ahead of you." She sipped her drink then held her head back and finished the glass.

"I thought my husband would be an ambassador by now. Dudu." she called into the other room. "Get me another drink, for God's sake. Do I have the laziest maid or what?"

Sarie just smiled and kept trimming her hair. It wasn't up to her to make judgments about her clients. She actually felt sorry for this American who was so unhappy with her life. As far as Sarie was concerned it looked like a pretty decent life to her. The American diplomat families lived in the nicest houses, and this one came with a beautiful swimming pool. Besides, the Americans were good tippers. She wondered if this woman tipped her for her styling or for her silence.

"So Sarie, what are you going to do with your life? Are you just going to stay in this pathetic little place? Don't you have any aspiration to get out and see the world?" Dudu brought Madam a new drink and quietly left the room. Working for this American wasn't an easy job, but unemployment was high, and Dudu couldn't take any chances of losing her job.

"Whatever you do, Sarie, marry a man with some backbone. My husband has turned into such an insipid little man."

She swirled her glass and shook the ice cubes around to cool the drink.

"Marry a REAL man. You know, somebody with some muscle and testosterone. God, I would love to have a man hold me tight.... just have his arms around me and really act like a man. You know what I mean?"

Sarie thought about the guys at the hotel the other night. They were a lot of fun. That American guy, Brian was somebody she would like to know better.

The doorbell rang while Sarie was drying the American woman's hair. Dudu opened the door and came into the kitchen.

"Madam, the roses have arrived. Where do you want them?"

"Where do you think I want them, Dudu? Put them on the dining table where they always go. Get me a cigarette off the coffee table while you're in there. Gees, do I have to do everything around here?"

"Those are beautiful Swazi roses." Sarie remarked.

"Yeah, yeah, it's the one thing I do like about this place." Dudu brought her a tray with cigarettes on it. She handed Madam a cigarette and lit a match for her.

"You know there's a woman in Manzini who grows them, and hers are really exceptional." The American woman inhaled a long puff and let it out slowly. "She's just a maid, but she can really grow roses.

You know her daughter is a hairdresser, too. Of course, I wouldn't go to her. She's in Manzini. I think she just specializes in fixing hair for the locals. Maybe you know her, her name is Lindi."

Sarie did know Lindi, of course. She remembered that Lindi had never talked about her family or her background. How did Lindi ever get the money to own a business?

"Uh, Sarie, a little more concentration, please; your mind seems to be wandering and so is my hairstyle. I'm starting to look like a goddam freak here. What's going on with you?"

"I'm sorry, Madam. I was just thinking about the roses and Lindi. Yes, I did know her awhile back, but I haven't seen her in a long time."

"Well, I'm sure it's not important anyway. Yes, that's better. Now I'm starting to look like a diplomat's wife. Whatever the hell that is!" She waved her hands when she spoke, and Sarie smiled. She thought this American woman was amusing, in a sad sort of way.

"Do you know how many days I have to stay here before I can go home?" Sarie shook her head. She didn't see what was so wrong with being right there. "I think I counted like, four hundred lousy days until we're out of here."

"Then do you go back to the US?" Sarie inquired.

"God, I don't even have a house in the US." The American replied. "Sometimes I feel like a gypsy with a fancy passport." She held her hand mirror and looked pleased with her appearance. "Dudu, I need you again. By the phone there's a list of people who are coming for the dinner party. Call the embassy and give the secretary the names."

"I met an American the other day." Sarie said proudly.

"Who on God's earth did you meet around here?" The diplomat's wife looked skeptical.

"He's a young man in the Peace Corps. Maybe you know him. Is it possible he's coming to your party?"

"Peace Corps?" The woman threw back her head and laughed. "I wouldn't even talk to one of those grungy people much less have one of them in my house." Sarie took the towel from around the woman's neck. She was surprised to hear an American talk like that about another out of country American.

"You see, Sarie, dear. Everybody wants to be part of the embassy. I don't know who they think they are, but they can't just walk in here and pretend they're one of us. That's just sick. You can rest assured; we don't entertain Peace Corps kids."

Sarie finished the diplomat wife's hair and packed up her tools. She was glad to be finished with that customer for a while. At first she felt sorry for the American. Then she started to find her amusing. By the time she left she was sick of her ramblings.

She passed Mark in his car on her way home. He honked at her and waved her over to the side of the street.

"Okay, beautiful. Do you want to get to know that American better? You know, that Peace Corps guy, Brian?"

Sarie couldn't help but feel a little excited to hear his name again.

"Sure, but why would I want to get interested in somebody like that? Don't those people just live in squalor and are poor?"

"Well, not this guy. I hear he comes from a nice family in the US. I think he's from Boston. He joined the Peace Corps to do some good deed for mankind."

"I knew I should have learned geography in school. Where is Boston anyway?"

"Come down to the disco tonight at 9:00, and let him tell you."

With that Mark drove off and left Sarie to wind herself back onto the street to get home.

She and Tess dressed up and met the guys at the disco that night. Sure enough, Brian was there, and it was clear that he liked her. She learned about his family, his education, and she even learned where Boston was on a map. It looked very far away from Swaziland.

They started to talk on the phone, long distance. Sarie felt badly about that, because she knew how expensive it must have been for him, and after all, Peace Corps people didn't have much money.

One afternoon she and Tess went to their favorite Portuguese restaurant for lunch.

"Tess, I'm going to break it off with Brian." Sarie looked down at her plate and pushed the curry around with her fork.

"Are you out of your mind?" Tess was shocked. She wished that Brian had been interested in her instead. "Sarie, you're a fool. What do you want in a husband? This guy is crazy about you. And, do I have to add…he's American?" She realized she had raised her voice and tried to whisper to her friend.

"So what is it about Brian that you don't like?"

"I don't know." Sarie said shrugging her shoulders. "I just can't figure it out, but I think he's not right for me."

Tess couldn't believe what she was hearing. The entire time Sarie and Brian had been seeing each other Tess wondered what it would be like to marry an American.

"Sarie, listen to me, dearie. Now you think about this." Tess moved her plate of curry to her side and leaned over the table to emphasize what she was about to say.

"This guy is WONDERFUL. He's handsome, kind, smart. And, I repeat, American. Can you imagine living in New York?" She looked Sarie in the eye, and Sarie tried to look down at her plate.

"Don't you watch American television? What about those women on those soap operas? They live in gorgeous houses and wear beautiful clothes. I think everybody in New York must be a zillionaire. She leaned back and put her hands on her cheeks in disgust. Then she leaned forward again. "Sarie, listen to me. Grab this handsome American guy and get on the plane to the US."

"Sure, I watch American television." Sarie said. "I watch those chat shows where everybody is married to somebody's brother, and then they all jump up from their chairs and start hitting each other. That's America, too. But that's not the problem, Tess."

They could hardly speak to each other for a minute. They both ate their curry and prawns in silence. Tess didn't know what to say at this point. She honestly didn't understand what Sarie's problem was with that cute American guy. She didn't even have a boyfriend, and Sarie was throwing away a promising one.

"You know, Tess." Sarie started talking again after she had a minute to think about it. "He's just so different from what I'm used to."

"And that's a bad thing?" Tess was incredulous.

"Well, it's not a good or bad thing. But I have always thought I would be with a man; well, more like my father. I know that sounds silly. But my papa is a real man. He's strong; he's steady. I know my parents have always been happy. My father was demanding, but we all knew where we stood. It just doesn't seem like American men have that...I don't know...maybe it's that bush spirit I'm used to."

She spoke softly now like she was starting to sort it all out in her own mind.

Tess was quiet, too. She knew what Sarie was talking about. She noticed at the bars and clubs that the South African guys seemed so in control of the place, and the American was much more reserved and quiet.

"You know, Sarie. Mark has really liked you for a long time." Tess realized she was planting a new idea in Sarie's mind. She hesitated to bring up a new guy at this point, but she knew her friend well enough to know that it was over between Sarie and Brian.

"Oh Tess, I don't know. Maybe I'll never get married. I can stand on my own two feet very well."

Sarie and Brian met for a final time. It was hard to tell Brian how she felt, because she could sense that he didn't understand. Finally, all she could tell him was "We are from other sides of the world, and I belong in Swaziland. When I drive around the mountains I know that this is my home, and my life is here. I can't even dream about what life is like in your world."

"Sarie, I love you. Believe me, you would be happy in the States. I know I can make you happy there if you just give me a chance." Brian was heartsick for her. Yes, he was lonely away from home for two years, but he really loved Sarie. He loved her spirit, her sparkling blue eyes and her independent attitude.

"It will never work." She replied softly. She kissed him long and held him close to her. Brian held her and tried to keep her with him.

"I will always love you Sarie. Even when I'm 10,000 miles away, I will still love you."

$$\Longrightarrow \Longleftarrow$$

Sarie was styling the hair of a European woman one day when she noticed Mark standing outside the salon.

"What is he doing out there?" She whispered to Tess.

"He doesn't want to come in, Sarie." Tess whispered from her station over to Sarie.

"Well, I'm too busy to see him right now. What does he want, anyway?"

"You know what he wants." Tess laughed.

The petite Belgian client smiled. Mark looked curious standing outside the glass partition.

"Go now. See that boy." She said. "He looks lovesick to me, and my hair can wait a few minutes. My taxi driver, Dumisani isn't coming for me for another half hour. It's okay, go, go on now."

Sarie excused herself for a moment and went to the front of the salon.

"Mark, what are you doing here?" Sarie put her hands on her hips and waited for his answer.

"Sarie, you know, love, I just have been thinking that we should know each other better."

"Look, Mark. I don't have time to talk right now. Can't we go for coffee later?" Then she looked at him quizzically. "What do you mean know each other better?"

"Tell you what, love. I will be around after work, and we'll talk some. How's that?" He gave her a quick kiss on the cheek, turned and left.

Sarie stood without moving for a second. He had left as quickly as he had come to the shop. She felt her cheek. Tess had been saying for quite some time that Mark liked her, but she hadn't paid much attention. It had taken some time for her to come to terms with breaking off the relationship with Brian. There were still times that she wondered if she had done the right thing. Brian was such a smart person, really smart, but he just lacked something she knew she wanted in a man. She wasn't even sure she knew what that was. Perhaps Mark had it.

Mark came over to the flat that night. He surprised her with a bouquet of Swazi roses that he had hidden behind his back. "You know I'm not usually one for giving flowers." He smiled "But you're as pretty as a rose." Sarie was amazed. She opened the door and surprised herself by giving him a quick kiss." Mark grabbed her in his arms and kissed her long and hard.

Tess reached around and took the flowers out of Sarie's hand. "Why don't I just put these in some water, and maybe it's time for me to run to the grocery."

=⇒ ⇐=

A year later Sarie planned her wedding to her old friend, Mark. Her family was very pleased with her decision. They knew all along that he was the right match for her. He had a good job, too. He was the lead supervisor at Swazican in Malkerns.

Sarie and Mark bought a comfortable home in the valley close to the canning factory. One weekend Helmut, Ingrid and Dinusha drove up from Big Bend. Helmut and Mark built a brick braai in the backyard. Sarie watched her father and future husband working side by side. It was a beautiful spring day, and there was a soft breeze in the air. She felt complete seeing them getting along so well. Mark was such a handsome man. He had the blue eyes of her brother and the strength of her father. While the men were in the back building the braai, Ingrid and Dinusha helped plant a garden of hydrangeas in the front yard and a vegetable garden in the back.

"Sarie, you've done a good job, dear." Ingrid took off her sun hat and smiled at her eldest daughter. Then she waved the heat away from her face and pushed the loose tendrils of hair behind her ears.

"Papa and I like Mark so much. He's a good solid man, and he is a God fearing, one, too, I should think."

Sarie just smiled back and thanked her mother. To tell the truth, she didn't think that Mark was very God fearing at all. She guessed that one of the things that impressed her was that he didn't seem afraid of anything alive, dead, on earth or in the Heavens. She watched him lifting the bricks while Papa laid the mortar.

The wedding was a casual affair. Sarie never liked formality. She wore a long floral cotton dress and flowers in her hair. All of their friends and family came for the big braai. Katie flew up from Stellenbosch, and her brothers drove from Durban and Pretoria, South Africa. It was such a joyous festival. There was live music and dancing and so much food and drink that all the guests were totally satisfied. A lot of their friends camped out at their house for the next three days. The Castle Beer was delivered and the bottles of South African wine were spread out across a long table. Helmut proudly cooked steaks and boerewors. He reminded anybody who would listen, that he had built the brick braai himself. Ingrid brought out the wedding cake that a friend had baked. Then, as a special treat, she carried out a mammoth platter of homemade koeksisters. Katie danced with several of the young men at the party, but it was clear to Sarie that her little sister had moved on with her life. Katie was so beautiful and sophisticated. Sarie knew that Katie would never be comfortable again in Swaziland after living at the Cape. Tess danced, too. She enjoyed sampling every type of wine at the party. She pulled Sarie aside and hugged her friend. "Well, my old married girlfriend. You made a great choice in a man. I always knew he was the right one for you. And that's not all…." Finally, she fell asleep on Sarie's sofa.

It took them hours to clean up the mess after everybody went home. "My little Sarie, Papa and I have to go back to Big Bend, and it's a long drive. Will you be okay with the rest of this?" Ingrid hugged her oldest daughter, and she felt so warm and motherly to her.

"Oh Mama, I'm so very happy, and the rest of this can wait until the maid comes in the morning. Drive carefully, and thank you so much for everything." She hugged Ingrid and kissed her cheek.

"Let God run your house, and everything will be right for you." Ingrid reminded her. With that Ingrid, Dinusha and Helmut got into their 4-wheel drive utility vehicle and sped down the dirt road outside Sarie's house. She waved to them as far as she could see the car through the dust. Then she walked back to the house. She kept thinking about what Tess had said in her drunken state.

A month later she got home from work later than usual. Mark was standing by the gate in front of the house. Their two oversized and imposing dogs stood next to him.

"Baby, I've been so worried about you. Where have you been, girl? Why didn't you call and tell me you would be so late tonight?"

"What's the matter with you?" Sarie asked. "It's not that late. I just had a customer come into the salon at the last minute. What's the big deal with that?"

"Ah, it's nothing, love." He put his arm around her neck and they walked into the house together. Once inside he bolted the door behind them.

"I heard talk at the plant that there's some political trouble. The labor people are causing unrest."

Sarie felt so protected at that moment. She knew Mark loved her, and his concern confirmed that.

That night when they went to bed Mark loaded the rifle and put it along side of the bed. He put a small pistol under his pillow. He kissed her goodnight and stroked his hands along her body.

She rolled over and smiled. When Tess was drunk at the wedding party she had told Sarie that Brian was now a Ph.D student in engineering at Purdue University. She didn't even know where that was, but she knew it wasn't as though it was in New York or any famous place. Here she had a husband who would protect her and love her. How could marriage be any better than that?

Chapter 3 – Elizabeth

Rolilahla broke down the door in a jealous drunken rage and waved his finger into the face of the new mother. His wife, Bawinde, lay on the kraal mat on the floor holding her infant daughter in her arms. Her head was propped up with rolled blankets, and the baby was wrapped in a faded towel.

"That is not my child." Rolilahla screamed at her.

"How can you say that?" Bawinde whispered through her weeping. "This is your baby daughter. See how beautiful she is. Come, please, look at her."

"She doesn't look like me. I know you have cheated on me." He continued his tirade. "You will never be forgiven for what you have done."

"I have done nothing. You must know that you are the only man I have been with." She cradled the baby who was starting to cry and held her breast for the newborn to suckle. "Please, you are frightening our daughter."

"That is not my child. She looks nothing like me."

"How do you know? She is just born and only looks like an innocent baby." The mother started to yell, and she held the baby closer to her.

"She is not innocent. She is of your body. I will name her 'bastard child.' She must pay for your unfaithfulness."

"No, you cannot do that." The young mother screamed. She gripped her stomach in excruciating pain and nearly fainted.

"That is her name, and I will register it with the chief. It will be your punishment forever."

Rolilahla ran out of the hut leaving the new mother and tiny daughter both crying. Bawinde swayed, the baby in her arms, while she nursed the new life with her thin breast.

"There, there, don't cry little one. You are special, and no one will say otherwise. I will name you Elizabeth. You are Elizabeth named for the Queen of England who rules Swaziland with the paramount chief, our king, King Sobhuza II."

And so Elizabeth was born into the world and the tiny Kingdom of Swaziland.

As soon as Bawinde was strong enough, she took Elizabeth to the Roman Catholic Church in Manzini to have her baptized. She was adamant that in the eyes of God this child would be known as Elizabeth. No mortal in a poor dirty village could be more important than God, and she would make sure everyone knew it.

Elizabeth was very young when her mother divorced Rolilahla. Bawinde could not tolerate the abuse, beatings and drunkenness any longer. Divorce was rare in the kingdom. She paid a heavy toll for her independence. Not only was it against the church to have a legal divorce, but it was against Swazi culture as well. Women's needs were not important, and if there was discord in the marriage the husband had the legal right to walk away or take another wife. After all, legal authority came from the chiefs, and they were all men. The term adultery applied simply to women having sex outside the marriage. Men could have relationships with any woman other than another man's wife.

Elizabeth had an older brother, Thomas, and someday he would serve as her guardian. A Swazi woman was always under the protection, or some would say dominance, of a male. Elizabeth's father wanted nothing to do with her.

When Elizabeth turned five years old Bawinde went to Rolilahla and chided him into paying for her education. There has never been a policy in Swaziland for free public education. Bawinde put on her best tshweshwe and wrapped her hair in a colorful scarf. She would not appear to beg him for anything. She had to be strong and independent. Taking care of his children had nothing to do with asking for charity. She felt it was his responsibility.

"Whether you believe Elizabeth is your blood is not important." She had grown strong in her resolve to take care of her daughter. "This child needs to go to school. If you don't pay her school fees the whole village will know that you are a bad father."

"I don't care what anyone thinks of that." He sat at the table across from her and leaned back in his straight wooden chair. "You are the one who left me. You want to do everything. You take care of her. It is hard enough that I must educate our true son Thomas. He is my obligation."

Bawinde looked straight at him. She was no longer afraid of the man who had terrorized her years earlier. "Everyone will know that you are poor."

"How dare you!" He rose to his feet, and the chair fell over behind him. He looked as if he would strangle her. "You know that is not true. I have a good job, and everyone in the village knows I am respected."

She was not about to back down now though she could feel the blood racing through her heart. She swallowed her rage and spoke with calm authority.

"Yes, you can tell the other men whatever you like, but when your daughter is shoeless and can't read they will draw their own conclusions." She breathed slowly so that her voice wouldn't tremble. She had the upper hand, and she used it cleverly to her advantage.

"Tell them what you like. Brag about yourself. But they will know that any man who doesn't pay for his family must be hiding his poverty."

$$\Longrightarrow \Longleftarrow$$

Elizabeth's mother was named Bawinde, which meant she was a winner. She won the fight, and Elizabeth did attend school. Elizabeth was a remarkable student, who grew to be a beautiful cheerful girl with a ready smile and high cheekbones. Bawinde was an excellent seamstress, and Elizabeth always wore stylish dresses. No one would diminish her daughter. She did whatever she could to give Elizabeth a future that would belie her meager circumstances.

They lived in Ezulwini, a tourist mecca in the valley between Mbabane, the capital of Swaziland and Manzini, the industrial city. During the years of apartheid the valley was a playground for wealthy white South Africans, or Afrikaners, who could not gamble in their own country. There were posh hotels complete with golf courses and casinos. Employment was not difficult to find.

Bawinde was an outcast as a divorcee in the village; though she worked hard, she was never able to overcome her status. Elizabeth and her brother, Thomas, attended school, but Bawinde had no extra money from her husband. He made sure that Bawinde suffered for the embarrassment he believed she caused him. She took a job as a maid for a South African family in the valley who required her to keep residence there during the week. Elizabeth and Thomas stayed with their gogo, Bawinde's mother, so that they could walk to school. On the weekends Bawinde taught Elizabeth how to embroider, a skill that she hoped would set Elizabeth apart from ordinary village girls. Thomas played soccer at school and was an average student. He was well liked, but he was never as bright as his younger sister. Elizabeth adored Thomas. He was her protector, and he took her everywhere with him.

Elizabeth was ten years old when King Sobhuza's royal decree ravaged the schools and villages. This horrific event occurred just after Swaziland gained its independence from Great Britain in 1968. King Sobhuza II ordered a decree that the Swazi children should open up their ears to their culture and listen to their king. The king demanded that his subjects recognize him as their supreme ruler. He was no longer the paramount chief. Now he was their monarch. The decree was taken literally by the chiefs. The chiefs were loyal to the crown, but moreover, they served Sobhuza out of fear as well as respect. Soldiers throughout the country were ordered to slash large holes in all of the Swazi children's earlobes. They broke into Elizabeth's classroom pushing her teacher out of their way. The children scattered in terror. Her teacher pounded one soldier on his back, but he threw her violently against the floor. It was a simple routine. One soldier held a child down while another soldier took a long rusty knife and carved a hole into each of the child's earlobes. Then that soldier pushed a dirty stick through the earlobe to keep open the piercing. Elizabeth screamed and attempted to jump out the window of the classroom. A soldier grabbed her leg and dragged her back. The task was accomplished. Elizabeth was left sobbing and bleeding on the floor.

Her head was throbbing, and her face was streaked with dust, tears and blood. She ran home and into the arms of her gogo. Fortunately, it was Friday. Bawinde came home for the weekend. When she saw what had happened to her children she was furious. She was horrified at the abuse and control of children by the hands of the government.

"Nobody will hurt my children." Bawinde said in anger as she pulled the sticks out of Elizabeth's earlobes.

"Bawinde, you mustn't do this." Gogo whispered quietly. "You could create terrible trouble with the chief, even the royal government could come down on us for this." She pulled Bawinde aside and held her by the shoulders. "Don't do anything to bring trouble to this house. I beg you. Already people think you act too proud for your circumstances. You know how jealous people become. They could bring the muti into this house." She was serious and frightened. She knew the way their culture treated people like her daughter. She had heard of people who had died from being given weevil tablets, or rat poison. Poison was such simple muti, or witchcraft. "Please, Bawinde. Be careful of the things you do and say in the village."

"I will not let anyone harm my child. I don't care who it is. This is not right." She pulled the last stick out of Elizabeth's earlobe. Elizabeth shrieked and pulled back in pain.

"Stop that, Elizabeth." Bawinde ordered. "Let me finish. Now you wash your face, and don't talk about this with anyone."

Elizabeth's earlobes never closed properly, but she always credited her mother with the fact that they weren't as damaged as the other children in her generation.

Elizabeth came home from school one day to find her mother seated with Gogo. It was Wednesday, and her mother should have been at the Afrikaner's house. The two women were speaking softly and drinking bush tea. "Elizabeth, where is your brother? I need to talk to both of you. It is important."

"He's playing soccer after school today." Elizabeth was now twelve and took pride in her academics. Her teacher felt she was one of the smartest students she had ever taught and frequently sent letters home to Bawinde complimenting her daughter. Elizabeth could speak, read and write in English as well as siSwati.

"Why are you here today, Mama? You never come home in the middle of the week." She bent over and kissed her mother. "Is something wrong?"

"Elizabeth, this is something I have to talk to you and Thomas about together. It will affect all of us. When will he get home?" Bawinde got up and looked out the door to see if he was walking down the path.

Elizabeth was curious; she tried to get more information out of her mother. "He will come soon, but what is going on here?"

"Okay, so I will tell you since you will not be satisfied until you know the truth." She stood up and offered Elizabeth a chair at the table. Gogo poured her a cup of tea.

"Gogo, please, I don't really like bush tea."

"Be quiet. Drink your tea. Now, you listen quietly to your mother." Gogo didn't take nonsense or backtalk from children.

Bawinde continued by taking Elizabeth's hand in hers across the small wooden table.

"Your daddy is dead." She said the words softly as though they would have meaning to Elizabeth. The news didn't move Elizabeth. Rolilahla had never cared for her the way a father should. It was difficult to feel any emotion other than surprise.

"Dead? How could he be dead? I never heard that he was sick. Did he have an accident?"

Elizabeth was more curious than concerned.

"Your father went to the low veldt with friends last week." Bawinde began to relate the story to Elizabeth.

"Tell her the truth." Gogo said. "Don't hold back. She may as well know everything now. Maybe if she hears more about her father she won't make the same mistakes you have made."

"Please, Mama." Bawinde turned and gave her mother a stern look. "Someone has died. Don't speak cross about him now. He was still the father of my children."

"So, Elizabeth" she continued. "Your father went to the low veldt in the south, because it is marula season." Bawinde stood up. She felt disgusted having to tell the story of his death. Here was a man who was a parent. He had a responsible job. Why did he have to drink the marula like some teenage boy?

The marula fruit is well known to have fermenting properties. It grows on large trees and is the size of a small orange. In the summer when it ripens the fruit falls from the trees, and local people concoct a beer from it. It is not our traditional mealy beer. They celebrate for days drinking the liquor it produces. It is well known that animals enjoy the fruit as well. In the bush veldt monkeys bite it and toss the remains out of the trees. The fruit then ferments in ponds and lakes. The elephants drink from those watering holes and become intoxicated from it. A staggering elephant is a dangerous sight in the bush.

"Your father drank the marula and became ill. They tell me that he became sick very quickly. He was taken to the hospital, but his cholera was too advanced for their medicine, and he died."

"Mama," Elizabeth looked skeptical. This all sounded very strange. "How does marula kill someone? That is not a poisonous fruit. I don't believe this."

"They said that the marula was brewed with water, and the doctors say the water was contaminated. It was not only your father who was infected. There were other people who developed cholera and died as well."

"Now, doesn't that tell you how childish that man was?" Gogo added her thoughts and advice on the subject. At the time Elizabeth thought Gogo was cruel to hurt her mother any further by condemning him. Later in life she would be forced to respect the teachings of her gogo. "This is not the first year that people have died from the cholera in the low veldt. It is not the second or the tenth year. Every year people drink the marula liquor, and some of them die from bad water that brews with it in the pot. I have no pity for him. I have no pity at all." Gogo was a bent over old woman who was wise from her years of life and decades of hardship. "I warned your mother many years ago about that man. The heart has no common sense." She looked Elizabeth directly in the eye and squinted demonstrating a strong emphasis of sincerity. "Do not listen to your heart little one. You have been named for a queen." She pointed to her head and then her breast. "Use your brain and not your heart to do your thinking." Gogo moved to a spot in a dark corner of the room and let Bawinde finish her story.

Bawinde sat close to Elizabeth and hugged her daughter. "I know you never felt a closeness to your father, but there are many problems that will come to us because of his death. Now that he is dead I don't know where we will get the money for you to continue in school."

Elizabeth was horrified. She loved school. It was the only time in her childhood when she escaped poverty. When she was at school she could learn about the world outside of her little village. She would read history, geography, and literature, then close her eyes and try to imagine herself in those places.   She couldn't believe that the only satisfying part of her life would come to an end. She was only 12 years old, and she felt that her life was finished.

"Please, Mama. Tell me that I can go to school. Maybe Papa's family will help us."

"I'm sorry, my child. I talked with them earlier today, and they said that they will only educate your brother."

"See." Gogo was on her feet again. "See, I told you they are evil people. They know that it is our culture for the father's family to take care of his wife and children if he dies. They are bad Swazis. They are dogs to abandon their granddaughter."

"Mama, please." Bawinde attempted to calm her mother. "You must stay out of this now. You know I am divorced, so they have no obligation to me. As for Elizabeth, they have never accepted her. There is nothing I can do about that anymore."

"I will never love them." Elizabeth whispered quietly. "But why are they taking Thomas from us?"

"He is the son, and they regard him as their blood. Do not worry. We will see him on the weekends." Bawinde patted Elizabeth on the leg, stood up and sighed. Life was hard, but it was definitely going to be much harder now. She put off telling Elizabeth the rest of the dilemma for a few more days.

Finally, Bawinde confronted her daughter. Elizabeth would not only leave school, but she would have to go to work as well. At twelve years old Elizabeth accompanied her mother to the house of the South African family who agreed to employ both of them. Bawinde told Elizabeth that Madam was very generous to hire her. She even suggested that if Elizabeth could save some money working for the belumbi, the white woman, she might get to go back to school.

This dream never came true, and Elizabeth's future was altered forever.

≕ ≕

Her education was abandoned, and all her friendships came to an end. She was expected to work along side of her mother, so it became her job to iron the napkins. To most people this wouldn't seem to be such a terrible job, but the South African family used an abundance of cotton cloth napkins. Every day there was a new pile of just washed, wrinkled napkins. Every napkin she ironed represented the worst aspect of Elizabeth's life. She would be doomed to this kind of mindless activity and would never learn anything academic again. In the afternoons she stood at the ironing board and looked out the window of the laundry room. She tried to remember everything her teachers had taught her and imagined all the places they had talked about in school. Surely, there had to be more to life than this, but there were only napkins in the basket to look forward to the next day and every day after that.

On the weekends Elizabeth and her mother went home to Ezulwini to stay with her mother's family and Gogo. Elizabeth spent every weekday looking forward to that time, because it was her chance to be a child again. Sometimes she was able to see Thomas, but his grandparents made it increasingly difficult for them to be together. For two days she would shut out the ironing job that lay waiting for her Monday morning. She walked up the red clay road to the top of the hill where the mission school stood and looked through the dingy windows into the empty classroom. The sight and smell of the school brought back memories of happiness and security. She imagined herself sitting once again in the third row of the classroom. There were books to read about a world she would never see. Someday she would marry a good man from a better family. He would take care of her, and together they would build a life where her children would never suffer as she had. She walked back to Gogo's house and ate dinner with her mother. "Yes," she thought, "I will never be reduced to such poverty as this. I will marry the right man."

= =

The cloth napkins eventually faded, became threadbare and were replaced, but Elizabeth and her mother remained. She kept working for the white family while she dreamed of her future with children, a house and a wonderful husband.

Elizabeth was fifteen years old when Bawinde reminded her that the date of the annual Reed Dance was approaching. The annual Umhlanga Reed Dance is one of the most important festivals in the kingdom. This is the celebration where the maidens in the country pay homage to the queen mother, the Ndlovukati, or she-elephant. The queen mother co-rules Swaziland along side of her son, the king, the Ngwenyama, or the lion. In truth, the Queen Mother is actually regarded as the Mother of the Nation and its people.

The Umhlanga is held annually at the end of August or the first part of September. Every year the date is slightly different, because it is determined by the position of the stars. All the adolescent virginal maidens in the kingdom gather special reeds and present them ceremoniously to the queen mother. The reeds have to be a special variety, usually the red bushwillow, and they are used to repair the royal kraal. Thousands of young maidens gather singing and dancing for days at Ludzidzini, the royal kraal. They dance for the queen mother and the king. The king often selects a new wife from the thousands of dancing girls.

"Mama, I don't want to go to the Reed Dance. I can't believe I have to parade like that in the valley with thousands of girls."

"Elizabeth, you shouldn't talk like that. This is an important part of your heritage and culture. Why, if you don't dance for the king everyone will think you have something to hide. They will wonder if you are not a virgin."

"Mama, I don't have any babies. So anyone who is interested will know I'm a virgin. Why do I have to dance bare breasted for the world to see me?"

Gogo laughed with an open mouth that showed off her missing teeth. Then she leaned over the supper table. "I remember when I danced the Reed Dance. It was a warm sunny day. I felt like I could be a princess. I made my skirt myself." She gazed up at the thatched roof and smiled. It was clear to Elizabeth and her mother that Gogo was filled with memories they couldn't share. "Every girl in this country should celebrate our culture and participate in the dance. This is the way we show our respect to the Queen Mother. The rest of your life you will remember the excitement of that day."

"I remember when I danced the Reed Dance." Bawinde sat back and reflected on her past. It was rare for Bawinde to pause and honor her memories. "I felt so proud to be a Swazi. It is a time that will live in my heart forever. Isn't it amazing that you will dance for the same king that I danced for so many years ago?"

"Can you believe it? I, too, danced for the great King Sobhuza. In my day he was so young and handsome." Gogo smiled and sighed. " Such a strong man with so much power. God has blessed us with a ruler who has led us bravely through so many years of struggle."

"That is just another reason why I don't want to go to the Reed Dance." Elizabeth remarked. "The king is a very old man. I can hardly believe that he will still take another wife, and who would want to be married to such an old wrinkled man? I would hate to be chosen as a bride. He already has so many wives. I heard that no one even knows how many there are in his different palaces. Some people say he has 100 wives. He probably doesn't even know some of these women. Who sleeps with such an old man as that?" Elizabeth spoke with the carefree confidence of youth.

Bawinde was usually patient with her independent daughter, but this was blasphemy. She was furious that Elizabeth would speak about their king in that manner. She drew her hand back and slapped Elizabeth across the face.

"You must never speak against your king and country like that. It is wrong and unSwazi to do that. I won't hear you talk like this anymore. You will dance in the Reed Dance and do what you are told!"

Elizabeth held her stinging cheek and said nothing. She would have to obey. Over the next month she picked and dried special grass in long lengths. Then she carefully wove her Umhlanga costume. Her skirt had to be designed with specific details. It was crafted from woven grass. It hung from her hips but rested just above her thighs. Nothing was worn underneath. The buttocks had to show beneath the scarlet pompoms that hung from the tiny skirt. The definition of a virgin in Swazi culture is a woman who has not conceived a baby. So the breasts were left bare to signify that the girl was still a virgin. The bare buttocks were shown so that anyone could see that the girl was amply endowed. The red pompoms drew attention to that part of her body. Girls wore wool streamers hanging from their skirts. The different colors signified whether or not they were already betrothed. Only the royal maidens were allowed to wear red feathers in their hair. The costume was complete with a handmade necklace and unique ankle bracelets. The ankle bracelets consisted of seeds that were threaded on a heavy string.

These created a wonderful rhythmic sound when the maidens danced barefooted.

Elizabeth memorized the special songs of praise that she was required to sing for the event. She gathered all her reeds making sure that none of them ever snapped or broke. Everyone knew that if a maiden broke one of the reeds she was carrying it would prove that she was not pure and that she was only pretending to be a virgin. The elderly women would then beat the girl and send her home.

The Umhlanga Reed Dance was a huge success. Elizabeth discovered that she enjoyed the comradery of being with other girls her age. Her costume was constructed perfectly, and she sang with pride presenting her reeds to the Ndlovukati. It was far more amazing than she had expected. Thousands of maidens presented themselves to the king's wives, and the royal children greeted the singers. The Queen Mother that year was not the king's true mother. King Sobhuza's natural mother had died many years earlier. This Queen Mother was his mother's sister, his aunt. The Ndlovukati sat on a velvet throne near her nephew, the king. The dancing girls could not appreciate the difficult political decision to place the King's aunt on the throne. Until King Sobhuza's reign the king had always died before his mother, the Queen Mother. During King Sobhuza's 62-year reign five different women would be appointed to the position of Queen Mother.

It was a humid summer with an unrelenting sun, but Elizabeth didn't notice the weather. She was proud to be a Swazi that day. The king was indeed, a very old man. Some people said later that he ruled for more years than Queen Victoria had ruled Great Britain. Historians remarked that King Sobhuza II was one of the longest ruling monarchs in modern history of the world. He certainly appeared regal as he sat erect in front of his subjects. When he died several years later in 1982 the royal council estimated that he had possibly 100 wives and several hundred children.

The Umhlanga Reed Dance came to an end, and Elizabeth returned home to her mother and Gogo. She hung up her skirt and ankle bracelets on a protruding stick that was embedded in the wall. The Reed Dance turned out to be another example of everything she was missing in the outside world. So many of the other girls were finishing school; they were discussing parties, gossiping about boyfriends, planning their graduations. As she sat down on her mat to go to sleep she gazed back at the costume. She hummed to herself one of the songs of praise, blew out the candle and fell asleep.

$$\Longrightarrow \Longleftarrow$$

By Monday morning Elizabeth was back at her domestic job with her mother. They took the rickety bus to the white South African family's house and proceeded with their usual chores. Elizabeth was already planning her weekend. The hours and days in front of her seemed endless and mindless.

She met her future husband two years later during one of those weekends home to Ezulwini. She was walking down a dirt road to the market when she heard him whistling behind her. She had to shop for the mealy meal and milk for supper. That was her favorite way to eat mealy meal. She loved it when Gogo boiled the mealy meal to a thick paste. It would get so thick that she had to use a sturdy wooden spoon to stir it. Even with that the mixture would stick to the bottom of the pan. At the end Gogo would stir in emasi milk. The emasi, sour milk, added such a creamy texture and tart flavor. After all, mealy meal was just mashed white corn, so it required extra flavor. Sometimes Gogo would cook beef or chicken if they could get it. Then she would serve the mealy meal with thick meat gravy. The whistling continued, and Elizabeth was annoyed that someone was interrupting her thoughts.

"Why are you singing?" she asked. As she whirled around she saw a handsome colored Swazi standing in front of her. She had never seen him before and was surprised by his appearance. He was, indeed, a colored man. He had the white man's blood in him leaving his skin the color of cinnamon. He could not be considered a true black African. Indeed, his skin was much lighter than hers. He was tall with very broad shoulders. He had a different look from all the other boys in her village.

"Why not sing? But, pretty lady. You don't hear that I'm whistling?" He laughed at her, and she turned away embarrassed. She didn't want him to see that she was impressed with him. "So where are you off to this fine sunny morning? Do you have church? Are you shopping? I can walk with you and carry things."

"You are too silly." Elizabeth still looked away from his face. She didn't want to make any eye contact with him. "I went to church this morning. Now I am going to the market, and I can take care of myself."

James liked the spunk of this girl. She reminded him of his own mother. He pursued the conversation and insisted on walking her to the store. Then he walked her home from the store. The next weekend he was there again ready to walk her anywhere she wanted to go.

Elizabeth felt complimented to have his attention. She asked all around the village for information about James. The old women in the village were the ones who knew everything about everybody. They would sit outside their huts and gossip while they prepared the meals.

"That boy James," one of them said as she spread her long skirt in front of her knees. "He has a Swazi mother and a white father."

"The father is Dutch." Another one remarked. "James lives farther down in the valley, but he comes here to see his mother's family. I hear he is close to his gogo."

"Never trust a Dutch man." Another old woman wagged her ancient finger at Elizabeth. "You must stay away from someone like that."

"Those white people think they are better than we are. They pretend to be nice, but they are not for us."

"Only a fool lets a colored man like that into her heart." The old woman held onto a stick and slowly rose to her feet. She looked Elizabeth straight in the eye. "Now you listen to me. This man can only bring you trouble. He is half white, and he will think less of you."

"That is the problem with you, Elizabeth." The first woman was still sitting on a low stool by her doorway. "You are proud like your mother. If you are not careful you will end up like that. She thought she was clever, and now she has nothing."

These women were considered to be a wise and elderly group in the village, but their words injured Elizabeth. She loved her mother, and she hated it when people accused her mother of having false pride. She wondered if she was falling in love with James.

On the weekdays she and Bawinde worked for the South Africans, but as the weekend approached Elizabeth was anxious to get home to see if James had come to visit his gogo in the village. There had been weekends when he didn't come around, but now he was staying more often. It was common knowledge throughout the village that he was infatuated with Elizabeth.

Elizabeth's mother was enraged. She wished her daughter would never marry anyone. What kind of life did marriage provide a woman except to be owned by a man? Once a woman was married her husband had total control of everything she did and all the things she had.

Swazi law prohibited a woman from having a bank account or passport without the consent of her husband. She could never have total claim to any property. Her mother shook her head in disgust. This colored man had such arrogance; how could Elizabeth expect to be happy? She was sitting outside of the little mud house shucking corn when Elizabeth strolled out in a floral print blue dress and black shoes.

"Where are you going?" Bawinde demanded. "I am telling you now that he is wrong for you!"

Elizabeth didn't want to argue with her mother, but at that moment she realized she was in love with James. She would defend him to her mother and all the other women in the village; it must be love. She kept walking and heard her mother behind her.

"You come back here. I forbid you to see that man." Her mother started chasing her down the path.

Elizabeth ran and could feel her mother behind her. Bawinde had a long thin stick and waved it to catch Elizabeth and beat some sense into her. At one point Elizabeth screamed as it whipped her in the back of her legs. The switch left a permanent scar on the calf of her leg.

"You will never make me leave him. I know my heart." Elizabeth cried as she kept running in the direction of his house.

James saw her coming and grabbed her up in his arms. "Elizabeth, my love. No one can hurt you now. I love you, and you are mine."

As he held her Elizabeth could feel her heart pounding against his chest. She felt protected and loved. That night she crept quietly back to her kraal. She lay down on her mat without making a sound, but she kept remembering him saying 'you are mine.' What did he mean by that?

She married James against everyone's advice. She knew they were all wrong. James had a good job and earned a decent income. He was the head chef for the finest casino hotel in the country. Elizabeth worked for a new South African family and stayed with them during the week. When she became pregnant she continued to work full time for them. She gave birth to a healthy son, Peter, and she continued to work. She often cleaned their house with Peter strapped to her back. Together James and Elizabeth were able to have the things they needed and even saved money to build a new house.

Peter was still a baby when Bawinde died suddenly. Elizabeth felt in her heart that her mother was poisoned by the muti. She knew that there were people who were jealous of her mother, and jealousy in Swaziland was a dangerous situation. Muti was powerful witchcraft and held in great respect. Bawinde came to Elizabeth's house and was visibly sick.

"Elizabeth" She said weakly at the door. "I am sick. Oh my God, I think I am going to die. Yesterday I was well, and today I will die. Someone has put the muti on me. Maybe she was jealous of me. I don't know. But, Elizabeth, please help me. Oh God, help me."

Elizabeth rushed to the door and helped her mother into the candlelit room. She gently laid the shaking woman down on a mat on the floor. Elizabeth didn't hate her mother for the things she had said about James. James was a good husband and provider, and that was enough proof Bawinde was wrong. Peter cried in another part of the room while she comforted her mother.

"Mama," Elizabeth began to cry. "You cannot die. Here, you can stay with me. Please, you must take this water and rest."

She held her mother's head, but it fell limp in her arms. Elizabeth broke out in a loud shriek.

"Oh Mommy, I love you. I do forgive you. I do understand." She fell onto the dead woman's breast and wept.

$$\Rightarrow \Leftarrow$$

Peter grew and Elizabeth kept working for the South African family. When he was about four years old she left him in James' care during the week. It was not appropriate for him to stay around the white people's house while she worked. Besides, it was time for him to start school. With great pride she enrolled him in the local Catholic mission school. Elizabeth was satisfied that she could raise him in the faith that she had loved and thought she understood. Peter had new clothes and just the right shoes. He carried primary books and took a bus to school.

Elizabeth wasn't feeling well. She attempted to complete her work, but she was so tired and nauseated she had to rest in the afternoon. Finally she had to admit to Madam that she was pregnant. The South African belumbi was furious. How could Elizabeth do this to her? Elizabeth obligingly offered to have her cousin, Dudu, take her place temporarily.

"Please, Madam," she begged. "I need to take some time now, because I am too sick. But I know from having Peter that I will feel better in two months." She continued uninterrupted. "My cousin, Duduzile, will work for you now, and I promise I will be back."

She walked three miles to the bus stop. After a bumpy, steamy bus ride she walked another two miles down a tree lined dirt path to her home. She felt comfort seeing the candles glowing in the windows, because she knew James was home waiting for her. Duduzile would continue her work for now, and everything would be all right.

The next week there was a stir in the village. Madam drove up the red clay road to her house. She got out of her car and slammed the door. "Elizabeth" she called in a tone of authority. "Where are you? I need you out here right now."

Local villagers started gathering to investigate the commotion. It was rare for any white person to come to the area.

Elizabeth emerged from the house and walked over to the car.

"You have the maid's uniform, and I want it back. Did you think you could steal it from me?"

"No, of course not, Madam." Elizabeth said looking down at the ground. This was such an odd encounter. "I told you I would come back in two months."

"Well, you are not welcome back. Your cousin, Dudu, serves me well now, and I don't want any more disruption in my household."

Elizabeth felt sick as a wave of nausea poured over her, but she wouldn't give Madam the satisfaction of her misery. She walked slowly, very slowly, to her house and brought out the blue uniform. It was washed, pressed and hanging on a hanger.

"Elizabeth, you will find other work in the future, but I need a maid now, and you are not able to fill that position. Good luck to your family."

With that the white woman drove straight backwards out of the little driveway leaving a fog of red dust behind her.

<hr>

Angela was born six months later, a healthy baby girl. Everybody in the village said she looked like Elizabeth. But it was her third child Mondi, born five years later, who resembled her spirit and brains.

Elizabeth was known in the area as an excellent maid who was honest and hardworking. The only housework she begrudged was ironing napkins. In her village she had a reputation for being smart and capable. Her chief asked her to be a spokeswoman for the people in the village.

She adamantly declined the offer. "I cannot do that." She replied in horror. "People don't like to be told what to do. If I say something they don't want to hear, they could put the muti on me. Look what happened to my mother."

$$=\!\!\!= \quad =\!\!\!=$$

Over time she worked for a British family who resided in the country for just a year. They treated her with respect and paid her well. With her money she sent Peter and Angela to school. They wore the proper clothes and had the necessary books and pencils in their backpacks every day. James reveled in his position at the hotel. His ego swelled as he became acquainted with some of the most influential people in the kingdom. At night he and Elizabeth continued their plans to build their new house. It was to have three bedrooms, a dining room, living room and a kitchen that was inside the house. The hand drawn papers were spread out on the dining room table, and they examined them carefully by candlelight on the weekends.

The British family left, and Elizabeth never heard from them again. She knew this was the order of life, but it was painful. She also knew that good employers were rare and wondered what she would do for employment.

James contacted other restaurant owners in Ezulwini and found a new job for Elizabeth. She took a position in the kitchen of an elite German restaurant where she prepared salads and vegetables. The restaurant was popular with an excellent reputation. It was an elegant gathering place for diplomats, tourists and royalty.

The work in the kitchen went well for her. In fact, it went so well that the German owner, Karl Ruskin, called her into his office with a new proposition.

"Elizabeth, I have noticed that you are working very hard." He spoke in English with a deep German accent. Sometimes it was difficult for her to grasp everything that he said.

"So, I want to make an offer to you. Here is the idea." As he leaned back into his chair she heard it creak under his weight. "My wife needs a maid. Our maid has left, and we have no one at the house to help her at this time. How does that sound to you?"

Elizabeth was speechless. She had no idea he was planning a new job for her. She quickly thought about it and agreed. She was getting tired of working at the restaurant with all the other people. Everyone gossiped, and that was something she avoided. She always made it a policy to avoid situations where anyone could say something against her. Life was hard enough without having others interfere in her business. Anyone could inflict the muti on her at any given time. She knew to be careful, to take care of herself and her family, so that no person or spirit was angered.

"Of course, I would be happy to be your wife's maid." She responded in a cheerful voice. She didn't feel that she could question why their original maid had left the job. Work was difficult to find and leaving a job was unusual. "I have worked as a maid many times. I know well how to take care of a house."

Elizabeth showed up for work early on the first Monday of the new month. She had never met Karl Ruskin's wife. She rang the doorbell over and over, but there was no response. Elizabeth was about to leave when she heard a soft voice on the other side of the door.

"I'm coming. I'm coming. Don't go away." The Madam opened the door with a cigarette in her hand. She was dressed in a white negligee and made no attempt to cover herself. "Are you the new maid? Oh, you must be Elizabeth. Come in, come in." She waved her cigarette in a welcoming gesture. "My husband told me you were going to come."

Elizabeth didn't know what she should say. It was clear the woman was not prepared to have guests or even a maid for a visitor.

"Excuse my appearance this morning. After you're here a while you'll understand why I don't just jump out of bed at the crack of dawn." She started to walk back to the kitchen and motioned for Elizabeth to follow her. "Here is the kitchen. My husband told me that you are excellent in a kitchen. That is absolutely essential for us. After working all day in a restaurant the last thing he wants to do is cook, and I can tell you right now. I'm no cook." She blew the cigarette smoke into the air. "Believe me, he didn't marry me for my domestic abilities. If you know what I mean."

Elizabeth wasn't sure she had heard all of that correctly. This woman had a strong accent, too, just like her German husband. She certainly seemed different from other people Elizabeth had worked for over the years. She kept an open mind in the hopes that they would get along with each other. At least Madam Ruskin seemed to be a friendly sort of person.

The German madam, Greta, was young and attractive. Her blond hair flowed in waves past her ivory shoulders. She had striking blue eyes, just like the Afrikaners, but her smile was softer. She was tall and thin and moved like a graceful bird through the house. Greta met her husband, Karl, in Frankfurt, Germany a couple of years earlier. He was home on vacation and was regaling everyone at a party with his stories of life in southern Africa. Greta was at the party, too. Initially she cast Karl off as merely an old bachelor. She was so much younger, and he looked old enough to be her father. As he continued with his stories she was drawn to Karl's life of adventure. It all seemed so exciting, unusual, and amazing. He stood in the host's living room bragging about sleeping alone under the stars with wild animals surrounding him in the bush. He shocked the guests when he recounted his experience with a curious hyena that came too close to his campfire. They believed every detail of how he shot the hyena just as it was attacking him. Greta found herself caught up in the fantastic details of his life. She wasted no time marrying Karl, and she flew back to Swaziland with him.

It didn't take Greta long to discover that he was just a raconteur, and his stories were simply inventions of his imagination designed to entertain friends at a party. Life in the kingdom was dull, and her husband was the dullest of men. He ran a successful restaurant, but at home he was not up to the challenges of satisfying a young woman with a fierce libido. He compensated for his inadequacies by lavishing her with gifts. His time, energy and interests were devoted to his restaurant.

Greta never visited the restaurant. She acquiesced that she was stuck in this kingdom and would make the best of it. There wasn't anyone waiting for her back in Frankfurt, and if she retreated to Europe people might laugh at her foolishness. She wondered if the other guests at the party in Frankfurt had seen through Karl's stories. Was she the only one who was more amazed than amused?

Greta set about to create her own adventures. These had nothing to do with camping in the wilds, and she never bothered to include her impotent husband. She started to frequent hotel bars where she could meet European businessmen. Then she met some available local South African men. Soon she became brave enough to invite them to her house.

Elizabeth was totally unprepared for the job that lay ahead of her at Greta's house. The first day of work Elizabeth went directly to the laundry room. She knew that the clothes would have to be washed early in the morning so they would have a chance to dry and be ironed by the end of the workday. As the clothes were soaking in a tub she headed for the kitchen to wash the dishes from the night before and start the midday meal.

Madam was in her bedroom and let Elizabeth work uninterrupted. Greta was bored, and she spent most of her time lounging. The phone in the front hall rang, and Greta hollered for Elizabeth to answer it.

Elizabeth answered the phone and a man responded. She knew it was a South African accent. It was certainly not Karl's voice. At first this didn't mean anything to her. After all, anyone could be calling. Perhaps, it was someone from the restaurant. She had no interest in Madam's personal life.

Another week went by. Elizabeth enjoyed the work, and she liked her new madam. It was an easy and beautiful house to maintain, and Greta was kind to her. Elizabeth and James started to build their home. They broke ground and celebrated on Saturday night with a bottle of cheap wine and some leftover steaks James had brought home from the hotel.

The next Monday Elizabeth hung Madam and Master's clothes on the line in the back of the house. She finished the chore and came back into the house through the kitchen door. As she came down the hallway she could hear strange laughing. She knew that Madam was alone in the house and wondered what she was laughing about in the bedroom. Elizabeth approached the bedroom and knocked on the door.

"Are you all right, Madam?" She inquired.

The laughing stopped. No sound came from the bedroom for a minute.

"Elizabeth, don't worry about me. Just go on with your work."

Elizabeth did what she was told. She was puzzled and shook her head as she walked back to the kitchen.

A little while later Elizabeth heard the laughing again. This time she continued washing the dishes and didn't venture back down the hall. None of this made any sense to her, but she figured that it wasn't any of her business to question the strange ways of white people.

The dishes were finished, and she turned to go into the living room to do her dusting. Suddenly she came face to face with a stranger. He was a tall white man with blond hair, and he was attempting to walk out of the front door.

Elizabeth was so shocked she screamed. Greta came running out of the bedroom. She was scantily dressed in a thin camisole.

"Elizabeth! What's the matter with you?"

"Madam, this man is in your house. I think he must be a robber!"

Greta laughed in relief.

"Elizabeth, this man is a friend of mine." Greta stood so close to him that her breast pressed up against his shirt. She tossed her long blond hair out of her face. "You know about friends, don't you, Elizabeth?" Greta lifted up her leg slightly and rubbed his trousers with her bare foot.

The gentleman caller stood on the spot in the front hallway. He was anxious to get out of the house. He said nothing as the two women stared at each other.

"Now, dear Elizabeth, you wouldn't want to hurt a friend's feelings would you?" Greta was so beautiful and tender hearted. She smiled sweetly and laid her head on the man's shoulder.

"Let's not worry about this. Okay?" She fluttered her hand in the air as if brushing away an affair was like brushing away a fly.

Elizabeth nodded without speaking. She never expected to see white people act like this.

The caller left, and Greta put her arm around Elizabeth.

"Can you understand how hard and lonely my life is in this country, dear? Nothing has turned out the way I planned it." Greta sat on the sofa and pulled a cigarette out of the case on the coffee table. Elizabeth reached for the lighter and lit the cigarette for Madam. "Oh, Elizabeth, why did I believe all those lies Karl told me about his adventures in Africa?" She inhaled the cigarette and rested her back against the soft cushion.

"Oh well, what difference does it make now? I suppose I love him on some level, but right now I can't think of what that would be." She gazed at nothing on the wall. "So I make my own happiness." Greta pulled Elizabeth's arm down to her level on the sofa.

"Please, Elizabeth. You're a woman. Can't you understand how I feel? Please, help me. Please keep my secrets."

Elizabeth was speechless and confused. She felt sorry for Madam, but she wasn't sure she should keep such a confidence. Finally, Elizabeth rationalized that Madam was a kind and lonely woman. The salary was excellent. She and James needed the funds to continue building their house. Yes, she would stay and work for Greta Ruskin.

Every weekend Elizabeth and James spent all the daylight hours building their house. Her brother, Thomas, and his wife joined in to help. The walls were constructed of strong cinder block. The glass windows fit into the places designed for them. The windows were large with lattice bars behind them for security. It took several men in the village to place the tin roof and hammer it neatly on top of the structure. Elizabeth was so happy she broke out in song when the roof was in place. She hugged her children tightly, threw her head back and laughed.

⇒ ⇐

Greta had more friends than she had initially confessed to Elizabeth. Elizabeth turned her head and minded her own business as various men streamed in and out of the house.

Secret friends, though, should be careful coming to someone's home. One day as Elizabeth was dusting the living room she looked out the picture window and saw Karl's BMW driving through the gate. Greta's secret friend was in the bedroom.

Elizabeth felt a pain like an assegai spear stabbing through her breast. She was terrified. The master of the house was arriving. What if he should see the 'friend' in the bedroom?

She dropped her cloth and sped to the bedroom. Elizabeth pounded on the bedroom door until her fist was stinging.

"Madam, Madam, please hurry." Elizabeth was breathless and terrified. She heard the gardener outside greeting Mr. Ruskin.

Apparently, Greta heard him too. She threw open the bedroom door with a look of desperate panic.

"Quick, Elizabeth. Get him out of here." She threw her man friend right out of the bedroom and tossed his shirt to Elizabeth. His trousers were partially up one leg, and he practically fell into the hallway.

Elizabeth had no time to question Madam about where this friend should go. She heard the Master unlock the front door. She pushed the man friend down the back hallway and out to the garden. She threw his shirt and shoes out after him.

Elizabeth's heart beat rapidly up into her throat. She gasped for air as she heard Karl call for Greta when he entered the house.

She was stunned to see Greta wrapped in a Chinese silk robe float calmly out of the bedroom.

"Oh Karl darling, I have had one of those evil headaches. It has been such a wretched day for me." She reminded Elizabeth of a snake as she slithered up to him and loosened his necktie.

Karl loved any attention Greta showed him. He wanted to return her lust, but he resigned himself that he was too old to please her.

"What brings you home in the middle of the day, my love?" Greta inquired as she continued to fuss over his tie, then his suit coat.

"I forgot some important papers that I need from the study. I won't be here long, dear. I'm sorry you are so ill." He gently kissed her on the cheek and straightened his tie.

Elizabeth had already washed the kitchen floor, but she washed it again just to keep busy while they were in the living room. She didn't want to go in there. She didn't want to know what they were talking about. Her head felt like it was going to burst from anxiety and stress.

After Karl left Greta felt her face where he had kissed her. She craved a real kiss from him, and at that moment she didn't feel guilty anymore. She figured that it was his fault that she had so many secret friends. If he had been a real husband, she wouldn't have so many problems.

= =

Elizabeth's house was almost completed. The bills were paid, and the children were doing well in school. She shopped for a kitchen table and chairs to put in her new house. She and James built a pen for their 18 pigs and a kraal to keep the cows from roaming. Elizabeth cared for their cows as if they were an extension of the family. Each cow had a name, just like a child, and each was groomed and nurtured. The cows were more loved than the family's dogs. Dogs were designed for security, but cows were 'money in the bank.' Some day, Peter would be able to marry a healthy woman from a prosperous family, because they had acquired a sufficient lobola.

Working for Greta was stressful, but Elizabeth rationalized that she was an honest employee who was competent and trustworthy. Her family needed her income, and she earned her wages.

It seemed that Greta made new friends on a regular basis. More than once Elizabeth had to rush one friend out the back door while another waited impatiently in the parlor. Then, Greta would breeze in to greet her guest with such ease that Elizabeth was in awe of her.

Elizabeth felt like she was developing an ulcer from the constant deception in the house. She was uncomfortable being an accomplice to Madam. She pitied Madam for her loneliness, but she could not forgive her for the dagga. Elizabeth noticed one day that Madam's bedroom had a familiar bittersweet odor wafting under the door. She recognized the smell as the smoke from marijuana, or dagga. She knew that people used dagga for recreational purposes, but to her that was immoral. Smoking dagga was an ancient ritual in the Swazi culture. The effects of marijuana brought the individual in touch with his spiritual ancestors. While smoking dagga one could get advice, see into the future, and understand his past. This was a special rite that should never be abused.

At first she tried to ignore the odor from Greta's bedroom. Elizabeth's house was being wired for electricity and plumbing. She needed her salary to make sure that everything went as planned for her home. Then one day Greta asked a favor that Elizabeth should have refused.

Elizabeth was ironing the master's shirts in the laundry room when Greta ventured into the room. She rarely came back to that part of the house, and Elizabeth was startled to see her.

"What can I do for you, Madam?" Elizabeth inquired. She was almost afraid to ask what Madam needed.

"Elizabeth, I wouldn't do this normally, but I have a bit of a problem."

Elizabeth was accustomed to Greta's style of speaking sweetly to get her way. It was easy to see through her manipulations by now. Nevertheless, she liked Madam and still felt an obligation to do what she asked of her.

"Elizabeth, I have this little packet, and I need for you to take care of it for me. My husband is a little suspicious. He has even been checking through the house for evidence." Her voice was as soft and smooth as the velvet in the fabric shop.

Elizabeth stood silently. She wondered what had taken the old man so long to get suspicious, but what evidence could he be looking for around the house?

"Elizabeth, dear, my good confidante, if you could just take this little packet to your house for the weekend it would really help me. By Monday all this nonsense will blow over, and you can bring it back again." She lowered her head and placed the packet of dagga in Elizabeth's hand.

"You are such a dear. I just don't know what I would do without you."

This was more than Elizabeth had bargained for, but she wasn't sure how to handle the situation. How could Madam ask her such a thing? She said nothing. She thought of her family. They had recently moved into their house. She accepted the packet.

All the way home that evening she felt tightness in her chest and churning in her stomach. Not only was it immoral to use dagga for recreational purposes, it was illegal to have it as well. She did something that she believed was not right, but she rationalized that she needed her job. Still, how much could an employer ask of a maid? What were the boundaries of protection for a woman like Elizabeth?

She hid the packet under a rock behind her new little house, and walked into her new living room through her polished front door. She always loved the front door. It was varnished wood with a full-length piece of glass placed vertically through the middle of the door. The glass was tinted the color of amber. Elizabeth felt prosperous and content.

James was working late again at the hotel. He stayed away a lot lately, and she assumed that he was working overtime to provide for the family. She and the three children ate by dim candlelight, but her stomach was so upset she could hardly swallow. The bile rose up into her throat and left her choking. After the children were in bed Elizabeth walked by candlelight down the hallway to her bedroom.

"Soon I will never have to carry these candles down a dark hallway. When they connect our wires to the transformer we will have electricity in our home." It was a comforting thought as she slipped on a simple cotton gown and lay down on the bed. She blew out the candle and fell sleep.

It was an agonizing night for Elizabeth. The stress of building the house, Greta's secret life, and the dagga under a rock in the backyard were too much for her. All night she dreamed that her ancestors were visiting her. Gogo and Bawinde, both long deceased haunted her sleep.

"Elizabeth, can you hear me?" Gogo's voice was very clear in the darkness. "What are you doing stupid child? Can't you see that you are running your life in a bad way?"

"My little baby, my Elizabeth," Now Bawinde spoke to her. "You must change your ways. You have angered the spirits. That is why you are sick in the stomach."

Elizabeth tossed and turned, but the voices were still there. She could not ignore them.

"Elizabeth, get away from this trouble. You are traveling down the wrong road. Look at your family. Didn't I warn you not to follow that man, James?"

With this Elizabeth sat up in bed with a start. Her nightgown was wet with perspiration. What did this mean? She understood that the work she was doing for the Ruskins was not in keeping with her morals, but what did her mother's spirit mean by her reference to James?

Elizabeth reached over to nudge her husband, but he was not in the bed. He had never come home that night.

=≡ ≡=

On Monday morning Elizabeth took the packet of dagga back to the Ruskin home. She knew she had to resign from her job. It was not a difficult decision. Her deceased mother and Gogo had spoken in her dream, and their advice was right. James never came home that weekend. Her concern grew into suspicion. It was clear that her family needed her at home.

Greta appreciated Elizabeth's anxiety about the stress of the job, and Elizabeth told her that she was not well enough to continue working for her. Before Elizabeth left Greta's house she asked a simple favor.

"Madam, would you mind if I used your telephone to call someone?"

Greta was kind and obliging.

Elizabeth called the hotel where James worked. She asked to speak to him, and he was called to the line. She spoke in siSwati, because she didn't want Madam to know that she had marital concerns of her own. Elizabeth had never met a white person yet who could speak siSwati. There was a European priest in Manzini who had lived there for over 30 years, and even he didn't know the language. He prayed for and nurtured the sick, the unfortunate, the poor and the dying, but he never learned the language of the people he ministered.

"James, where are you?" She said in her native tongue. "We are very worried about you."

"Elizabeth." He answered in a shocked voice. "Why are you calling me at work? You can't do that. I'll get in trouble. If I lose my job it will be your fault." His voice was rapid and agitated.

"I want to know who you are spending the night with when you are not in our bed." She said carefully.

"Why are you accusing me?" He was angry. It was clear by the defiance in his voice he had something to hide.

"I know you are cheating. Come home to your family so we can work this out together." She spoke quietly into the phone. She knew that Greta couldn't understand her, but she also appreciated that the tone and timber of a voice is its own language.

"I'll be home soon. Do not call me again." He hung up on her with a loud bang.

Elizabeth thanked Greta and left quickly. Her stomach felt like it was exploding. Her mind was racing, and her head throbbed. She walked up into the hills where her new house sat peacefully, and her cows grazed casually in their kraal. She stood at the beautiful new front door with the amber glass in the middle and hardly had the strength to open it. Once inside she sat on her little sofa in the living room and laid her head against the back of it. She noticed the intricate electric wiring on the ceiling set in place just waiting to be connected to the transformer. At that moment Elizabeth knew that her dream of electricity would never come to pass, and she would be destined to live by candlelight the rest of her life.

James didn't come home that night. He didn't come home that week or the next. Elizabeth became gravely ill. She developed severe ulcers and suffered from migraine headaches. The days drifted into weeks, and she couldn't raise her head off the flimsy pillow on her bed. Peter stepped in as the caretaker of the family. He was 15 years old now and took it upon himself to look after his sick mother and two little sisters. Every morning he prepared the porridge for them and got them off to school. Then he tried to get Elizabeth to eat something and drink some Rooibos bush tea.

One morning he brought the tea to Elizabeth and noticed that she was sitting up and looking stronger.

She smiled when he entered the room. "I never liked bush tea. Gogo always made me drink it whenever there was a problem." She laughed and adjusted herself against the pillows. "I suppose Gogo was right." She sighed and continued. "Mama was right, too. I have been a fool, Peter. Your daddy is the man she warned me against years ago. She knew, and Gogo knew, too. They tried to tell me he would break my heart, but I was too young. I was too much in love to listen to them. You see this?" She pushed the covers away and bent her leg to show Peter the scar on the back of her calf.

"This is where my mother whipped me with a stick to stop me from running into his arms." She rubbed the thin scar. "That is a permanent badge of my stupidity." Her son sat on the edge of the bed and stirred sugar into the cup. He couldn't bear to see his mother in this condition. Elizabeth was a beautiful and vital woman. She was smart and responsible. How could she have been treated so badly by his father? He hated his father for doing this to the family. A boy should be able to look up to his father and learn to be a man through his eyes. Peter was angry and confused.

"Mama, please. You must be strong. We all need you now. Little Mondi is growing so fast, and Angela is at an age where she needs your guidance. Please, you have to get well, and be our mother again." He had tears in his eyes as he finished his sentence.

"We have lost Daddy. Please don't let us lose you, too." He leaned forward and kissed Elizabeth's cheek.

Elizabeth starting to weep, but as the tears came she couldn't control them anymore. She cried and sobbed from a broken heart. Peter cradled her in his arms. This was the woman who had nurtured all of them. She protected her family and sacrificed for everyone. He would not let anyone hurt her again.

As Elizabeth drank the pungent tea she reflected on her situation. She remembered the dreams she had about her mother and Gogo. She sent Peter off to school and got out of bed.

She laid out her clothes and washed herself. She dressed in a conservative black dress with a decorative vinyl red belt. Then she added her black shoes. Before she left she checked her purse to make sure she had some money, but there were only a few pennies. On the way out she grabbed her umbrella. The sky looked ominous and the rains were coming. Elizabeth locked the front door and headed up the dirt path into the mountains.

"Perhaps I have angered my ancestors with my foolishness." She reasoned to herself as she walked. "That must be the reason I am sick and in pain. I should have listened to my mother, and now her spirit is angry. Gogo, too, knows I am a poor wife and mother." She held her stomach as she walked. The hill was steep and the searing pain was unbearable. "I must see the sangoma. He will know what to do to please the spirits and make me well again."

Sangomas, traditional healers, have the answers for everything from spells to hexes and cures. A sangoma can put the muti, or spell, on someone and control his thoughts and life. When a person is bewitched a sangoma can give an antidote. When someone has angered an ancestor the sangoma can reconcile the problem with a sacrifice, usually the client's wallet.

As Elizabeth walked up the mountain to the sangoma's house she kept thinking about her life and the mistakes she made. Suddenly she stopped abruptly. "Wait a minute." She broke her silent thoughts and said aloud. "I am not wrong. I have been a faithful wife and a caring mother. I worked my whole life and gave all the money I had to James. I gave birth to three children, and they are strong and healthy. James is the one who is wrong. He is the one who is crazy."

Elizabeth turned around with a new resolve. She practically raced back down the mountain. She knew where Nomalanga, James' new girlfriend, lived, and she decided to face her. This woman stole her husband and ruined her dreams. Nobody could do that without a fight.

Elizabeth stopped as she neared Nomalanga's house. She took off each shoe and poured the pebbles out of it. With her shoes back on, she took a deep breath and walked up to Nomalanga's front door.

Nomalanga answered the door and was shocked to see James' wife standing in front of her. Elizabeth was surprised to meet Nomalanga. The woman was not particularly attractive. She had extensions braided into her hair in an attempt to appear alluring, but all Elizabeth could see was that she was young. More than that, she was visibly pregnant.

"We must talk, you and I." Elizabeth said in a firm voice. "You have someone who needs to come home to his wife and three children."

Nomalanga was not impressed. "Is that so?" Nomalanga answered with a sly voice and a sarcastic smile. "I think that I have someone who belongs to me now. You just want him back."

At that moment James came up from behind Nomalanga. He gave Elizabeth a vicious glare. He put his arm around Nomalanga and said. "Go home, Elizabeth. What's the matter with you coming over here without an invitation? You are pathetic."

Elizabeth's head felt like it was splitting into pieces. Her stomach twisted into a tight knot. She was so distraught that she lunged for Nomalanga. She grabbed Nomalanga's braided hair and pulled it. The pregnant woman screamed and tried to shove Elizabeth off of her. James moved between them to break up the fight.

"You poisoned my husband with the muti." She screamed at Nomalanga. "I know you put a spell on him to love you, but it won't work. You will see. He is a colored man. He is mixed race. God knows that when you mix the races you get a man with a crazy mind."

Elizabeth was screaming so hard that her throat hurt, and her voice was hoarse.

"That's enough, Elizabeth. Stop acting like this. You're such a child. What made you think that I would never take another woman? I am a Swazi man. It is my culture. I have a right to take another woman. Nomalanga and I are together. As you can see she is going to have my baby."

Nomalanga stood silently. She leaned up against James and gave Elizabeth the smile of a satisfied leopard after a kill. She purred against his chest, and rested her head on him.

"Take him then you foolish child. Find out for yourself." Elizabeth spat her words. "He will leave you, too, some day. If he thinks it is culture that makes him hunt for women, you won't be the last one to share his bed." Her strength was coming back now. "And you, James. You're a ridiculous old man looking for your youth." Elizabeth turned to leave and glanced back at the two lovers standing near the door.

"Don't come home. We don't need you. The children don't want to see you. My heart is dry, and my bed is cold."

≡ ≡

Elizabeth whirled around and dashed out of the house. She didn't look back to see if they cared or mocked her. There was still unfinished business. She had three children to feed. She knew from Bawinde's experience that James would never take responsibility for them.

The sky was turning darker and thunder roared above her. Her head was still throbbing as she turned onto a wide dirt road near her village. Suddenly the tropical rains of spring broke through the clouds and poured out their fury drenching the earth and turning the road into a river of mud. Elizabeth took off her black shoes and walked barefoot. Her shoes were too valuable to ruin in the rain. She put up the umbrella, but the wind beat against it. Step by step in the deep mud she made her way to her cousin, Duduzile's house. She knocked on the door and Dudu's husband answered.

"Typical Swazi man," Elizabeth thought as she looked at him. "Dudu is at Madam's working, and he sits around drinking beer. On the other hand, at least she knows where he is today."

"Is Duduzile here?" She asked.

"Dudu will be home soon." He answered and moved away from the door so that she could enter the little house. "Come in out of the rain. I was going to look for a job today, but the weather was so bad, I decided to wait until tomorrow. What difference is one day going to make in a lifetime?"

Elizabeth thought he was lazy and disgusting. She knew his rationale was ridiculous, but she didn't want to make Dudu an enemy now, so she just sat down and smiled. He sat in a chair and stared at an old television. There was no electricity in the house, but he was able to watch the Swazi network by hooking up the television set to a car battery that was proudly placed on top of a teetering table.

Elizabeth sat in her cousin's small house and waited. Dudu had a hard life, too. She had labored for years as a maid. Her first maid's position was working for the South African woman years ago. Elizabeth reflected on the day that she had given her job to Dudu when Elizabeth was pregnant with Angela. She wondered if Dudu ever wore the uniform that the Madam drove away with all those years ago. Dudu kept that job for a long time and was very grateful to Elizabeth. Now Dudu worked in Mbabane. She often complained about her American madam whose husband worked as a diplomat for the American Embassy.

Finally, Dudu came home. She slipped off her wet muddy shoes before she entered the house.

"Elizabeth. Unjani, how are you? What a surprise." She shook her wet jacket and hung it on a nail behind the door.

Dudu came over to Elizabeth on the faded and threadbare sofa. "Elizabeth, I was very sorry to hear about James leaving you." She took Elizabeth's hands in hers and spoke in a tone of sincerity.

"I should have guessed that you would know." Elizabeth responded looking down. "Everybody knows everything about each other's business in this small country. There seem to be no secrets, except those kept by a man from his wife."

"Other people knew about James running around with this woman." Dudu weighed her words carefully so she wouldn't hurt Elizabeth. "The wife is always the last to know where her husband sleeps."

"Duduzile, thank you for your concern, but I'm here on business." Elizabeth took her hands back from Dudu's embrace and continued. "I need to work. I must have a job to feed my children. If I can't care for them they will starve. Please," she looked pleadingly into Dudu's eyes. "Please can you help me get a job with an American family?"

Dudu wasn't sure what to say, but she knew that she owed a lot to Elizabeth. "Well, sisi. I will tell you the truth. The American madam that I work for is not very kind. I always hear people say that to work for an American is the best kind of job. This woman's husband works for the American embassy. They have a beautiful home and yet she is unhappy. She complains constantly. If you could see what she is like, you would reconsider working for an American."

"Yes, I have heard that, too." Elizabeth agreed. "But there aren't very many Americans in this country. Maybe you have a hard job, but at least you have one. Certainly, you must know of some American who needs a maid. Can't you ask Madam if she knows someone?"

Dudu drew in her breath. "I don't like to talk to her very much. You don't understand. This belumbi is rough on people. She complains and demands, and she does nothing in return. She sits around smoking and drinking all day. Then she mutters that she does all the work. I swear to you, cousin. I have never seen her lift a plate." Dudu rose from the sofa and paced around the small room. "Would you believe that she actually makes her hairdresser come to her house? Then when the white hairdresser leaves, I have to clean up behind her, too. I have heard that some Americans give their maids food, but this woman won't let me touch even a teaspoon of sugar for tea." Dudu laughed and said, "As if she would ever give me a cup of tea anyway."

Duduzile was restless. She knew she had to help Elizabeth. Many years ago Elizabeth had lost her job to Dudu. Now was the moment of repayment.

"Okay, okay. I will talk to Madam in the morning. I will not make any promises to you, but I will see what I can do."

Duduzile kept her word. On Monday morning she talked with Madam. The American madam had no interest in helping her. She said it wasn't her problem to worry about an unemployed Swazi. The US State Dept wife walked around her well furnished living room with her drink in one hand and her cigarette in the other. Finally, she gave Dudu the name of the Swazi secretary at the US embassy whose job it was to worry about these matters, or 'such trivia' she remarked.

While Madam took her daily afternoon nap Dudu phoned the embassy. She spoke with the 'trivia secretary' and fulfilled her promise and debt to her cousin, Elizabeth.

That evening Dudu made her way to Elizabeth's house.

"Elizabeth." She called as she came up the path. "I have the news you want to hear."

Elizabeth was feeding her 18 pigs in the yard. "It is going to rain tonight. The fog is coming in." Elizabeth remarked. "Look at this pen for my pigs. It is about to rain again, and the wall is starting to collapse. The mud will flow everywhere. How could that man leave me so poor?"

"Elizabeth sisi, you will be fine. Do you hear me?" She placed her hands on Elizabeth's shoulders. "Tomorrow you must come to Mbabane with me. I will loan you the bus fare. There is a couple from America who need a maid. I heard that they are truly desperate."

Elizabeth's face lit up. "Tell me more, cousin. Are they good people? What are they like? Are they young?"

"Stop it, Elizabeth. You mustn't be too happy yet." Dudu warned. The smell from the pigpen was strong, and she turned her head away. "I don't know anything about them. Madam wouldn't say much, because she said they aren't really embassy people. She said they are only a university professor and his wife, and they aren't very important. They don't even have a decent embassy house."

"It doesn't matter to me." Elizabeth finished throwing the scraps to the pigs and wiped her hands on her tshweshwe. "I will be the best maid for them."

"There is just one more problem with the American couple." Dudu waved some flies away from her face. "Madam said they are only here for one year. That makes it a short job, Elizabeth. Do you still want it?"

"A year is a long time away from now. I need work now. Today. Of course I want it." She hugged Dudu. "We will leave early in the morning for Mbabane."

That night Elizabeth heated a hot cast iron plate over a fire and placed the iron on it. When the iron turned red hot she pressed her dress. Later, all of her clothes for the morning were laid out carefully over the back of a chair. At five o'clock in the morning she awakened the children and prepared their porridge before they went to school. She packed a simple lunch of jelly sandwich and a hardboiled egg for each of them. After they left she bathed and dressed in her freshly ironed clothing.

Duduzile and Elizabeth walked for over a mile to reach the bus stop. They rode up Malagwane Hill to the city. Once they reached the city bus station they changed to another bus. The second bus took them several more miles to the Swaziland Government Institute. The bus stop was across a busy street. The little whitewashed house with a green tin roof stood in the distance.

"This is it, Elizabeth. You do the talking, and I will sit next to you during the interview."

Elizabeth was nervous. This job meant everything to her. If she were employed she would never have to beg her husband for anything. She could be an independent woman unapologetic to anyone, and certainly free of the man she had so foolishly loved and trusted.

The interview went well. The middle aged American couple hired her immediately. As the American woman spoke her smiling eyes convinced Elizabeth that God had answered her prayers, and the ancestral spirits were now satisfied with the decisions she was making in her life.

The couple appreciated Elizabeth's need to commute to work. The customary position required a maid to live in residence during the week and go home on Saturday afternoon to return on Sunday evening. Elizabeth could not possibly agree to this, because there was no one to look after her children. To her surprise, the Americans never requested such an arrangement. Elizabeth felt respected and appreciated for the first time in years.

⇒ ⇐

The Americans paid her well, and she was able to save some of her salary for small luxuries she had always wanted. She had her hair styled, and she bought cosmetics. When she was leaving work one day she said goodbye to her new American madam.

"You see, Madam." Elizabeth said. She had changed from her uniform into a cool summer dress complete with hose and new shoes. Her hair was set in a wavy style and she was wearing lipstick. "I am a poor lady who looks like a rich lady." She smiled proudly. She had a growing feeling of confidence that she had never known in her life.

Madam gave her extra money for the bus, and on Fridays she sent Elizabeth home with a chicken or beef for their Sunday dinner. Within a month Elizabeth had put on weight, and her headaches had ceased.

Elizabeth heard the rumor about Greta Ruskin from a neighbor in the village. She wasn't very surprised. Poor Greta. When Karl found out about her dalliances he was furious. Greta finally confronted Karl that he was the deceptive one, lying to everyone that he was a robust big game hunter. Greta packed up everything she believed he owed her and relocated to Cape Town. Karl grew despondent and depressed. He sold the thriving restaurant and retreated to Europe.

⇒ ⇐

It was early November, and the American couple had employed Elizabeth for two months. The summer evenings were warm and humid, but the darkness came late allowing her to reach her home before nightfall. As the bus approached her stop in the valley she noticed that her children were waiting for her. They often met the bus on Friday afternoons, because Madam sent Elizabeth home with treats for the weekend. It was always a surprise to see what Madam had packed in Elizabeth's bag. She would bake them cookies and cakes for special occasions. Sometimes there were candies, too.

Elizabeth loved watching her children at the bus stop. They were still in their school uniforms and looked so smart. Little Mondi, four years old now, waved to her mommy.

Before she could greet the three children Peter ran up to her and exclaimed "Did you hear about the fire last night, Mother?" He was breathless and excited as he spoke.

"What fire are you talking about, Peter? I haven't heard anything about a fire." Elizabeth looked confused.

"It's a fire about Daddy. The kids were talking about it at school today."

"They told me about it, too." Angela chimed in. "They said that Nomalanga's old boyfriend was jealous of Daddy. So he set fire to Daddy's car."

"They said the car burned all night and made a huge fire. Even the tires melted!" Peter said in amazement.

Elizabeth was momentarily horrified. Years ago she and James had purchased an ancient green Nissan. It never ran very well, but it was transportation to town. They were both proud to have a car, but James never let her drive it. Somewhere in his heart he must have known that Elizabeth was smarter and more capable than he was. He made an occupation of subordinating her, so that he would appear to have the upper hand.

Peter and Angela kept rambling about the burned car. As they walked the two miles to their house the summer rain started to pour. Elizabeth ignored it and laughed. She took Mondi's hand in hers and skipped through the puddles.

"Mommy, aren't you listening to our story?" Angela called to Elizabeth.

"I hear you." Laughed Elizabeth. She turned around to see Angela and Peter running to keep up with Mondi and her. "Isn't this wonderful, children?" Elizabeth danced in a circle with her head back catching the raindrops in her eyes.

Angela caught up with her mother and joined hands with Mondi to form a circle. They danced in the middle of the muddy road as the thunder roared through the mountains around them.

"Mother, why do you think this is so wonderful?" Peter asked. He didn't dance with them, and he wasn't laughing. Life had become so serious for him. At fifteen years old he was already feeling the stress of a responsible much older man. This was another sign that his father's foolishness had hurt the family.

"Peter, can't you see?" Elizabeth stopped dancing and hugged her son. She was completely soaked, but her eyes glistened with contentment. "Tonight James is also walking in the rain. I have walked so many miles in the cold, in the heat, in the rain, and he never cared. I have walked miles with babies on my back while my arms were full of groceries and my head balanced bags of mealy meal. Do you think he ever offered to ease the load for me? Tonight he is walking, too.

I never drove that car a single time, so it is no loss for me. But it is a lesson for him. God knows, and all the ancestors see the things he has done. They watch him, and they are punishing him. It is not wise to anger the spirits. Come, children. Let's hurry home now and see what Madam packed for you this weekend."

⇒ ⇐

On Sunday Elizabeth put the boiled chicken on the table for dinner. She prepared it with onions and garlic and plenty of pepper. Peter carried water from the stream for washing. Angela stirred the pap on the fire, and Mondi set the table. The American professor had given Elizabeth a small battery powered radio, and they all listened to gospel music as they settled down to eat. The table was set with pumpkin greens, squash, the chicken and pap.

Elizabeth directed the dinner prayer, but before she could finish there was a loud knock. She got up from her seat to answer it. "Don't touch the food until I serve you." She ordered. Elizabeth always rationed out the food to make sure that everyone was fed and equally satisfied. She sang the gospel tune on the radio as she walked to the door. She peeked through the amber glass and saw that James was standing on the threshold. The three children stayed in their seats. They had not seen their father in several months though he worked only two miles away.

"Elizabeth. You look fit. You actually look nice and healthy now. Those Americans must treat you well." He walked past her into the house. "Unjani, my children. Do you miss me?"

Mondi was the only one who got out of her seat to greet her father. James lifted her up in his arms and kissed her cheek.

"At least someone in this house still loves me." He sat down at the table with the family.

"Are you hungry?" Elizabeth inquired. Peter shot her a puzzled glance. "We have plenty of food today."

Elizabeth was beyond anger now. She had come to terms with the reality that in Swaziland there would be no retribution for an unfaithful husband. She recognized that if she wanted him to continue paying the children's school fees she would have to pretend to be nice. If he knew she had laughed about the car he would retaliate against her. Elizabeth remembered a recent story about a woman who was beaten to death by her husband. The man was tried for murder and released with a suspended sentence. As the judge gave his ruling he advised the man that "When you beat your next wife, don't kill her. You must beat her about the body, not hit her in the head. The object is to teach her a lesson, not to kill her."

It was a strangely normal dinner for the family. Elizabeth silently grieved for the loss of this way of life. She sat back in her chair and could see how much her children ached to be a family again. James entertained them with stories about the important people his restaurant had served. He made them laugh with his renditions of the white tourists staying at the hotel.

After dinner Elizabeth sent the children to bed, and she cleaned up the dishes. James followed her to the kitchen and spoke first.

"That was a delicious meal, Elizabeth." He started to hug her, but she pulled away from him.

"It was only a dinner, James, but I think our children enjoyed it. You can see how much they need you."

"Elizabeth, I have something to tell you. It is a bad story." He hesitated and then continued. "Somehow our car was burned. It is so strange the way it happened."

Elizabeth was surprised that James was volunteering this story. She didn't acknowledge that she knew anything about the car.

"I was at the hotel and there was a big storm. I heard a loud crash and saw that a tree was hit by lightning."

"Oh my, that must have been terrible." Elizabeth looked down at the sink. She could smell a lie, but she had to appear naïve and concerned.

"The tree fell over and hit the car." James spoke rapidly. He knew that if he took a breath he might forget the story he had invented. He waved his arms around in a lavish presentation.

"When the tree fell it burst into flames from the lightning. Then the car was on fire, too." His eyes were wide; he seemed amazed with his accounting.

"Oh James, how lucky that you were not killed in the blaze." Elizabeth kept washing the dishes so he couldn't see the smile on her face. She had to concentrate on her work so that she wouldn't laugh out loud. As he kept talking she thought about him having to walk to work.

"The car is completely ruined." James looked down at the kitchen counter and continued. "You know we never had insurance on it, so I can't replace it." He was quiet at that point and waited to hear Elizabeth's reaction.

"These Swazi storms do get out of control don't they?" She composed herself long enough to look up at him. "It's a shame when outside forces step in and make life so uncertain and difficult."

James stared at his wife. He wondered how much truth she knew. He had plotted that story all weekend, and yet, he was bewildered by her reaction. He expected her to be angry or scream at him or cry. He expected anything but the response she gave him.

≡ ≡

Elizabeth reveled quietly in the few moments of happiness that God granted her. She knew that evil was always lurking in the distance waiting for an opportunity to strike. It would sneak up on her and laughingly peel away any vestiges of contentment she would feel. Don't ever get too comfortable. It was the curse her father had inflicted on her when she was born, and it would plague her entire life. Her mother swore that Elizabeth was not the bastard child Rolilahla pronounced her to be, but truth was not as valid as impression. It had to be true. She was cursed from her first breath.

Within a month of James' outlandish tale regarding the demise of their car, the curse struck Elizabeth again. She came home from work one evening and noticed a strange stillness in the air around her house. It had been a good day for her at work. The weather was warm with a pure blue sky and her spirits were high. She sang radio gospel songs from memory as she walked down the red clay road.

She knew immediately what was wrong as she approached the path that led to her house. There was no sound. There was no movement. All her cows had disappeared. Elizabeth was panic-stricken. She dashed up the path and threw open the amber glass door. Peter, Angela and Mondi were sitting nervously in the dim living room. They looked terrified, too. For a moment no one spoke. The cows were missing. Twelve cows had vanished from the tiny kraal while she was at work that day.

Elizabeth caught her breath and screamed out "The cows! Where are the cows?"

Peter rose and put his arm around her waist. "Mother, the cows are gone, but we have also been robbed."

With that Elizabeth raced through the house down the narrow dark hallway to her bedroom. She slipped her hand under the mattress. Nothing. Again, she stretched and reached her arm under it as far as she was able. Nothing. She finally used all her strength and lifted the entire mattress throwing it away from the bed. Still nothing. The 300 emalangeni she had saved for months were gone. She didn't notice until she dropped the mattress back onto the bed that even her blanket had been stolen. In terror and fury she ran around the house searching for things that might be missing. Everything of any value was gone. There was a glass vase that Madam had given her. It was gone. The radio that she loved was gone. Her wristwatch that she kept in a sisal basket by her bedside was missing, too. Whoever did this had spent a lot of time during the day while the house was empty picking through her belongings.

She threw herself down on the living room floor, buried her head in her hands and wailed. "Who would do this? Why must the Devil always take my life apart?"

Mondi wrapped her arms around her mother and whispered. "We know who did this, Mommy. It wasn't the Devil. It was the cow herder."

"What? You mean that boy I hired to herd and wash the cows? He was only 13 years old. He worked for me a long time. Why would he do this to me now?"

"I know the answer to that, Mommy." Angela sat on the floor next to her mother. "This is not good news, but you have to know it." Angela related the events.

When the children came home from school a neighbor told them that James came earlier in the day just after Elizabeth went to work.

With the blessings of the chief James took all the cows away. When he came for the cows he paid the young cow herder to drive them to the home he shared with Nomalanga. The young boy knew that he would have no job now, so he took the opportunity to rob Elizabeth of anything he could carry out of the house.

Elizabeth was emotionally crushed. She was so protective, so proud of her cows. They were Peter's lobola. They were like a bank account to her. Just a week earlier Madam queried Elizabeth about how people identified their cows.

"Elizabeth, there are cows everywhere." Madam said. "Some even roam freely down the highway. The Swazis never brand them or mark them. How do you know which ones are yours?" The American madam asked her.

Elizabeth replied with a smile of satisfaction. "Madam, you recognize your children, don't you?"

So now Elizabeth's 12 cows that were like children to her were stolen away in an act of hate and spite. For several minutes Elizabeth stayed in a heap on the floor. She didn't have the strength to get back on her feet. She was defeated once more. It would be pointless, she reasoned later, to approach the chief. Man to man he and James had worked out an arrangement. She could picture in her mind how those men settled the deal between them. It would take a small tribute from James to get the chief to turn his head. If the chief still felt uncomfortable about the theft, James would remind him that there is no such thing as robbing your own property. Certainly, all the property belonged to James, anyway. So the cows were his, too. Finally, James would advise the chief that it would be impossible for Elizabeth to care for the cows the way he could. Her resources could not match his, and it would be in Peter's best interests to have the lobola safely in James' care. It didn't really matter who was right or who had the best explanation for the chief. Elizabeth had no bribe to give him, but far worse than that, she was only a woman.

Finally, she dragged her worn body to bed and thanked God that it was summer, so she wouldn't freeze that night without her blanket. She loved that blanket so much. She bought it with her first paycheck from the Americans. It cost many emalangeni, but it was large and soft and full of colors. She would have to save for a long time to replace all the things that were lost to her. She would never be able to replace the cows, and they were never returned.

⟹ ⟸

The American couple was shocked to hear Elizabeth's story the next day. She arrived at their house in the morning, and her eyes were still red and swollen from crying all night.

"Oh Madam, I have a big nginga. You know, I have a big problem. I am sorry to say, I always seem to have a problem."

The American couple had a wall safe in their house, and they proceeded to give Elizabeth the key.

"Keep anything you want, money or valuables in here. We never use it, and we know that you are not legally allowed to have a personal bank account. Please, consider it your space in the house."

With that Madam gave Elizabeth a handful of emalangeni to help replace some of her money that was lost. Elizabeth immediately put the money in the wall safe.

⟹ ⟸

Elizabeth gained a sense of independence and confidence that she had never felt. In spite of James' cruelty and the curse she seemed to suffer from, her life was taking a new turn.

Christmas came, and there were gifts from the Americans. In addition to presents for Elizabeth and her children, they gave her a large chicken, a Christmas cake and a month's salary as a bonus. She took the bus home on Christmas Eve and put the wrapped treasures away for the morning. Before she prepared the holiday dinner she walked down the red dirt road to her cousin Dudu's house.

Dudu greeted her at the door. "Come in, sisi, blessings of the season of our Lord Jesus' birth to you."

Dudu's husband was sitting in the same chair he had been sitting in months ago. Elizabeth laughed to herself that the man was probably glued to the seat of it. The can of beer seemed to be mysteriously attached to his hand.

"Unjani, sisi." She hugged Dudu and entered the house. "I want to give you a Christmas gift. Then I must get back home to my children." Elizabeth opened her purse and pulled out a small Christmas card that contained some of her Christmas bonus. She handed the card to Dudu.

"You helped me when I was desperate, and I have wanted to thank you for a long time. The American professor gave me a Christmas gift, and I want to share it with you."

Dudu was stunned. Her American employer had given her a fraction of Elizabeth's gift. There were no other gifts or food from those Americans.

"Thank you, thank you, cousin. You are the lucky one."

That comment surprised Elizabeth. No one had ever told her that she was lucky in her entire life. She walked back to her house in the warm summer evening. That night she prayed to God that the

American professor and his wife would change their minds and stay in the kingdom. She prayed every night that they would stay in Swaziland, but in her heart she knew that Europeans and Americans rarely stayed in Africa forever. What would become of her without them? There were times when she was able to put the dread of their leaving in the back of her mind. Those were the best days. She sang as she worked in their kitchen, laughed with their day guard, Themba, as she washed the clothes. She and Madam had wonderful discussions about their lives and feelings about the world. It was obvious that Madam was very homesick for her family back in America. Then she would grow sad too, because that was a clear sign that they would leave as they had planned from the beginning.

The year went by so quickly that Elizabeth was shocked when she saw the packing boxes in the hallway one morning. The unvarnished truth of life lay before her. The Americans were going home, back to America, the land of wonder where everyone was happy with a full belly and plenty of money.

She considered a new idea and approached madam.

"Please, Madam. I have been thinking lately. If you could consider taking me to America with you I could work very hard. Then I could make money and send for my children." There were tears in her eyes, and when she looked at madam she noticed tears there as well.

"Elizabeth, dear Elizabeth, I would do anything for you. But that is something that is not possible. Do you remember when I came to Swaziland that I was crying for my family? You would be crying for your children, too. The biggest problem is that neither your husband nor your chief will give permission for you to have a passport. Your children need you by them." She held Elizabeth's hands in hers and said softly. "We are going to write you the best reference letter, and we will make sure the United States Embassy hires you and looks out for you."

Elizabeth took her hands away and dried her eyes. "My brother, Thomas, says that if I can get a job with another American family and stay with the embassy I will be taken care of here. Do you believe that?"

The American madam wanted to believe it, but she was skeptical. She smiled at Elizabeth and said, "We'll do our best."

The American professor and his wife left Swaziland, just as they promised they would a year ago. They gave Elizabeth all the household goods they had accumulated. There were pillows, sheets, towels, pans and dishes. It took Elizabeth a week to carry home all the items they packed for her. One day she remarked to madam. "I cannot take all this on the bus today. I will have to carry some home tomorrow. If people see me with too many things they will be jealous. Then they will put the muti on me. I cannot risk any more trouble."

Along with piles of belongings they gave her a stellar letter of reference. Elizabeth cried when they handed it to her. The embassy told Elizabeth that someone was coming, a single American man who needed a maid.

It all looked perfect to her. Perhaps the curse had been broken.

Two months after the American couple returned to the United States they received their first letter from Elizabeth.

Dear Master and Madam,

Greetings is my first word that I can say hello to you. Madam and Master I can always remember you. Madam, I got the job, as you knew when you left me. The American man took me to his embassy house. He is not a nice man. He don't have a wife. He don't have a child.

Madam, to this man there is nothing what I am doing that is good. All is wrong. Every day I am wrong. He won't give me even tea. He told me that he wasn't come here to Swaziland for feeding me. He lets me only drink water from a used yogurt container.

He gives me 300 emalangeni a month. (The equivalent of $45).

Madam, I remember. I think that you can also remember when I told you that I would never get some people like you again. He is American, but there are things what he is doing to me that is not American.

Madam, I remember the professor when he cook coffee and says to me…Elizabeth, come and have coffee. I also remember you, Madam, when you ask me what I want to eat and what I want when you go to town. Madam I still not believe that I will never see you again, because you were all to me. My children still think that when I'm coming they will get cakes and sweets everything that you bake for them. Madam, now I think that if you can come and take me with you to America, please.

Love,

Elizabeth, Peter, Angela and Mondi

A second letter followed a month later.

Dear Master and Madam,

I miss you too much. Since you left me my mind is always hurting. Madam, thank you for all the money you send to me. God can be with you wherever you are. Madam I think if you can return back to Swaziland again I can be happy. It is hard if you have been in good hands and then come out of them. My heart is hurting everyday. The way you was taking care of me I was like a child to you.

I am sorry to tell you that the American man I work for, he don't care about me. One day Peter was sick with the asthma. You know he has a problem. I came to the man and say my child is sick. I think if I can work a half-day to go and see him. The man says to me, 'if you want to go back, go. If you want to work, work. That is not my problem. I don't care about your children.'

Every day, Madam, I came to work. I left Peter even when he was sick. And then one day the man, he fired me. I am feeling so sorry to tell you, but he says one thing, that I am not good enough to work for him. Then, Madam, I tell myself how stupid I am and I beg him 'please, please. I am very, very sorry with that I am not doing as you want. I will try to do better than before.' But he would not talk to me.

Madam, please don't forget that I am always remembering you.

I thank God for giving me the time to write this letter to you.

Please do not forget me.

Love,

Elizabeth

The American professor and his wife often sent Elizabeth money, but they could not send her hope for a better life. Perhaps she was cursed from her birth, but more likely she was an intelligent capable woman trapped merely by her circumstance and culture.

Elizabeth was, indeed, the blossom of a perfect rose that was littered with thorns.

Chapter 4 – Busisiwe

Busisiwe walked up the path to her house. The document she carried in her hand was the most important piece of paper she had ever held. She was so excited to show it to her family, but she wasn't sure how to approach them.

Busisiwe knew that her father, Musa, would be impressed. She always felt that she was her father's favorite. When she was born he had named her 'blessed' and she liked to live up to her name. It wasn't easy being the third daughter, and life became more complicated when her father took a second wife. For that reason she always worked very hard to get Musa's recognition and approval. Sometimes she enjoyed life in a large family. There were many parties, and Christmas was a wonderful celebration with gifts and food for everyone. On the other hand, being one of 10 girls and 2 boys was difficult most of the time. The jealousy between the two wives was bad enough, but the children were all relatively close in age. They not only had the normal sibling rivalry, but they broke into maternal factions as well. Life was also complicated by the fact that the second wife had delivered both of the sons. That gave her more status than Busisiwe's mother felt the other woman deserved.

As she walked up the steep hill in Mbabane Busisiwe pulled out the paper and read it again. It was a document from the Ministry of Foreign Affairs in Swaziland. She had just been awarded the honor of going to the United States of America to be the secretary to the Ambassador from Swaziland.

"Sawubona, Busisiwe." A young man whom she knew from school called to her from his car. "Do you want a ride to your house?"

Normally she would appreciate a ride home. The hills of Mbabane were steep, and her shoes were always covered with a thin layer of red dust. Today she needed the time to think and plan what she was going to tell her family.

"No, I think I'll just walk today." She replied. She must have been smiling, because the young man smiled back and nodded. She could feel herself smiling. How could she go into the house and look humble to the whole family? It would take some preparation on the way home.

Busisiwe was petite, thin and attractive. Her large brown eyes and delicate features completed her appearance. She was smart and well liked at her office. She had always been an excellent student. Grace, her mother, worried about her, because she studied so hard. Sometimes it seemed that Busi liked to read better than eat, and that was a concern. Musa was an important man in the royal government. He was well educated, and very respected throughout the country. Her mother, too, had a college degree. Grace was regarded as an excellent nurse in the city. Musa and Grace expected their daughters to be well behaved. After all, their father was a very high profile man.

When Busi was a young teenager her father took a second wife. As a man of means and stature it was expected that he would develop a larger family. The two women hated each other. They both knew that having more than one wife was natural in their culture, but that didn't mean they had to like it. When Musa was having dinner with the second wife Busi would hear her mother complain that they would all be forgotten and left hungry. When Musa had dinner at their house Grace complained that the other wife had more food on the table, because she didn't have to feed a wayward husband. No matter what Musa did, there were always problems at both houses.

"I'm never getting married." Busi thought on the way home. "That way no one will ever break my heart or hurt me. Besides, I have to take care of my own needs now. When I go to America I'll be totally independent. America...the United States of America, yes, I like the sound of that."

Interestingly, Busi had never lived away from home. Though she was in her twenties, she still lived with her mother and sisters. The government house provided for them was simple. It was a one-story building constructed of cinder blocks. The structure was painted white while the tin roof that completed it was painted brown. It was a larger home than most other government houses, because Musa was well connected in the political system, but they still had to share bedrooms, three to a room. Musa's second wife lived on the other side of town. Busi's mother was comforted by the fact that the other woman's house was not furnished as well. She never went there on her own, but her children told her all about it.

Busi finished high school and continued her studies at the Swaziland College of Technology. She had good organizational skills, she was reliable, and she knew she could get a good job in a government office. After she was awarded her diploma at the college for business, her father arranged appropriate interviews for her in better governmental departments.

On her way home, Busi remembered the day she first walked into the Ministry of Foreign Affairs. She wore a dark suit over a simple blouse. She was so thin that Grace had sewn a tuck into the side of the skirt. Her new shoes pinched her toes as she walked.

She passed all the typing tests demonstrating with ease that she could run an office. Of course, these skills were essential, but with her father's political connections the job was hers before she walked through the door. The thought of that did not please her. She wanted to prove that she was able to get her own job and make Musa proud of her. With that in mind she had worked harder than ever in the Ministry. That was five years ago. Now her hard work had paid off, and soon she would be bound for America.

Busi reached the house, and her nieces were there. Her older sister, Lindiwe was married and often brought the children by to see her mother, their gogo, in the afternoon.

"Sawubona, sisi." Her sister called. "You look so happy that I think you must have a new boyfriend."

The little girls squealed with delight when they saw Busi. She was their favorite aunt, because she would bring candy and treats after work.

"No. I don't have time for a boyfriend." Busi called back. She hugged the little girls and handed each of them a wrapped piece of candy. Then she kept walking up to the house. She was still holding the letter in her hand.

"I received this on my desk at work today. What do you think?" She passed it to her sister to gauge her reaction. That would give her an idea of what to expect when she told her mother.

Lindiwe read the letter and threw her arms around Busisiwe. "You are the lucky one. They should have named you Inhlahla for luck."

"You know that not everyone in the family will be so happy for me." Busi remarked. She stood outside on the step waiting to go into the house.

"Who wouldn't be happy for you, sisi? I know that sometimes people wish bad things on each other, but you have worked hard for this appointment. The worst part for us will be that we will miss you so much. The little ones will miss you, too. No one gives them candy and treats like you do."

Busi laughed softly and hugged her sister. Then she took off her dusty shoes and went into the house.

"Busi, I'm glad you're home. Your father is gracing us with his presence tonight, and I need help with the table." Her mother breezed by Busi gave her a light kiss on the cheek and kept talking. "Change your clothes and come back to the kitchen. Cecile is cooking the meat, but she needs help stirring the pap. You know best how your father likes it."

Pap was something that Musa enjoyed every night for supper. It was mealy meal corn that was cooked until it was very stiff. It was eaten with meat and gravy. Both wives knew that he liked to have a large hot meal especially with plenty of meat, and they would compete with each other to cook something really special for him. A clever wife is one who can grant her husband favors and in return get presents and extra household money from him. The maid, Cecile was in the kitchen trying to prepare the dinner for a large group. Busi walked obligingly back to the kitchen and stirred the pap for supper. Busi was glad that Musa would be home that night. He would be proud of her. He wouldn't let anyone make negative comments about her going to America.

The dinner was ready, and Musa finally came home. Busi's sisters and the nieces were also there. In all, 10 people sat around the table. The commotion was so loud that Busi didn't want to break into it for fear of losing her train of thought. After dinner Musa approached her. "Busisiwe, I heard something about you downtown today. Don't you have something you want to share with the family?"

Everyone suddenly became silent. They looked in her direction. Her face grew red and hot, and she felt embarrassed.

"Today I received a letter from the Ministry." She said softly. She looked down at the table. It was respectful to turn away. "I have been chosen to go to America to be the Ambassador's secretary in Washington DC."

To her astonishment everyone seemed happy for her. This was something she was unaccustomed to experiencing. In such a large family there was always a problem or a jealous sibling. Tonight they celebrated with her.

A month later Busisiwe was in her bedroom packing her suitcase. Her younger sister watched as Busisiwe folded her new clothes in neat piles.

"If you're lonely I could come and be good company for you."

"Oh, Shirley" Busi smiled at her sister. Her younger sister liked to go by her English school name. It made her feel more modern and westernized. "I won't be gone that long. Maybe I will only be there for a year or two. It won't be that long. I assure you."

"But, Busi, I'm doing nothing here in Mbabane. I don't have a boyfriend, and I don't like going to the tech school. Can't you take me with you, just for awhile?"

"No, Shirley. They only gave me enough money for one ticket. As it is I'm nervous about going. After I said I would take the position I started reading about America. I think it's going to be much more expensive than I thought in the beginning. What if I run out of money? What if something happens to me and nobody cares?"

"Oh you are so funny." Shirley fell back on the bed and laughed. "I hear that everybody in America cares about everybody. They would never let someone go homeless or hungry like people in our country. Once you're there, you'll see. You will probably never want to come back here."

Busisiwe finished her packing. Musa had bought her two new suitcases for the trip. They even had wheels on the bottoms, because he said she would be walking through great airports. She had never flown on a plane before, and now she would be taking one of the longest nonstop flights in the world. Grace had bought her a new suit for the job, and her sisters had gone in together to buy her a smart pair of new shoes. Her sister, Lindiwe had just learned that she was expecting her third child.

"Busi, I wish you were going to be here. I need your help and guidance with these girls of mine. I think three children is a good-sized family, don't you? This will be my last child. Already my husband says we shouldn't have anymore. Our house isn't very big, and children are very expensive to raise."

"Oh sisi," Busisiwe smiled at her sister. "You know that all men want sons. I'm sure you will have many children until your husband feels he has one that looks like him."

As she headed out the door with her suitcases her mother came running out one last time. "Busi honey, now you must take care of yourself. You never eat. You have to eat a lot while you are away and put on some weight. Don't you think that men like a woman with some meat on her?" She patted Busi's hip. "I don't know what American food is like, but you will have to eat it regardless of how bad it is." She adjusted Busi's collar and ran her hands over her cropped hair. "One last kiss for luck, baby. Stay fit until we see you again."

With that Busisiwe got into the waiting taxi and was out of sight down the road.

The trip to Washington DC was terribly long and exhausting. First she had to fly to Johannesburg. From there she had to change planes and board the biggest plane she could imagine. She felt like a monster swallowed her when she boarded the South African Airways Boeing 747 jet. The flight to the United States took 17 hours. She knew she was over the Atlantic Ocean, but she couldn't see anything out of the window. She kept praying for her safety and for God to guide the pilot. She finally landed in New York and changed planes again for Washington. Her father was right. These airports were massive and confusing. She had not slept well on the flight over, and the jet lag was taking its toll. She fell asleep on the final leg of the journey and awakened to hear the flight attendant remind the passengers to fasten their seatbelts. "If you look out the right side of the plane you can see the Washington Monument." The woman continued. Busisiwe could not believe what she was seeing. The city below was so enormous and elaborate. She could see all of the monuments as the plane banked and turned toward Reagan National Airport. It was thrilling and yet terrifying.

As she walked up the jet way into the airport she saw someone holding a sign with her name on it. The Swazi ambassador's chauffeur had been ordered to pick her up at the airport. She was relieved to see a welcoming Swazi face, but she was too tired to talk. He drove through the Capitol with ease, while Busi sat in the backseat staring out the window at this strange new world.

The driver was a friendly jovial man. It was obvious that he felt fortunate to have this assignment in the United States. Busi wondered what his political connection was back home in Swaziland. To be a chauffeur required responsibility and trustworthiness. As he drove he explained a lot about life in the States. He told her about his own adjustment to living in a western culture. He reminded her that Americans are expected to put in long work hours, and that they are never late to meetings. They have too much stress. When he came to a red light he stopped the car and turned around to look at her. "Don't worry." He smiled a broad kind smile. "You will love this country. It takes some adjustment, but you will never want to go back to Africa." Then he laughed as he started driving again. "You would be amazed to learn how many Africans live right here in the Capitol. Maybe some of them shouldn't be here. Their visas are finished, and they should go home. Maybe the American government knows that and turns its head. Maybe the government doesn't even know how many people are in the city. But here they are, and they believe they are American now. I tell myself that this is a country built by immigrants, so they won't mind a few more now and then."

He pointed out the local grocery store and showed her where the metro station was located. "You won't even need a car here. There is a lot of public transportation."

Finally, he arrived at her apartment. It was a small, simple flat, but it was clean and comfortably decorated. Fortunately, it was one of the perks of her job, or she would never have been able to afford it. It didn't take her long to realize that apart from loneliness, the worst part of living in the US was the expense. The chauffeur unloaded her suitcases and handed her the apartment key. "I have to go back to the embassy now. You need some rest. Tomorrow morning I'll pick you up and drive you to work. After that you will learn your way around."

He drove off, and Busi was suddenly alone, tired and hungry in a metropolis she knew nothing about. She started to unpack, but she was so exhausted that she fell onto the bed and went to sleep.

≡ ≡

The embassy driver was right about everything. The work was much more extensive than anything she had done at the office in Mbabane. The phones were ringing constantly, and she had a hard time remembering which line was available. There were faxes, messages and memos. Every single item seemed to be essential and urgent. After work she would pick up some 'take away' on her way home. They called it 'carry out' in America. Even the language was new to her. One evening she ordered a pizza for take away, and the young woman behind the counter just stared at her without moving. Finally, Busi heard someone else put in an order, and she realized that English wasn't as straightforward as she had been taught in school. Many of the words and phrases were foreign to her. Learning the American accent was also very complicated. The Americans spoke in drawn out syllables. She often had a difficult time understanding people when they called on the phone to the embassy. A colleague in Mbabane had warned her before she left home that Americans don't speak English; they speak American.

There were nights when Busi sat in her little apartment eating 'take away' in front of the television, and she wondered why she had ever left home. The culture shock was consuming her. The nights were filled with dreams of home followed by uncontrollable tears. One night when she was lying in bed consumed by loneliness and fright she came up with the idea that maybe life in the US would seem easier if she wasn't so alone. Didn't her sister, Shirley, wish she could come to America? She got out of bed and wrote down a plan complete with a budget to bring her sister from Africa to be with her.

Shirley was ecstatic when she received Busi's letter. She was working in a job that she hated and felt had no future. Many people in Mbabane would have been happy to take her place as a receptionist. In Shirley's mind there was a fascinating world waiting for her outside of the tiny kingdom. She, too, worked out a plan to get to the United States. It would take time to raise the kind of money needed for the plane ticket, but she would find a way. Shirley knew that she would have to curb her taste for new clothes and other amenities, but it would be worth it. A new dress shop opened in the Swazi Plaza downtown, and Shirley prided herself in resisting the temptation to walk into it. "I will get to America." She said to herself as she walked across the street away from the shop. "I will get an education there. Then I will get a good job and become an American."

Busisiwe had a simple plan to have her sister keep her company, but Shirley had no intention of anything so provincial.

⇒ ⇐

Busisiwe had worked at the embassy for over a year when a Swazi man whom she had never seen before appeared in front of her desk. He was dressed so well she thought that he had to be someone important and wealthy. He walked into the office and immediately was attracted to her.

"So," he picked up her nameplate on the desk and read "Busisiwe, you must be the blessed one." He put down the sign leaned over her desk and winked at her. "Is this the way our beautiful Swazi women have chosen to spend their lives? You must be one of those modern independent girls."

He shuffled some papers around on her desk.

"Please, sir." She tried to rearrange the papers that he had touched. "Are you here to see someone?"

"Yes, I am." My name is Albert, Albert Dlamini." He placed his business card on the desk in front of her. "I'm studying at the university here, and I want to introduce myself to the ambassador."

Busisiwe was not impressed. It was hard to be as impressed with this man as he was with himself. "The ambassador is very busy this morning. You will have to make an appointment and come back another time."

"I don't make appointments." He looked straight at her. "Can't you see that I'm a prince? I will see the ambassador if I choose to do so. But let me make a deal with you. You know that's what Americans say. Then they always say they have an offer you can't refuse."

"Yes, I've seen those gangster movies, too." Busisiwe was getting annoyed with him.

"Here is the deal. I will make a real appointment and come back another time if you will go to dinner with me tonight."

"I never go out at night." Busisiwe said in a matter of fact voice. "I work hard all day, and I'm too tired." She didn't want him to think she was that easy, and she wasn't interested in him.

"Lunch, then. That's it. I'll come back at 1:00, and we'll have lunch at the little Italian restaurant down the street. He started to turn towards the door and looked back at her and said "I never take no for an answer."

"You haven't made your appointment with the ambassador yet." She called after him.

"Who needs to see the ambassador? I want you to show me around town."

And that was that.

After he left Busi wondered what she had done. Why didn't she tell him 'no' right on the spot? She couldn't have been attracted to a man like that, could she? She wondered. She asked herself why she hadn't refused and thought that maybe it proved just how lonely she was 10,000 miles away from home.

$$\Longrightarrow \Longleftarrow$$

Albert and Busisiwe went to lunch at the little Italian restaurant in the area. Later it became their favorite quiet spot together. Busisiwe felt like a new woman. Albert made her feel wanted and feminine. He understood her so well. They shared a background and culture that no one else in the area could appreciate. They were two lonely people far away from home, and they decided they were in love.

Busi had to admit finally, that she was more than a little impressed that Albert was a real prince even though he was a very distant cousin to the king. He had a lot of money and enjoyed spending it on her. Everywhere they went he made sure that she ordered the best food on the menu. They always ordered wine and even pudding, or dessert, as Americans call it. He had impeccable taste in clothes, too. He made her feel like a princess when they were together.

The first time Albert stayed over night seemed innocent enough to Busi. She had cooked a large dinner, and they had shared a bottle of wine. The snow was falling softly outside. The streetlights illuminated the slick snow on the road in front of her building.

"It's really cold and late, Busi." He came up to her from behind, put his arms around her tiny waist and kissed the back of her neck. If you want me to leave I can, but won't it be simpler if I just sleep on your sofa?" He turned her around to face him, and he kissed her in a strong embrace. He kept holding her with one arm while he stroked her breast under her sweater with the other. Busi felt weak and soft and fell into his arms. She returned his affection, and he never slept on her sofa.

Life was turning around in America. Busi started to feel comfortable and happy again. She made some friends with the people in the apartment building. The most important thing, though, was that Albert loved her. That made life in America perfect. She stopped thinking about him as a prince, and thought of him as the man she loved, the man who took care of her; the man who made her smile again.

⥱ ⥳

She dreaded her birthday. Sitting at her desk she remembered all the times she would count the days until her birthday. There were so many children in her family that her birthday was something that was hers and only hers. It was a special day that she didn't have to share with anyone. The family would have a big dinner with a cake. It was one of the better parts of belonging to a big family. She knew that birthdays in the United States did not compete with that. Suddenly in the afternoon Albert appeared at the embassy with a bouquet of flowers. "I know it isn't Swazi roses, but this is America, so I found the best substitute." The bouquet was colorful and fragrant. Busi came around from her desk and gave Albert a brief hug. "You are so good to me. I'll see you tonight. Come to my place later."

That night she waited for Albert to arrive. She lit candles and played soft music on her stereo. She waited and waited. She started to feel angry, but she stopped herself and questioned "what if something has happened to him, and I'm sitting here angry and self pitying?" She talked to herself as she blew out the dripping candles. She sat up until late at night. There was no phone call and no word from him. She stuffed the cork back into the bottle of wine, turned off the stereo and went to bed.

"Busi, Busi, honey." Busi was half asleep. Albert was on the other end of the phone line. It was 9:00 on a Sunday morning. "Busi, I'm so sorry I couldn't get over to your place Friday night. Something came up. It was business. It was so important. I couldn't even get to a phone."

"It was my birthday." She answered annoyed. "You said you were coming. I was worried. Are you okay?" She cuddled back down into the bedcovers.

"I'm okay, honey, but my life here gets so hectic. You know how much studying I have to do. Well, there was a study group. It went on longer than I expected. I'm so sorry. Please forgive me."

Busi was still half asleep. She wanted to be angry, but she knew that Albert had trouble in his studies at the university. He did have a lot of schoolwork, and he wasn't getting very good marks. If he performed badly at the university, she would blame herself. She couldn't let that happen. "It's okay." She answered sleepily. "Will I see you today?"

"Oh sure, I'll come over, and we can have a late breakfast together. How does that sound? Thanks Baby, thanks for understanding. I don't know what I would do around here if it weren't for you. Oh, by the way, I hate to ask you a favor. But I have a term paper due tomorrow. You know I worked on it all last night. Do you think you could type it on the computer for me?" His voice sounded so kind and innocent. He had been really good to her. Typing was something she did well, and she was happy to return a favor. "Why don't I bring some Chinese take away, and we can eat before you type the paper?"

"Sure, that sounds like a nice idea." Busi responded. By now she was awake. She felt so guilty for being angry. Albert was a university student who had to study hard, and she knew that his success in school would benefit both of them.

That afternoon Albert came by with the Chinese food and a very flimsy rough draft of his term paper.

"What's this?" Busi asked. "This isn't what I expected. I can hardly read your writing, and the pages are so scribbled. I don't think I can type this."

Albert was dishing out the food, and he laughed at her. "Come on, girl. You know writing's not my thing. Just put it together any way that makes sense to you. Now let's eat before this noodle stuff gets cold."

Busi worked all afternoon trying to decipher his work while Albert watched a soccer game on television. Finally, she finished the paper and printed it out for him.

"There." She handed him the finished paper and sat on his lap. She wrapped her arms around his neck and buried her face into him. "Now you go back to that professor and tell him you want an A in his class." She slipped his shirt away from his neck and kissed his smooth chest.

Albert gave her a quick glancing kiss while he continued to focus on the game. When the game was over he got up and gathered up his schoolwork. "Thanks Busi, baby. You're such a good girl."

That remark struck her very strangely, but she washed the dishes from the Chinese noodles and put it out of her mind.

⇒ ⇐

"Shirley! I'm over here." Busisiwe stood at Dulles International Airport and waved to her sister as she came into the terminal.

"Busi!" Shirley called back.

They ran and hugged each other right in the middle of the hallway.

"I can't believe you're finally here. Oh, sisi, I have been so lonely in this country. Now we can be here together. It will be the most wonderful thing in the world having you in America."

"I can't believe I'm here, either. That trip is horrible. All those cramped planes, and I'm so tired. I need a shower badly."

"That's no problem. Let's take the metro to my, I mean our flat, and you can get settled there."

They arrived at the apartment, and Shirley looked out the windows and down the street. "Sisi, this is perfect. The university is so close. They are giving me a small grant to study, and I can walk there from here."

"You will have to study harder than you think here, Shirley." Busi said. "Albert is having a real struggle. He said that his education in Swaziland didn't prepare him to study here. He studies so much he hardly has time to see me anymore. I want him to do well. I know I don't want to feel guilty or responsible if he fails in this country. What would people think of me if I were the cause of his failure? In fact, he gave me another paper to type for him." She picked up the scrawled work on the dining room table and looked disturbed. "He doesn't write very well, but I don't mind helping him."

Busi showed Shirley where to put her clothes and which bed was hers. "Look, Shirley. I have to type this work for Albert. Why don't you take a shower, unpack and relax. After I finish typing I'm going to surprise him by delivering it to him." She sat down at the computer. "He always comes over here to get his papers, but I know that takes away from his studying time." She looked up at Shirley and smiled. "This time I'll do him an extra favor by delivering it to him."

Busi worked for hours on the paper. After it was finished she put on a flowing red dress. Albert always told her how vibrant she looked in red. She dabbed on cologne that he had given her. She checked herself in her bedroom mirror and adjusted the collar of her dress.

"Don't wait up for me, sisi." She called to Shirley. She could hear her sister laughing in the background. She was so glad to have Shirley in America with her. It was like having a little piece of home.

She took the metro to Albert's street. Then she walked another several blocks. She never squandered her little bit of salary on taxis.

When she got to his door she straightened her dress, licked her lips to make sure her lipstick was on, and she knocked.

She heard Albert coming to the door and felt her heart skip a beat.

He swung the door open and looked shocked. He was in a silk robe with almost nothing on underneath. He pulled the sash around his waist and inquired, "Busi, what are you doing here tonight?"

"I finished your paper, and I wanted to surprise you with it." She replied. She felt confused and squinted her eyes to look past him into the living room. It was dark with candles lit around the room.

"Oh, that's nice of you. Look, this really isn't a very good time for me. I've just been working so hard on my math problems." He started to close the door behind him and he walked into the hallway. "If I don't get all this math right I may not be able to pass the course."

Busi felt awkward. How could he be studying in a dimly lit room? She was about to speak when she heard a woman's voice coming from inside the apartment.

"Albert, sugar, who's there? Come back to bed, sweetie."

Albert looked embarrassed, and Busi felt sick.

"So this is the studying you've been doing? You mean I've been typing for you so you could have time to entertain someone?" She ripped the paper in pieces and threw the shredded assignment at his chest where it fell all over the floor.

"Baby, honey, don't be mad. Let me explain." He pleaded with Busi.

"I am not your baby, and thank God, I will never have your baby, either."

She turned and walked, without running to the front door of the building. She would not let him think that she was fleeing. Once outside she leaned over the railing and sobbed. She refused to let him see her cry, but now she felt like she would vomit. Her heart was pounding. She felt like her body was about to burst from pain and rage. On the way back to her apartment she kept running events through her mind.

"Oh Busi, you stupid fool." She thought to herself. "Why couldn't you see what was happening?" She rested her head on the hand bar of the metro. As the subway car roared through the tunnel she caught herself talking aloud, and the tears were streaming down her face.

"Little girl too far away from home. You must be crazy." She said under her breath. "Silly little Swazi girl. He must have laughed to see you do all that work while he was bedding an American woman." She got off the metro at her stop and walked home slowly. She was nauseated, and her stomach felt like knotted rope. "How dumb you were to think that he was just too overworked to care about your birthday."

Suddenly she remembered that Shirley was upstairs. Her sister was in America. At last she had someone to talk to that she could trust. Shirley would understand. Busi ran up the stairs and threw open the door.

"Shirley, are you still awake?"

Shirley came out of the bedroom in her nightgown. "I'm still up. I was reading this magazine they gave me on the airplane. Did you know that the Washington Monument and the Lincoln Monument all line up in a row in front of the round Capitol Building? We just have to go see those places." Shirley looked up and saw Busi's face. She was still crying and looked terrible. "Busi, what happened to you? Did someone hurt you tonight?"

"Yes someone hurt me. Someone who should never have hurt me, and he planned it all along. It is my own fault. I was such a fool to think that he was a decent man." She sat on the edge of her bed and pounded her fist into the covers. "Maybe I was just lonely. You'll see. This is a beautiful country, but sometimes I just wish I could be home where I belong. I should have known he would do this. All the signs were there, and I was just too stupid to see it."

She dried her eyes and explained the situation to Shirley. Shirley was dutifully angry, too. "Here is the way it is, sisi. He thinks that if he tells these American women he is a prince they will be impressed. He probably tells every woman he meets about his royal blood just to get her in bed. Just because he's a prince doesn't make him a good man or an honest one. Back home you would never have been attracted to him."

"Back home in Mbabane, he would never have looked twice at someone like me. I'm just a lowly secretary. I'm nothing special. I'm just another conquest to him."

"You can do better, little Busi."

"I am never going to humiliate myself like that again." Busi stood up and walked around the room. "From now on I take care of myself. I won't be fooled that way again. Oh, Shirley, thank you for coming." She wrapped her arms around her sister's neck. "We can do everything together, and neither of us has to be lonely anymore."

⇒ ⇐

The time passed quickly with Shirley staying at the apartment. They were avid sightseers and went to every museum in the Smithsonian.

They loved shopping in America. Payless Shoes was a favorite, and they knew every aisle of the nearby Wal Mart. With Shirley around Busi didn't skip meals anymore. They loved to eat American hamburgers and huge salad bars at local restaurants. Work went well for her, too. She understood the demands of her job, and it became natural to answer several phone lines and send faxes to other officials. Shirley enjoyed going to the university, and she tried very hard to keep up her scholarship. Busi stopped thinking about Albert. He made it easy for her. He never tried to call or make amends. He simply moved on to the next impressionable young woman.

⇒ ⇐

It was a spring Monday morning, and Busi got to work at her usual time. She had learned that in America when someone says 8:00 he means it, so she was never late to the office. On her desk was a large official looking envelope. It was brown, the color of official Swazi government mail. The front of it read 'His Majesty's Royal Government of Swaziland.' She sat down and stared at it. It was definitely addressed to her, but she was afraid to open it. She had a strong premonition of what was probably inside the brown container. She brewed the coffee and read all the other mail on her desk. Finally, she had to face the large brown envelope. Inside was the letter that she had dreaded for quite some time. After six years in the United States her term was ending. She was ordered to go home the first day of the next month.

She debated the entire day as to how she would break the news to Shirley. By now they were both feeling more American than Swazi. They had made friends with some of the students at the university and had created a regular social circle. Most of the students they knew were from other countries. They would often sightsee as a group to the

Smithsonian museums. Busi had her favorite artists in the National Gallery. There were special places they liked to meet for coffee. How could she walk away from this life and go back to her tiny country in southern Africa? What would Shirley do if Busi left?

When Busi walked in the door after work Shirley was there excited.

"Busi, the new Mel Gibson movie is starting tonight at the theatre. I know it's a weeknight, but let's go anyway. We can be the first ones to see it. Let's not even eat any supper. We'll just have popcorn and Cokes in the movie." She looked at Busi's somber face. "Well, it's not that bad. If you want to go next week I guess we can do that instead."

"It's not the movie, sisi. In fact, that sounds like a good idea. Maybe that will cheer me up right now."

"What's the matter with you? Did something bad happen? Don't tell me that horrible Albert had the nerve to show his face again."

Busi laughed and sank into a chair. "No, Shirley, we'll never have him to worry about again. I'm not sure if he is even in the States anymore, but that is what I have to talk to you about."

Shirley sat down on the sofa and leaned forward with a concerned grimace on her face. "Something terrible must have happened today. Was it at work? Did something happen at the embassy?"

"Oh, yes. It was at work, and it was terrible. Come on Shirley, let's go to the movie. I'll talk about it with you on the way."

They grabbed their jackets and rushed out the door. On the way Busi told her sister about the letter.

"They can't do that to you. You've done a great job at the embassy. How can they just send you home like that?" Shirley was incredulous and furious.

"Sisi, you can't be cross about this. I knew when I came here that it was temporary. They kept me here longer than most people get to stay. I suppose I should be grateful for that." She turned up the collar on her jacket to keep out the wind as they walked.

"I'm not angry with anyone. I just don't know how to leave America. I have to admit that I'll be glad to see the family again after all these years. Just think, I have two more nieces now than when I left."

Shirley threw back her head and chuckled. "Isn't it funny that our sister, Lindiwe, named her third daughter Zanele thinking she would be the youngest child? Then she went on and had two more children." They both laughed thinking about a child walking around with a name that meant 'youngest child' and everyone knowing that she was the middle child.

"I'm sure she will use her English name when she grows up." Busi replied. Then she went on "Shirley, what will you do when I leave? Are you coming home with me?"

Shirley was quiet for a minute and held her head down against the cold air as they kept walking. Finally she answered softly.

"Busi, I still have my grant to go to the university. It doesn't offer much, but I want to stay here and finish."

"But Shirley, when I leave you will lose the flat we are living in. The next secretary will come from Swaziland, and they won't let you stay there. Where will you go?"

"You know we have made many friends here. I'll ask around and see if I can stay with one of them. I know I'll have to pay some rent, but I can work it out. Maybe I can get a part time job to help with my expenses." She stopped walking and looked at Busi.

"I can't go home. I have things I want to accomplish here. I really need to stay in America. Besides, what is there for me in Africa?"

They both stood cold and shivering in the night air. "Swaziland doesn't have anything to offer me. What will I do if I go back, marry some poor Swazi man and have too many children I can't feed?" She started walking again, and they approached the theatre. "No, Busi. I'm not going back. At least I'm not going back now."

≡ ≡

The month passed quickly, and Busisiwe packed her belongings. There were things to ship, things to carry back, and things that she left for her sister. Busi was amazed at the amount of clothes and shoes and number of items she had accumulated over the last six years. She shopped for gifts to carry back for everyone in the family. She was careful to remember both mothers, all of her sisters and brothers, and every single niece and nephew. She brought her father a special gift, a Lucite cube paperweight with American coins embedded in it. As her departure date drew closer she felt actually excited to see her family, mostly her parents, again.

Shirley found two female students from Nigeria to room with near the university. They were glad to have another person sharing the rent. Their apartment wasn't as nice as the one she shared with her sister, but she would adjust. Busi had left her the television, stereo and other appliances that she couldn't take with her. After all, the electricity and electronic equipment was much different than that in Africa. It would be pointless to send it home. On the other hand, she had skillfully bought an expensive VCR that would play both European and American tapes. That special purchase she shipped back to Mbabane.

Busi and Shirley said their goodbyes at the airport. It was strange separating at the same airport where they had once joined each other. Shirley was sad to see Busi leave, but she intended to get on with her life. She was more sorry for Busi having to leave such a great country than she was to be left behind in America.

By the time the Royal Swazi jet landed in Matsapha Busi was exhausted. She looked out the tiny plane's window and saw her family waiting and waving from the airport. Seeing them made her glad to be home again, and she couldn't wait to get off the plane. She navigated through customs and then moved into the small main terminal. Everyone rushed over and grabbed her and hugged her. All the way back to Mbabane the children were questioning her. What did she bring them? Did she like being home? What was America like? Is Auntie Shirley ever coming back?

Her luggage was taken to the bedroom that she had shared with her sisters since her childhood. It was awkward and strange to put her American clothes and shoes and belongings in that house. Her mother prepared a meal of all Busi's favorite foods, but Busi wasn't used to eating those things anymore. The thought of eating pumpkin leaves with peanut butter and mealie meal with gravy made her feel ill.

"You're so kind to go to all this trouble for me, but I think I really need some rest." She excused herself away from the dinner table.

One of the children followed her, but Lindiwe stopped her. "Let Auntie rest. She has had a long journey, and she is going through a lot of adjustments."

Busi went to her bedroom and lay on her bed. She buried her head in her pillow and tried to sleep. I know I'm happy to be with my family." She thought to herself. "Why am I feeling so sick?"

"Busisiwe, wake up." She felt her mother nudge her leg over the bedcovers. "Busisiwe, we have been letting you sleep for the last two days. You have to get up now. There have been many phone calls from the government office, and your daddy has answered them for you. It is embarrassing for your father to have to take your calls." Her mother sat down on the bed beside her, and Busi turned over to look at her. "Are you sick?" She put her hand on Busi's forehead, and it was cool.

"Well, I can't see what could be wrong with you. You have certainly had enough sleep. Now you have to get up, take a bath and get dressed." She pulled the covers away from the bed and forced Busi to react.

"Okay, Mama. I know you're right. It was just such a hard trip. And everything feels so different to me."

"Of course it does, dear." Mama had a way of understanding people. That was probably one of the reasons she was such a good nurse. "You are part of two worlds now." She stroked Busi's forehead and hugged her. "These worlds have very little in common for you, but this is where you belong in the world. This is your home; we are your blood. Come now, Cecile has breakfast on the table, and you need to eat. You are still so thin. Didn't you eat anything in America?"

Busisiwe thought about the wonderful food she ate in Washington, and all the restaurants she enjoyed while she was there. A wave of depression swept over her as she put on her American denim jeans and went out to the dining room.

"Busisiwe, you know we don't dress like that around here." When have you ever seen women wear clothing like that in Mbabane? You can wear it in the house, but please, don't go outside looking like that. It is so unfeminine."

"I wish I had a pair of those." Her niece remarked.

Mama was disgusted and everyone laughed. Busi was glad for the distraction.

⇒ ⇐

It didn't take long for Busi to figure out what she wanted. She knew that she had to have her own place. She had been independent for six years, and the idea of living under her mother's roof was out of the question. The Swazi government accommodated her with a job when she came back to the country, so Busi was able to establish herself emotionally and financially. They gave her the position of administrative assistant to a high-ranking government official at the Swaziland Government Institute.

Since she worked for the government she was given a government house. It wasn't elaborate, but it was large, and it was very close to her new job. That was essential since she had no transportation. She thought about buying a car, but it was impossible to save the kind of money it would take for her to own a decent car. Most of the people who worked at the institute were women. Busi had no trouble making new friends. No matter how gratifying her new job was, though, she missed her life in America. When she walked home on the red dirt path she remembered the times she walked home from the embassy in Washington. There were so many little 'take away' cafes and shops. Here there was just a dirty road down a steep hill to her brown square house. The equipment at the new job didn't compare with the sophisticated office supplies she had in Washington. There were computers and copying machines and fax equipment, but they were outdated and often needed repair.

"Busi, did you hear about the new shop across the street?" One of the instructors at the institute caught up with her as she climbed the hill to go to work. She had just gotten off the bus from Manzini.

"I remember hearing you mention that you got your shoes at Payless in America." The instructor, Thembekile, was so excited that she was breathless trying to tell Busi all about it on the way up the steep incline.

"Someone from America, someone in a religious mission got shoes from that place, Payless, and they are selling them real cheap in Sidwasheni. You know, that industrial area."

Busi was amazed. "Let's go during our lunch hour." Busi said. "That sounds wonderful."

During lunch they walked to the warehouse that the American mission had rented. Sure enough, inside were rows and rows of boots and shoes for men and women and children. Payless Shoes had donated their surplus to the mission. Then the mission sold the shoes very cheaply. The mission was able to accomplish two feats with this plan. They made a profit that they could use at their discretion, and they outfitted people with good quality shoes at a reasonable cost.

"Oh Busi, I just have to have this brown pair of heels. Don't you think it would look smart with my suit?"

"Yes, and I think I will get these black ones. These dirt roads are ruining the shoes I bought in America." Busi replied.

On the way back to work Thembekile said, "Busi, why don't you ever go shopping in Manzini? They have so many more places to look for things than Mbabane. I love Manzini. I can't even imagine living in a dull city like Mbabane. Mbabane is just a city of government offices and Europeans. Manzini is alive with excitement. The selection in their stores is so much nicer. Why don't you go there on Saturday and see for yourself."

"I don't like to go to Manzini." Busi responded. "I have to take one of those crowded buses, and it's such a long hot ride." They kept walking and Busi thought about it some more. She had been back in Mbabane for almost a year, and she was still making comparisons to the United States. Her mother had tried to counsel her about getting back to her culture. Her father had talked to her about accepting the good side of life in Swaziland. None of it was sinking into her mind or her heart. She was so envious of Shirley who was still studying in Washington. All of Shirley's letters were so positive and happy. How could she be comfortable again in her own country? She would have to force herself to be content; this was her home, and that was the way it was going to be. She had heard people talk in the government offices about the rarity of opportunities in the United States. They weren't allowing staff to go there for such long periods of time anymore. Once she overheard an institute faculty member on the phone complaining that students who go to the US to study never come back. "We are losing our best and brightest to America and Europe. What is the point of that?" He complained. "They can receive any education they need in South Africa. It is a waste of money to send students abroad."

"You know, Thembekile. I would like to shop in Manzini sometime. That is a good idea. When I get paid at the end of the month I'll make a trip down there." Her friend, Thembekile was pleased. She was glad to have an impact on Busi. Everyone at work liked Busi, but they were tired of hearing her talk about America. Secretly, Thembekile wished she could go to America. She wanted to study for her doctorate degree in history. She wasn't fussy about which university in America. It was all one big paradise in her mind.

The end of the month arrived. Busisiwe paid her bills and put some money aside to take on her shopping trip. She boarded the bus from the bus stop in the heart of Mbabane and sat near the front. The bus was so crowded. It seemed as if everyone in the country got paid on the same day. There were too many passengers on the bus. People were sitting three to a seat, and they were pushing people out of their way. The ride took almost an hour. Normally, it would have taken half that time, but everyone on the bus was shouting to stop at different locations along the way. The bus driver warned them that he would not stop on Malagwane Hill so don't ask. As the bus went down the steep hill Busi wished she hadn't been sitting in the front. She felt like they were going to career right over the side. When she looked to the back of the bus it was so packed with people and bags that she knew she wouldn't have been able to breathe if she had sat there. She looked down at the floor and was silent the entire trip.

Once she arrived in Manzini she got off the bus and looked around. She hadn't been to Manzini since she had arrived home from America. It was an exciting city. There was so much commotion on the main street. There were so many little stands where women were selling things. They had stands with vegetables and fruit wrapped neatly in little plastic bags that hung colorfully from sticks on either side of the table. There were stands that sold hot food and fat cakes. There was a particular stand that sold a variety of fragrant roses. She bought a fat cake to eat on the way, and she bought a bundle of roses. She didn't notice the man behind her as she reached in her bag to pay for the roses. The street was so congested that she headed down a side street to avoid bumping into someone as she ate the fat cake.

Suddenly she was face down on the pavement. The man came from behind and leveled her against the ground. Before she could scream he hit her on the side of her face. He hit her with a club against the back of her head. She tried once more to lift her head, but he kept hitting her back and legs and sides.

"Hey you! Get away from her." Busi heard another man's voice, but she couldn't move. She was in so much pain she just laid, face down, on the concrete. "Get away. You get out of here." The man yelled as he picked up a rock and threw it at the mugger. The mugger was easily frightened and ran off down an alley.

"Are you all right? Can you hear me? Are you okay?" She couldn't speak. Her face was swollen, and the pain was searing through her head where the mugger had beat her.

The young man turned her over and lifted her head in his arms. "Can you speak?" He pulled out a handkerchief from his pocket and tried to wipe the blood away from her lips. "He's gone now. But I'm afraid he has stolen your purse."

Busi collapsed in his arms. The purse had all of her pocket money for the month. Worse than that, she was in extreme pain and felt like all her bones had been broken.

"Here, let me help you. I have a friend who has a car. We can get you back home. Where do you live?" He looked at this tiny bleeding and broken woman. "Don't try to talk yet." He held her in his arms and cradled her weak body. "I'll take care of you now."

He picked her up and carried her to the end of the block. There he found his friend who had the car. "What's this?" The friend asked. "What should we do with her? Do you know anything about her? Where does she live?"

"Don't ask so many questions. Let's just put her in the backseat so she can rest for a minute." He helped her into the car. Then he ran back and picked up her roses that were still wrapped in a piece of newspaper on the sidewalk.

Busi tried unsuccessfully to sit up, but she just lay against the seat in the back of the little car. Finally, she got the strength to whisper. "Thank you. I live in Mbabane. Could you take me home if it isn't too much trouble?"

She felt half conscious the entire ride back to Mbabane. Busi thought about going to her mother, but she was too weak to deal with the commotion in that house. The men took her to her government house, and they helped her inside.

"My name is Busisiwe. I don't think I know your name. Maybe it should be savior or something like that."

The young man smiled and brought her a glass of water. "Well, I guess you could say it's close to that. My name is Mduduzi."

Busi rested her head back on a pillow on her sofa. "Yes, that means comfort. You are like your name. I don't know how to thank you."

"Please, you should see a doctor or someone for medical treatment. Your head has a big bump, and you are very bruised. You might have a broken bone. Let me take you for some help."

Busi tried to sit up but she fell back. She laughed weakly and replied, "My mother is a nurse. I wonder what she will say about this."

"Well, we will have to call her and find out."

Busi's mother was frantic when Mduduzi called her on the phone. She ran over to Busi's house carrying her bag of bandages and medical supplies. Unfortunately, as happens in big families, everyone rushed over with her to check on Busi's condition.

"Little Busi. I think you are going to live." Her mother put antiseptic on the cuts and scratches and ordered the nieces to get ice for the bruises. "That's not enough ice." Her mother ordered the girls. "Go to a neighbor and see if anyone has some more. There are far too many bruises for that little bag of ice." She turned to Mduduzi who suddenly felt out of place in the room. "I think my daughter has you to thank for saving her life."

"You'll be okay now. Here are the roses you dropped." He placed them on her lap. "I picked them up. I thought they looked like you. They are beautiful and perfect. Those thorns, they are the hard times in life, but they never stop the rose from blooming. I'll call you again another time." The entire family gathered to thank Mduduzi for saving their precious Busi. He left quietly while she was sleeping.

Almost a week passed before Busi was strong enough to get out of bed and go back to work. She was still sore. Her body was swollen and she could hardly speak. Her mother had Cecile cook foods that didn't require much chewing, and after a few days of soup and mashed avocado Busi felt it was time to face her job again.

Thembekile was shocked and amazed when she saw what had happened to her friend. She felt terrible and responsible for suggesting that Busi should go to Manzini. She wasn't sure how to apologize.

"Please don't feel bad." Busi tried to speak. "It was just a bad day. Anyone could have been me that day. It will heal in time. A very kind man came by and saved me or the robber would have killed me. It was God's will for me to live that day."

A few days after she had been back to work the receptionist told her that a gentleman was waiting in the office. Busi limped to the front desk and saw Mduduzi standing looking for her. She could get a better look at him now, and his face was as kind as she had remembered. It wasn't just a dream or her imagination.

"You look a lot better today." He said gently. "Your mother told me that you were back at work. You know, she is still worried about you."

Busi had to laugh, though it made her back hurt. "My mother makes a career out of worrying about me. I haven't had a chance to thank you properly. Would you like to come to my house on Friday night for dinner? I wouldn't say I'm the best cook in Swaziland, but I can cook a big steak for us. Well, actually, would you like steak? I am not able to chew that well yet."

"Busi, It would be an honor to eat anything you feel like cooking. If you can't eat steak then why would I want to eat it in front of you? We can share a can of soup. How does that sound?"

"It doesn't sound very good." She laughed. "So we'll think of something else we will both enjoy."

Mduduzi left and Busi went back to her desk. It felt good to laugh again. She felt happy to be home for the first time. How odd, she wondered, to be happy now when she was so bruised and beaten.

≡ ≡

Mduduzi and Busisiwe seemed to belong to each other. Comfort and the Blessed One were truly in love and inseparable. Busi had never felt so complete and happy in her life. There was just one little problem. Mduduzi was unemployed. Not only could he not support her, he could never afford the lobola to honor her parents. Busi wasn't concerned about the money. She was earning an adequate salary in her position at the institute. The lobola was another matter, and she knew that at some point she would have to confront her parents with that problem. There was another issue, too, and she kept it a secret as long as she could.

It was her mother who confronted Busi first. It was late on a Sunday afternoon. The family had gone to church and finished a big dinner at her mother's home. Busi's father was not there. He had been with them the Sunday before, so this weekend he was at the other family's house. After everyone left Grace took the opportunity to discuss Mduduzi with Busi.

"Busi, we need to talk about your relationship with Mduduzi." Grace said as they sat together in the living room. "I'm concerned about his intentions. You have been together for quite some time now. Has it been a year already?"

Busi sat with her head down and listened. She nodded in response to her mother. Then she looked up at her. "What do you want me to tell you, Mama? I love him. He's so good to me. I know he doesn't have a job. If I waited to find a man with a job in this country I could be waiting until I'm an old woman. You know how hard the times are right now. I just read in the Swazi Times that the unemployment rate is almost 40 percent."

"I know, I know. But you see, dear." Her mother took Busi's hand in hers and spoke softly. "You come from an important family. How can this man pay lobola? If he can't even pay lobola how can he commit to taking care of you?"

Busi almost broke into tears, but she stopped herself and spoke with a knot in her throat. "First of all, Mama, I don't know if I want to be married. I have taken care of myself for a long time. Remember I was in America 16,000 kilometers from home. I managed well. I love this man just as he is, and besides," She felt her throat tighten and she could hear the words coming out of her mouth as if she was speaking in a surrealistic dream. "I am carrying his baby."

So there it was. She had said it now. Busi had been wondering for weeks how to tell her family that she was pregnant. There was never going to be an easy way to share that news. She wanted his child. This was the first man who had cared about her in an unselfish and loving way. It would be an honor to be the mother of his son.

Busi sat and waited for her mother's response. The two of them were silent, and it seemed an eternity until her mother spoke.

"My little Busi, my little one who has blessed our hearts and lives, It will not be easy to tell your father about this. But...what are we to do? You are right. You have taken care of yourself in every way. It seems as though this was not an accident. Did you plan this baby? Have you thought about how you are going to raise him and take care of him? Does Mduduzi know about this?"

They both knew that in their culture a baby was considered a joy and an honor. The idea of abortion was not only illegal; it was taboo. There would be no discussion of what to do about the baby.

"Yes, Mama, Mduduzi does know, because I love him, and I share everything with him. I don't want to be married right now. I know he doesn't have work, but some day he will, and when he does we will have a proper ceremony. Please, help me tell Daddy about this." She dropped to her knees in front of her mother. "Please help him to understand what I'm doing."

Grace lifted Busi's face to hers and smiled. Her face welled up with tears and she said softly, "Busi, you will be fine. We will all see to that."

≡ ≡

Musa and Grace took excellent care of Busi just as she promised, but they didn't have to worry. Mduduzi was a man of his word. He could not afford lobola and he still did not have a job, but he was a tender-hearted man. When the baby was born he took his rightful position as his father.

Busi delivered a very big and healthy baby boy. Everyone at the institute was amazed that such a petite woman could come through that experience with such fortitude and confidence. Her labor had lasted only a few hours with Grace by her side the entire time.

When the baby was a week old Mduduzi accepted his responsibility for naming his son. He held the tiny infant up to the ancestral spirits and declared that he was now to be known as Makabongwe; he was God's gift.

Busi was home on maternity leave for four months. That was the tradition and policy in Swazi government. She and Mduduzi grew even closer, and she agonized over going back to work. She had already planned to have someone on the premises at work take care of baby so that she could nurse Makabongwe during her work breaks.

Makabongwe truly was a gift from God. He was a beautiful boy with large brown eyes like his mother and a head full of curly hair. He walked at an early age and made everyone in the family laugh when he could speak words in English and siSwati by the time he was a year old.

Busi came home from work one afternoon and her niece was taking care of the baby.

"Auntie, you must call Gogo right away. She is very upset and needs to talk to you."

"What is wrong? Is this any way to greet me when I come home?" Busi came in the living room and picked up little Makabongwe in her arms. As she was snuggling him she asked more questions.

"What does Gogo need from me?"

"A letter came today from Auntie Shirley in America. Gogo was reading it, and she started to cry. Then she told me to come over here and get you. I told her that I was going to watch little Makabongwe this afternoon, so I would give you the message. You must call her right now. She is very disturbed."

Busi put little Makabongwe back on the floor where he had been playing. She picked up the phone and called her mother.

After she hung up the phone she looked at her niece and said "Let's go to Gogo's house now. Put Makabongwe's jacket on him, and get your things. We will have to walk so hurry."

They arrived at the house, and Grace was sitting in a chair in the living room. Cecile had brought her a cup of tea, but it was left untouched. In her hand she held the letter Shirley had sent from Washington DC. Busi approached her mother and hugged her. Then she gently took the letter and read it.

"I'm so sorry, Mama. This is my fault. I'm the one who encouraged Shirley to go to the US. Now she refuses to come home. She doesn't even want to be a Swazi. I'm so sorry."

Busi hugged Grace and Cecile took the baby into the kitchen for something to eat.

"Busi, why, does she love it there so much?" Grace looked up. Her eyes were red and swollen and her face was streaked with dry tears. "It says in the letter that her grant was finished, but she won't come back. Doesn't she love us anymore?"

"Mama, Mama. It's hard to explain, I know. I always had a feeling that Shirley wanted to be American even before she went to the US. It isn't that she doesn't love us."

"But read this Busi. She says she has no money and no job. She is living in a shelter for homeless people. How can that be better than living with her family?"

"I think that she has been there so long that she thinks she is an American. I don't know. I loved America, too." Busi reflected on her years in Washington. She remembered how hard it was to live there and then how painful it was to leave it. "Mama, you would be surprised to see how many Africans live in that city. They drive taxis; they work in restaurants. They do anything to stay there."

"That certainly doesn't impress me." Grace gained her composure and stood up with an air of resolve. "Shirley doesn't even work. She preys on the welfare of strangers to feed her. How can that country be so wonderful that she would sleep in a bed for paupers rather than be with her family? I will talk to your father, and we will send her a ticket to come home."

At this point Grace was feeling her strength return. She was over the shock of her daughter's letter, and she decided to fix the situation once and for all. "That's what we will do. Shirley is a Swazi. She should be proud of that. What is all this American business? My daughter will come home."

Busi read the letter again. "I'm afraid you are wasting your time and your money. Look at this line near the end." She held out the letter for her mother to read, but Grace didn't want to see it anymore.

"Don't read it then, but I can tell you that she will not come home. It will not matter what you do. I think we have to realize that Shirley is on her own and doesn't want us to interfere." She hugged her mother and tried to comfort her. "Maybe some day she will return to us. No matter what Shirley thinks, she will always be a Swazi."

Busi and Makabongwe stayed for dinner that night. It was a quiet meal, and Cecile made sure that she prepared food that everyone would like. At least they would have some feeling of peace around the dinner table. Busi knew that Shirley meant the words she wrote. Shirley had always wanted to go to America. She had fallen in love with Washington the minute her plane had landed. Busi felt responsible for opening the door to that country, but now Shirley had taken her future into her own hands.

≡ ≡

It was a cold winter Friday night in July. Busi walked home from work and was thinking about what she would prepare for dinner. The air was crisp, and she considered building a warm fire. She glanced up and could see the brilliant winter fires burning like streaks of lightning up the mountainsides. The farmers had been told not to burn the grass in the dry season, but centuries of culture were ingrained in their methods. They always burned the dead grass in the winter to enrich the ground for spring planting. She thought it was a beautiful sight, and one that she always looked forward to during the year. Mduduzi was coming for dinner. She knew a cozy fire and a hot meal would please him.

She walked in the house and put down her groceries. She had purchased a bouquet of roses from Thembekile for a centerpiece. Thembekile always bought the prettiest roses from an old woman named Anna who lived near Manzini. Makabongwe was spending the night at her sister's house. This evening was a special one for Busi.

She barely had time to arrange the flowers in a vase when there was a soft tapping at her door.

"Who is it? If it's you, Mduduzi, you are much too early for my presentation."

She opened the door, and Mduduzi stood at the threshold. He leaned against the hinge and was perspiring profusely.

"What's happened to you?" She enquired.

"I don't know what is wrong, but I am so ill. It is something with my stomach I think. Can I lie down somewhere?" He practically fell into her arms, and she tried to support him to the bed.

"What do you think is wrong? What can I do?" She was scared. She had seen him weak and tired recently, but she had never seen him like this.

He collapsed on the bed and moaned in agony. He drew up his legs and twisted into a fetal position on her bed. All night he writhed in pain while Busi put cool cloths on his head and offered him sips of water.

Saturday morning came, and she called her mother. She was growing desperate. Mduduzi was in more pain and grew weaker by the hour.

"Please, Mama. I don't know what to do. I have never seen anything like this. Ask Lindiwe to keep Makabongwe for a while. I think I need to take Mduduzi to Mbabane hospital."

"Let me go with you." Grace advised. "That is a busy place, and you will need the best doctor. I will come to get you right away."

They rushed to Mbabane government hospital. Busi had never seen a place like that. When she had sprained her ankle in Washington Shirley and she had gone to the emergency room that was clean and efficient. This hospital scared her.

There were people moaning and crying in the hallways. People were lying on the dirty floors, because there were no more vacant beds.

She overheard one nurse tell a family that they would have to pick up their relative that night and bring him back in the morning, as there was not enough staff during the night hours to care for him. Then she watched other people bringing food, water and soap to their sick family members. The hospital didn't provide those luxuries.

Grace was able to find the best doctor on call, and he met them at the casualty area. The nurses and doctor attended to Mduduzi throughout the day. Once in a while they would come out shaking their heads at Busisiwe. Grace sat with Busi and comforted her the entire weekend at the hospital.

By Sunday night Mduduzi was dead.

Busi's anguished cries could be heard throughout the corridors of the hospital. She would not let them take away his body. She was sure that he had to be alive, and that they just didn't realize he was sleeping or unconscious.

Finally, Grace convinced her daughter that it was over, and it was time for them to go home.

"Busi, honey, you have to leave. Little Makabongwe needs you at home. That is your concern now. Let's go." She put her arm around her frail daughter and laid Busi's head on her shoulder. Together they walked in silence through the dingy doors of the hospital.

Busi dressed for the funeral and noticed that the roses were still in bloom in the vase where she had happily arranged them just a few days earlier. She picked them up out of the vase and held them in her arms. Her father escorted her to the funeral, and Grace took Makabongwe by the hand. As the friends and family left the burial spot Busisiwe approached the place where her beloved was resting forever. She bent over and laid the roses on the grave.

"I am these roses, and my heart rests here with you." She wept.

≡ ≡

A month passed before Grace had the courage to speak to Busi about Mduduzi's death. Finally, Busi was coming for dinner, and she seized a quiet opportunity.

"Busi, Cecile is taking care of dinner preparations in the kitchen, and I have to talk with you."

"Okay, what is the problem?" Busi knew her mother's tone of voice well enough to know when she was concerned about something.

"Busi, the doctor never told us how Mduduzi died. This could be a problem for you." She weighed her words carefully knowing she was edging on a difficult subject.

"Mama, nobody knows what happened to Mduduzi. It is a tragedy. That is enough for me." She felt her voice grow weak. "My little boy will never know his daddy. That is all I think about now."

"Busi" Grace held firm in her resolve to complete her mission. "I am thinking that maybe you should be tested for HIV."

"What?" Busi jumped up in anger. "How can you even suspect such a thing? There are many ways to die in Swaziland. AIDS is just another way to die." She heard her voice grow loud, and she tempered it so Makabongwe wouldn't hear her. "Just last week someone at the institute almost died from cholera. Maybe Mduduzi had that." She paced nervously around the room while she spoke. "Just because somebody dies everyone thinks it's the AIDS virus. I won't let Mduduzi's honor and reputation die with him. I won't speak about this anymore."

"What would it hurt to have a simple test?" Grace leaned forward in her chair and pleaded with her daughter. If you are HIV free, then you don't have to think about it. If you are not there are things they can do for you."

Busi put her hands on her ears and cried. "I won't listen to this. Look at me. I look healthy. My baby boy looks healthy. I have seen those AIDS victims, and they look thin and wasted. That is not me. I will not speak of this anymore."

Grace dropped the subject. Busi was still too fragile to handle that information. Perhaps Busi was right. After all, the doctor did not declare that Mduduzi had died of anything specific. He just said it must have been an acute intestinal attack.

"I'm sorry, Mama." Busi regained her composure and hugged Grace. "There is too much on my mind. You'll see. We will all be fine. Little Makabongwe is strong and healthy and bright. Have you seen him point to his eyes and ears and nose?" Her voice trembled as she spoke. "He is learning English from his cousins. He is God's gift to me, and I'm not going to give him an English name. I will honor his daddy and keep his heritage strong."

That night she put her precious son to bed. She told him wonderful stories about his daddy. She stroked his head and whispered, "Daddy is here in your heart, my sweet baby."

She sat on the floor and laid her head on the bed next to her sleeping son.

"I have to be strong now to raise this little one to be a good man." She thought to herself. "Could Mduduzi have died from a bad piece of food? Could he have been poisoned with the muti?" She closed her eyes and felt the weariness of an old woman, but she was not even 35 years old. "Maybe I will get checked out like Mama said." She yawned and stretched her legs on the floor. "Of course, there couldn't be anything wrong with me; I feel perfectly fine."

Chapter 5 – Thembekile

Thembekile sat at her dressing table. She glanced at herself in the mirror, and reached for her lipstick. Her younger sister came from behind her and whisked the lipstick out of her hand.

"Where are you going tonight, Thembekile?" Her sister asked. "You don't have to tell me, because I know already." Her sister pushed her way to the mirror and applied the cosmetic to her own lips. "Mama says that you are dating a married man. Is it true?"

Thembekile was disgusted. She was in a hurry and didn't feel the need to explain her personal life to her 16-year-old sister, Nobantu.

"Give me back the lipstick, and mind your own business. Don't you have other things to do than wonder about my life?"

"He is married. That proves it!" Nobantu laughed and ran out of the room. Thembekile continued with her make up and gave herself a critical evaluation in the mirror.

"What do I care if he has a wife?" She whispered to herself. "I don't plan to marry him anyway."

Thembekile grew up in a family of loving and devoted parents. Her mother, Siphokazi, and her father, Mbulelo, met as students in college. Both of them chose careers as teachers. Her mother was a head mistress of an elementary school, and her father was a high school science teacher. There was never another woman in Mbulelo's life, and Sipho adored her husband. They named their first-born child, Faithful, or Thembekile, out of respect to their own relationship. Thembekile was a bright and hard working student. She graduated at the top of her class in high school, and she earned honors in her university courses. Now, she was involved in a relationship based mostly on lust with a man who did not hide his marital status from her. She met Jacob at a local disco and liked him immediately. He was five years older than she and had an easy sense of humor that made her feel comfortable. They danced and had drinks and left the club together. The first night they were together he told her that he was married. At first Thembekile felt embarrassed. She knew that this was not the type of man Sipho and Mbulelo anticipated for her future. She couldn't help herself. She had grown up conscientiously studying, reading, and achieving to please her parents. Now at 25 years old she had to admit it; she really wanted to have some fun.

Thembekile finished putting on her make up and rose from her vanity chair. She slipped her new dress over her head and touched up her hair. After spraying cologne all over her arms and neck she emerged from her bedroom.

"I suppose that scolding you and telling you the error of your ways is not going to matter is it?" Sipho sat in the living room with her newspaper in front of her. She barely glanced over it to see what Thembekile was wearing.

"Now, Mother, let's not go into that again." She leaned over and kissed the top of her mother's head. "I'll be back late tonight, so don't worry."

"Don't worry?" Musa's voice rose from another part of the room. "Our daughter is out with someone we do not approve of, and we are not allowed to worry? Why do you go out with this man? There is no future in it."

Thembekile kept walking to the door. "I'm late. See you later." She closed the door behind her and breathed a sigh.

It was a long walk down the path to the road where Jacob was to meet her. The air was fresh with spring, and the ground was painted with lavender from flowers of the jacaranda trees. This was her favorite season. The harsh dry winter had ended and the mountains were blooming again. She felt young and beautiful and free as she kicked her feet through the fallen purple flowers. The doves sang in cadence around her, and she whistled back to them.

Jacob was waiting at the end of the path in his car. As Thembekile waved to him she felt guilty for not having him come to the house. She secretly enjoyed her mysterious rendezvous and had never introduced Jacob to her parents. "They would only be critical of him." She thought. "What difference does it make anyway?"

Thembekile and Jacob often went dancing. They had dinners in touristy restaurants, and they spent hours in a quiet hotel room in Nhlangano, a city about an hour away from her home of Manzini.

⇒ ⇐

Spring turned to summer and the humid air barely drifted into Thembekile's bedroom. She felt a wave of nausea pass over her as she lifted her head off her pillow. The room seemed to sway in front of her, and she hesitated about getting out of bed.

"Why am I so ill?" She wondered. "I must have malaria. This isn't right, but I don't have a fever."

She gathered herself enough to stand up next to the bed. Then she doubled over and lay back down. It crossed her mind that she could be pregnant, but she pushed the thought away and considered more simple explanations for her nausea and fatigue.

"Thembekile, you are late for the university." She could hear her mother calling from the hallway. "I'm leaving for school. You need to get up now. Hurry"

Finally, Sipho came to the door and looked at her daughter curled up in bed with a light sheet covering her.

"Are you sick?" Sipho felt her daughter's head and gave her a critical look. "How long have you been like this, Thembekile?"

"I have been feeling very tired lately, but this is the first morning that I have been so sick to my stomach."

"I have my suspicions about this." Sipho stood next to the bed, gave Thembekile a stern look and folded her arms in front of her.

"Could you be pregnant?"

Thembekile was shocked. She was embarrassed that her mother could so easily guess such a dilemma. The look on her face gave away her own concerns, and Sipho sighed in disgust.

"That's what I thought. Didn't your father and I warn you that this was a bad relationship? Didn't we tell you that Jacob was not right for you? Now what will you do? He is married and will not leave his family for you. This is your own fault."

"We don't know yet if I'm pregnant, Mother. Let me go to the doctor and find out what is the truth before you condemn me."

"You're such a smart woman, Thembekile, but you make bad choices. How can someone with such a good brain that was given by God do stupid things with men?"

Thembekile started to cry. "We still don't know the truth. Please, don't say anymore until I know the truth."

Sipho hugged her daughter and left for school. She didn't know what to say at this point. If Thembekile was pregnant, then they would make the best of it and love the baby that God had fated to come into the world.

Thembekile crawled out of bed, bathed and dressed, but she didn't go to the university. Instead she sought the counsel of her gogo.

Themby walked out to the road and waited for the bus that would take her up into the mountains. The bus was hot and crowded, but it was not a long trip. It was the walk up the mountain that seemed endless. When she got off the bus she looked up the red clay road and eyed the long walk that was ahead of her. Gogo lived deep in the cracks of the mountains, and today the hike there seemed unbearable. It is customary and common for Swazis to walk many miles to their destinations. Even little school children walk several miles each way to school every day. Young children, five and six years old often walk alone along the sides of busy highways. Thembekile was a city child, and she never developed the appreciation for the long treks. Gogo always encouraged her to walk instead of riding on buses and driving cars. The elders in the villages believed that walking developed the soul and gave an individual the time and spiritual energy to meditate. In Themby's world there was no time for soul searching and meditating. There were too many obligations and appointments. This was a day she could use the meditation, but she didn't have the energy to enjoy it.

Themby found Gogo sitting on the stone stoop outside of her hut. The chickens scattered, and the mangy dog barked signaling Themby's arrival.

"I can tell by your walk, Themby. You have come to see your old gogo."

"Yebo Gogo, I'm here. There can't be many secrets with these animals around."

"Hah!" laughed Gogo. "Do you think that the chickens told me you are here? There are many things that give you away, and the easiest one is that very strong perfume you are wearing."

When Gogo lost her sight to cataracts she seemed to gain the wisdom of the ages. Her eyes were glazed in a tint of blue. She could not rely on facial expressions or other traits that sighted people lean on for their information. She knew a person's thoughts by the hesitation or strength in his voice. She had an intangible sense of judging human nature. Indeed, Gogo knew the ways of people, and she could feel their good or evil thoughts.

Gogo adored Thembekile the faithful one, so kind, so smart and so giving. She reminded her of Sipho as a child, loving yet precocious.

"Gogo, how is your back this morning?" Thembekile started the conversation with a respectful concern for her elder.

"Oh, my back is aching so." Gogo stooped over in exaggerated pain. "I don't know how long God will let this old woman see the sun rise."

It fascinated Themby that her grandmother always used terms of vision when she had no sight. The truth was that Gogo used vision to mark the sight of the mind and not the eyes. She had no need to use her eyes anymore. One day, a long time ago, Themby mentioned that she felt badly that Gogo couldn't see. Gogo's smile spread to the crevices of her wrinkled cheeks. She told Themby that she had seen enough of this world. Now she would rely on God's eyes to get her through life.

"Themby my child, come in, come in." Her voice crackled, and she reached for her granddaughter's face. Her ancient rugged hands felt like sandpaper on silk as she patted Themby's cheeks.

"Come, come, we must have a drink and talk. You haven't come to see me in a long time, Themby. What keeps you away?"

Themby knew it would be useless to attempt to deceive Gogo, and she needed her counsel.

Thembekile pushed the warped wooden door open and helped her gogo into the hut. For years Thembekile's parents tried to persuade Gogo to move in with them. She was much too independent, and she hated city life. They cajoled Gogo to find a more modern and suitable house. Again she refused.

Thembekile lit a candle on a small wooden table and remembered the argument her mother had several years ago with Gogo.

"This is my life. This is my culture." Gogo explained. "If I live in a fancy house like you the children will forget their roots. We must all remember where we come from. If everyone starts living like the white people what will become of our Swazi heritage?"

Sipho was disgusted. She told Gogo there were better ways to demonstrate Swazi pride than to live in a shack, tote water from a creek, and sleep on a kraal mat.

It was a heated argument daughter to mother, new ways to old. Perhaps Gogo did win, if staying in a musty dark hut was a prize.

Thembekile put out two carved wooden cups and poured Gogo's homebrewed beer. Then she presented the fatcakes she had brought in her purse.

"Aaah, I can smell the fatcakes. Now, it does not take the wisdom of a sangoma to know that you did not bake these."

Themby laughed. It was common knowledge that she could barely cook pap.

Thembekile always credited Gogo with influencing her to study and teach history. As a child she loved to sit by the fire listening to Gogo relate the tales of Swaziland. These were passed down orally through the generations. One of Themby's favorite stories was the battle of Sudwalla Cave. Andres Pretorius, the great Dutch South African leader attempted an invasion of Swaziland in the 19th century. The great King Mswati II fooled him. Mswati gathered his people into the mammoth cavern, and they threw rocks down on Pretorius's soldiers. They massacred the Dutch and won the battle. The Kingdom of Swaziland is named for this great ruler.

Themby didn't learn the rest of that story until years later in school. Pretorius survived the attack. He retreated, regrouped his troops and came back to the area. The white South African troops took their revenge killing hundreds of Swazis and taking their sacred cave for South Africa. Even today the Swazis are still trying to recoup their rightful land. The capital of South Africa, Pretoria, is named after him.

Gogo would never relate that ending to the story. To her all the Swazis were great warriors, and all the rulers were heroes. The rest was trivial.

"Oh Gogo, this must be the best brew you have ever made." Thembekile sipped her beer from a small wooden cup.

"Of course dear," Gogo pointed her arthritic finger at Themby. "I am experienced. It takes many years of practice to get the mealies to brew like this. You know, you must learn the method I use to make beer. I won't be here forever, and the tradition must be passed down." Gogo sipped her beer with enthusiasm. She loved the smell of fermented corn. She rose from her chair and poured some beer into a cup by the fire.

"Themby my dear, you must never forget to give the ancestors a tribute when you serve the beer. Always remember to have a kagogo in your house to honor your ancestors."

"Gogo, most people don't have kagogos anymore. The houses in the city don't have the room for a space for the spirits to visit. I think you are very lucky to have a special kagogo to honor them."

"You must always come here and honor our ancestors at my kagogo. Don't ever think you can run away from your past, child. Why do I think that you will ever learn the old ways? You do not cook do you, dear?" Without waiting for the answer that she already knew she continued. "You did not come here for my brew, Themby. What is troubling you?"

Themby leaned back in her chair and felt it wobble beneath her. She sighed and rose to be closer to her grandmother.

Gogo had become so short over the years that Thembekile felt she was towering over her. She kissed the top of Gogo's gray hair and sat down on the floor beside her. "Gogo, what would you say if I told you that I am going to have a baby?"

She related her dilemma to her closest confidante. Yes, she was pregnant. The father was a married man with three children of his own.

Thembekile started to cry. "What will I do? How can I take care of a child and work? I had hoped to further my education, but now what will I do?"

"You make me a very old woman, indeed, you know. Every baby is a gift from God and the ancestors. Your poor dead mkhulu must be smiling down on you from heaven to hear this news. He always loved you more like a daughter than a granddaughter."

"I know that Grandpa would have been happy to see a new life, but what do you think he would have said about the fact that I am not married?" Thembekile spoke softly. "I know it would not make him proud, but, Gogo, I would not want to marry the father even if he was available to me. I enjoy him; I like him, but I never had any interest in spending my life with him."

"Poor, poor Thembekile, you must not spend so much time thinking about the father. It is the baby that you will care for and raise, not the father. Sometimes, life is simpler that way." Gogo rose to her feet and poured herself another cup of beer. There was no doubt in her mind that Thembekile was the pride of the family. She was the first-born child to Siphokazi, her daughter, and from the day of Thembekile's birth everyone felt she was destined for great things. Thembekile had walked younger than any child in the village. She could talk by the time she was a year old. Aside from being precocious, she was a beautiful child who grew up to be an intelligent and attractive woman. At 25 years old, Thembekile had a college degree and was teaching history at the University of Swaziland. Gogo could think of nothing but positive things to say about Thembekile, the faithful one.

Thembekile sat before her grandmother and wept. The whole picture of her future became clear now. How would she manage to work, take graduate classes and rear a newborn? Who would ever care about her needs, while she worried about everyone else's?

"Thembekile, you silly child, don't you understand that bringing children into the world is the way of a woman? God loves children, and the Swazis are proud of their beautiful babies. I only want to see tears of joy from you when this little one is born.

If mkhulu was only here now, he would be so proud to see his little granddaughter grown up, educated like a scholar and still womanly enough to have a baby." She patted Thembekile's hand. "It is a good day, my little one. Do not ruin it with tears. In Swazi tradition we have a saying that 'every new life lengthens your bones.'"

Gogo patted Themby's head as it lay in her lap. "Now you think about that." She raised Themby's face to look at hers and continued. "Tell me if you know what that means."

Gogo was a great believer in proverbs, and Themby often used her examples in the classroom. Sometimes the proverbs were so cryptic they were hard to comprehend. How could a baby lengthen anyone's bones?

Thembekile walked back down the hill from Gogo's house and sighed with relief. She had a new resolve that she could manage without a husband. She laughed to herself when she thought of Gogo telling her that life was actually simpler that way. Sitting on the bus on her way back to Manzini she thought about Gogo's proverb. How did new life lengthen the bones?

$$\Longrightarrow \Longleftarrow$$

In the depths of winter Thembekile delivered her daughter. The delivery went smoothly at her parents' home. With the assistance of her mother, Nobantu and the local midwife the new life came into the world. Since Jacob was a married man with his own responsibilities, Mbulelo, Themby's father, took charge of the naming ceremony. There was much discussion over the name and everyone voiced his opinion, but Mbulelo was Themby's guardian, so the privilege belonged to him.

Thembekile insisted that they travel up the mountain to Gogo's house for the naming ceremony. Sipho appreciated this gesture, though she thought it was too hard on her daughter and one week old granddaughter. They borrowed a car from a colleague at the university, and the family drove together to celebrate the tiny baby's entrance to Swazi life and culture.

It was a feast of food and love. Gogo held the little girl in her arms and moved her withered hands over the infant's face. Instinctively the baby grabbed Gogo's finger with her tiny hand. With tears in her damaged eyes Gogo kissed the baby's forehead. They feasted on wonderful traditional food outside in the sunshine. The women in the village had killed several chickens and prepared them in curry sauces with rice. There was pap with gravy and salad made from potatoes and beetroot. Along side of this was a wooden platter of wonderful fruit. Avocados were cut open and eaten by hand.

After the meal the women chanted songs of their ancestors while the men sat and smoked under a tree. Thembekile found a spot in the sunshine where she could rest and nurse her daughter. She felt warmth throughout watching her family on this important day. Suddenly, she understood Gogo's proverb. New life doesn't actually lengthen bones. It strengthens and lengthens the linkage from the ancestors to future generations. It was clear to her now. She felt peace and pride as she laid back on the blanket and closed her eyes to the sunlight.

"Wake up, Thembekile." She heard Nobantu calling her. "Are you all right?"

"Of course, I was just resting after the big dinner."

"Father is about to announce the baby's name. Are you able to participate?"

"I wouldn't miss this for anything." Thembekile smiled.

Mbulelo took his rightful position and gathered the family into a circle. He took the child from Thembekile's arms and held her to his lips. He kissed her then raised her up to the spirits that surrounded them in the sky and in the mountains.

"Today it is an honor to welcome this most perfect child into the world. I will name her Nathi. We ask the ancestors to accept this child. Help us take care of her and watch over her. She is ours and we will always be here for her. Everyone will now welcome little Nathi, the one who is with us."

Thembekile welled up with pride and happiness. She was always interested in the Swazi culture of name giving. There were names that held historical value. Those names were given to people born during times of floods or drought or disease. There were names given out of rage or hurt that left the poor child cursed. Then there were the names given out of love and respect. Nathi was such a name. It signified that the family would stand by the baby; the baby belonged to all of them. In short it translated to "with us."

Jacob never attended the naming ceremony. After all, he had his own wife and family. What Thembekile did not know was that Jacob would use the birth of Nathi to garner more money from his employer to support his new child. Thembekile and Nathi would never see a cent of that money.

⇒ ⇐

Three years passed quickly while Thembekile continued to teach at the university. Since she didn't have a graduate degree she could be classified only as an instructor. She always felt less of a colleague because of that, and she wanted much more from her career.

The entire family took care of Nathi and each encouraged his own values upon her. Mbulelo insisted that she be a quiet and respectful child. Sipho encouraged her to come forward and request what she needed in life. Gogo would hold Nathi on her lap and sing the folksongs of their culture. Themby recognized the old songs and stories that she had listened to as a child.

One evening while Sipho was preparing dinner Thembekile came into the kitchen to help her.

"What an unusual event to have you in the kitchen. Are you finally going to learn how to cook the butternut squash?" Sipho asked.

Themby picked up the large wooden spoon and stirred the squash on the stove. She had been trying to find this time to talk to her mother for several weeks.

"Mother, I have something I need to talk with you about tonight." Thembekile hesitated in the middle of her sentence. She didn't know how to continue so she blurted out her prepared speech. "A few months ago I applied for a grant to study near Cape Town at the University of the Western Cape. I didn't think anything would come of it, in fact, I almost forgot that I had sent the application. It took so long to hear any news from them. Then, I received this."

She pulled out of her pocket a crisp document stating that she had been accepted in the history department to study at the Master's degree level.

"Before you tell me all the reasons I can't go and lecture me on my responsibilities let me tell you that I understand all of that. I truly believe that this is an opportunity that I may never have again in my life. The University at the Western Cape has such an excellent reputation. You know that Desmond Tutu, the university's chancellor, recently received the Nobel Peace prize. There are so many important things happening there. I would feel so fortunate to study history at an institution that is making history every day."

Thembekile knew she was talking too fast and her heart was beating, but she really believed that this avenue was right for her future.

Sipho took the spoon away from Thembekile. It was obvious that Thembekile wasn't interested in cooking anything. While she had been talking the squash was burning, and Thembekile was stirring it into mush with her excitement.

"Themby, watch what you're doing. Look at that squash. How can we serve that for dinner?" Sipho smiled at Themby and held her hand. "You can explain how the squash turned to pap to your father during dinner. Then you can tell him that you are definitely going to South Africa."

"Mother, Mother, thank you!" She almost picked her mother up off her feet as she hugged her tightly. "You watch. We can work out all the details. I'll ask the cousins and Nobantu and others to help take care of

Nathi so she won't burden you too much. Oh, thank you, thank you! You know that it's just a year, and I'll be home for holidays."

And so began Thembekile's adventure to South Africa a country crossed into by a small insignificant border. South Africa was a country that looked so much the same, but one that was totally opposite her own. No matter how much history she had learned, and how much knowledge she had of apartheid, she was not prepared for the lifestyle that awaited her.

≡ ≡

Thembekile recognized the difference of South Africa the minute the bus crossed the border. The mood was dark in the new country. She had read everything she could get about apartheid. The Swazi newspapers were full of articles on a daily basis relating stories of prejudice and separatism. It was common for Swazis to shake their heads in sympathy and disgust for their neighbors in South Africa. It was a totally different matter to see the problems firsthand. Gogo had been the only one who had tried to discourage Thembekile from going to Cape Town. Gogo told her that she lived in the best country on earth. God had created such a beautiful and safe country why did Themby feel the need to go anywhere else? It seemed a ridiculous argument. After all, Gogo had never been out of the kingdom in her life. She rarely found it worthwhile to come down from the mountain. Gogo did not know and did not care what was beyond the borders of her own country.

Thembekile settled into her living quarters at the university. She was handed a pamphlet as she arrived. The document advised her as to where she was able to walk without violating the codes of law for black people. It recommended certain restaurants and shops where she would be welcomed and outlined those where she would be arrested. The idea of being arrested for eating in a restaurant amused her at first. Then it terrified her, and she wondered what she was getting into in this new country.

She decided immediately that she was only in South Africa to study for her advanced degree. She didn't want to cause any trouble for herself or embarrassment to her family. The first month she stayed on campus and never left the security of the walls that embraced the institution.

The University of the Western Cape was a dynamic institution that was filled with energy in a country immersed in oppression. Where Stellenbosch taught all their courses in Afrikaans, UWC prided itself in teaching in English. The faculty at Stellenbosch was immersed in the culture of Dutch South Africa. The arrogance of that university nearby in the Cape served to create an explosive resolve of human freedom at the newly established University of the Western Cape. It wasn't long before Thembekile realized that she could not shut out the roar of revolution that surrounded her.

One day as she walked across the campus she became intrigued by a student anti-apartheid rally. Several students stood on a thinly constructed stage belting out their anger towards white oppression.

"This is our land." One of them shouted raising his fist. "What do the Europeans believe they can accomplish holding down the rightful owners of this country?"

The students cheered as the young man yelled into the crowd.

"Their plan will never work. It cannot last. We will rise up against the administration. We will take back our country, our jobs, and our land."

The crowd roared, and students raised hand painted signs above their heads.

Thembekile felt genuinely moved by the demonstration. She was a history major watching history come alive all around her. She felt an uncontrollable desire to meet the speaker. He had a charisma that she had never felt from anyone. She pushed her way through the crowd and found herself at the base of the speakers' stand. Thembekile stood staring and finally got his attention. When he realized that she was looking at him, he reached his hand down to hers to shake it. Thembekile suddenly felt uncomfortable and turned away. She tried to disappear into the crowd, but now the path was blocked with more students.

Suddenly, she felt a hand on her shoulder. "Are you interested in the movement?"

She glanced back and saw the young man standing waiting for her answer. It was an awkward moment, and she sputtered out a reply.

"I'm not sure. I guess I was just drawn to the crowd. I… well…. I really have to get to class now."

"Don't go." He took her by her shoulders and turned her to him. "Let's have coffee and talk. I think there is more to you than just schoolwork. You don't look South African. Where are you from?"

"Really, really, I have to go." Thembekile tried to get away, but she felt herself drawn back again to his charismatic voice. "I suppose I have time for one cup of coffee." She said quietly.

They headed for a small coffee shop in the main building of the campus. The roar of the rally continued with a young woman standing on the stage talking of racial bias and rights for women.

As the door of the building closed behind them the noise of the rally seemed diminished, and the mood felt calm. It was almost too quiet. Thembekile didn't know what to say. They both ordered coffee with milk and sugar and found a place in a corner to talk.

"So you haven't answered me yet. Where are you from and what brings you to our Cape Town?"

Thembekile stirred her coffee and looked down at the cup. She wondered how she had become so mesmerized by this man. Gogo would have told her that she was bewitched.

"Look, I know you aren't from here. You actually look Swazi to me." He kept watching her reaction as he drank his coffee.

His remark so surprised Thembekile that she laughed. "I am Swazi. That was a very clever guess."

"You think it was just a guess? I make it a practice to recognize people by their heritage. Everyone has a different look, a different speech pattern and a unique set of mannerisms. You, my dear, are very Swazi."

"How can you tell that in a few words in such a short time? I think you are guessing, and with a good guess you flatter yourself."

"Hah! This is what I love. I have found a woman with spirit. So, you have come to Cape Town to fight the good fight with us then? You know, we will gain our rights as equal South Africans in our own country."

"No." Thembekile suddenly felt freed from his spell and found her voice again. "I came here to study for my Master's Degree in history. Then I will go back home and teach at the University of Swaziland."

"So, that explains it. You are a history teacher, and you have come here to live history rather than to read about it." He slapped his hand on the table. "This is a smart move for you. What did you say your name is?"

"I didn't tell you my name, and it seems to me that you haven't introduced yourself."

He leaned back in his chair studying Thembekile's face and expression. "My name is Sifiso. I am Zulu born." He placed his hand on his chest as if he was pledging his allegiance to his ethnicity. "I am here expressly to help my people and all the black people, the real

Africans. I must be the voice of so many who have no voice. God has given me the mission to free our people. I will never stop fighting until all the 20 million true Africans in my country have the right to realize their true talents, potentials and freedoms."

As Sifiso spoke Themby felt herself drawn to him again. She could feel her heart racing and was afraid that he might see her attraction to him. She had never been so absorbed in a man's voice. Poor Jacob in Manzini would never have been able to capture anyone's attention so smoothly and quickly.

"Did you know" Sifiso continued his speech "that our revered Bishop Tutu had to have special permission to travel to Johannesburg through a white designated area? He was to attend his own investiture as the first black bishop of the Anglican Diocese of Johannesburg." Sifiso shook his head and leaned forward across the table. "It makes me furious to think of what they put that great leader through to reach his pulpit."

"Yes, well, I agree with what you are saying." Thembekile searched for words to convey what she meant to say. Apartheid was a horrible and cruel method of regulating black people. She didn't want to sound uninterested to Sifiso, but she wasn't sure she felt the same level of passion that he demonstrated.

"Do you? Do you really care?" He began to sound sarcastic. This was a young man driven by fury. "You will walk across this campus many times. You will move through the academic system here, and then, in the end, you will just take your piece of paper back to the security of your kingdom. Why did I think you would understand our cause?"

Now Thembekile felt her own rage. This man was insulting. He accused her of being apathetic, of being foreign to pain and hardship.

"You think that I haven't seen history moving through life? We have had our own political dilemmas in Swaziland. Only recently there was terrible conflict at home. When our great King Sobhuza II died in 1982 the country nearly collapsed. There was a rift in our government, because the new king was too young to take office. So, who would rule the kingdom? Would it be the young king's mother, the new queen mother? Would it be the sitting queen mother under the late king?" She squinted and leaned across the table. She related the drama as she would if she were teaching again.

"Oh, please. Your queen mother story does not impress me." Sifiso sounded sarcastic. "How can that possibly compare to imprisonments, beatings, and murders of our brethren in this country? We must rise up against racial injustices that plague this land?"

Sifiso sat back waiting to see what Thembekile would say. The spider had captured his prey in his web. He would let her squirm around until she was worn out and relinquished herself to his charms. Thembekile fascinated him, but he underestimated her. That was the part of her that he fell in love with that day.

To his surprise Thembekile rose immediately to leave. "Thank you for the coffee. I have many important things to do, the least of which is spending my afternoon with you." She gathered her books and purse.

"It may mean nothing to you, but in my country the death of King Sobhuza was marked with tragic arrests and political imprisonments. No one knew if he was safe from day to day. It was a period in time we would all like to forget, but so many people are scarred by it that the history books will have to sort out the rights and wrongs of the government's decision."

Sifiso stood up quickly, grabbed her arm and held it firmly in his hand. His voice was excited and his words were rapid. "Thembekile, come with me to the meeting tonight. You can be part of history. It is alive here. History breathes in our midst. Can't you feel the heart of the movement pounding in you right now?"

Themby felt her pulse racing, but she knew it wasn't caused by the anti-apartheid movement. Sifiso had pulled her so close to him that she could barely breathe.

"Tell me you will meet me tonight in the main courtyard. We are planning our next protest. Come, you know you want to be with us."

Thembekile agreed to meet him and finally broke away, but when she arrived back at her room the spell wore off, and she wondered again what she was thinking. Yes, Gogo would definitely say there was something bewitching about that Zulu man. Sifiso's name meant that his parents' wish had been granted. She wondered what his mother thought of her son now who seemed so full of rage and power. His eyes were direct and piercing. With an air of confidence he swept her into his world.

Thembekile quickly found herself immersed in a world of revolution and anger. She supported the anti-apartheid cause, and she believed in Sifiso. In her room there were large signs that she painted with epithets against the government. These were propped up against the walls waiting for another rally or demonstration. She attended the planning meetings. At night Sifiso proved to be as passionate a lover as he was a freedom fighter. Everything he said, everything he did exuded his strength and energy.

He had all the reasons and all the answers until Thembekile presented him with her own problem.

⇒ ⇐

Thembekile recognized the tell tale symptoms she had experienced with her first pregnancy. She felt more dread than fear when she woke up in the morning. How could she possibly consider having another child? She was guilt ridden that she was not raising the daughter she already had. The whole family kept busy caring for little Nathi while she was away having an affair in another country. Nathi was growing, learning and being loved by others. Those people took the responsibility off Themby's shoulders believing that they were advancing her career.

"Oh my God" she pushed her face into her pillow as if the lack of oxygen would erase the truth. "What am I going to do now? I can never go home and face that kind of shame."

For several weeks she pushed the whole matter out of her mind. She attended her classes more faithfully and stayed away from the rallies and demonstrations. She didn't want to see Sifiso again for fear he would bewitch her with his magnetic eyes.

"Thembekile, why are you avoiding me?" She heard Sifiso running up behind her as she walked to the library. When he reached her he was out of breath and anxious.

"I call you, but you never answer the phone. You are never at the meetings anymore. What is happening to you?"

Thembekile tried not to look at him. She couldn't afford to be weak minded now.

"You know it is almost time for me to go back to Swaziland. I only have one month here now, and I have to study for my final exams. Everything in my future depends on those test grades."

"I don't believe you." His voice was strong and concerned. He took her shoulders in his hands. It reminded her of the first time he had done that at the coffee shop. It seemed like years ago to her now. She felt so vulnerable and began to cry.

"I didn't want to tell you this, Sifiso. I know you have a lot of important things to do like saving the world, but I have important matters, too. I'm going to have your baby."

Sifiso stood in amazement. To Themby his blank star of disbelief seemed endless. It frightened her to think what was running through his mind. She had been down this path before with Jacob, but that was so different. Jacob was a married man from whom she asked little and was given nothing.

Suddenly Sifiso blurted out "My God, Themby…a baby." He swept her up in his arms and twirled her around the courtyard. "Oh my God! You know how much I love you. So this is why you are hiding from me?" Themby landed back on her feet with an unsettled feeling. Was she dizzy from his reaction or from the whirling he gave her?

"Here, look at me." He looked at her face, and she fell into his magnetic eyes. "We will talk all about this later. I have to be at a planning session for the demonstration, so I have to hurry now."

He pulled away from her and turned to run. Then he looked back at her, pointed his finger and exclaimed "I'll see you tonight. No.. wait…that won't work. I'll call you in the morning." He clicked his fingers as if he was trying to remember something and continued. "Oh, I forgot. I can't make it in the morning, there's the strike at the wharf and I have to be there. Maybe I can get in touch with you when I leave there, or something like that. Anyway, I'll call you."

As he ran off across the campus Themby's dreams fell apart. She knew in that second that his magnetic eyes had temporarily bewitched her heart. There was no future with a man who was married to a cause. She could never compete with something of that nature. She realized she would always be waiting for him to return from some critical meeting, some absolutely essential rally. He was a charismatic man wrapped up in his own agenda. She continued to watch him until he was out of sight. As she dropped her head and retreated to the library she wondered what would become of Sifiso when and if apartheid ever came to an end. Already the beaches were integrated and Blacks were starting to move through parts of the city where until recently they had been unwelcome. What happens to a freedom fighter when the war is over? She would have to study her history books for the answer. She never saw Sifiso again.

≡ ≡

The term finally ended and Thembekile finished her exams. She packed all the belongings she had accumulated and carefully put her new diploma in her suitcase. As she emptied out the dresser drawers in her tiny dormitory room she caught a glimpse of her new swelling body in the mirror. There were days she couldn't look herself at all. No one back in Swaziland knew anything about Sifiso or her involvement in his life, or especially about her unborn child. No matter how many times she rehearsed her confession to her mother, it never sounded right.

The bus stopped near the campus, and she boarded it with her suitcase. She kept feeling the other passengers' eyes on her and imagined the thoughts they must have had about her appearance. Of course, no one on the long bus ride knew that she was an unmarried pregnant woman with an illegitimate child at home.

Finally, after two days and three bus transfers she reached Swaziland and the area of her ancestral homeland in the mountains. She lifted her suitcase and heavy body off the bus and instinctively turned towards the hills. She felt her ancestral spirits were hypnotizing her, calling her to the mountains to receive the wise counsel of her gogo. This time it was a relief to walk up the mountain. Suddenly, she realized how lonely and homesick she had been in South Africa. Swaziland was so serene and beautiful. Winter was ending filling the hills with a patchwork of flowers against a backdrop of green velvet grass. The mountains seemed to sing with the sound of birds. When she heard the cadence of the doves she felt at peace. It was a comfort beyond anything Sifiso would ever be able to understand. Gogo would make it right. Gogo always knew how to view the world from a perspective that everyone could live and cope and feel comfort.

She didn't see Gogo sitting on her customary stone stoop and a second of terror filled her. What if something happened to Gogo? The thought had never occurred to her. Gogo was an institution and would always be there for her. She called out, and Gogo slowly emerged from her hut.

"Gogo, Gogo! I'm home." Themby dropped her suitcase and ran the rest of the way up the path to the hut. She wrapped her arms around Gogo's neck and kissed the top of the frail woman's head.

Gogo hugged Themby and laughed. "I see you have not come alone, my little one. Come in, we must talk."

Themby ushered Gogo back into the hut, and they celebrated with the traditional beer. Gogo served the spirits at the kagogo before she took her own sip.

"Gogo. I missed you so much. The year was so long and so lonely."

"Themby, child. My life is empty without your visits. Everyone is too busy to see me these days. But, sisi, it is true that you have not been that lonely."

Themby leaned back in the tiny wooden chair and sighed. Naturally, Gogo knew she was pregnant the minute she hugged her at the door. Being at her grandmother's always gave her a sense of complete security. She spilled out her story and her heart in the dim little hut.

Gogo was a good listener. She drank her beer and nibbled on bits of fried potato while Themby related the experiences of apartheid, of loving Sifiso, and how the whole year had gotten mixed up in her head.

Themby rose to light a candle and asked, "Can I stay here with you tonight, Gogo? It's still a long way home, and the night is already here."

Gogo stopped chewing and smiled. "I know your heart, Themby. Of course you can stay with me as long as you want, but you will still have to see Sipho and Mbulelo. Your parents have missed you very much, and you cannot insult them by staying away hiding up in the mountains. It is not your nature to lead a solitary life. So you will stay with me tonight, and tomorrow you will take responsibility and go home."

Themby and Gogo prepared a simple supper of mashed corn, and avocados. She was too tired to puzzle out the situation. There was no comfortable way to sleep in Gogo's hut, but she was so exhausted she dozed off immediately on a mat covered with blankets.

Morning came early at Gogo's. Gogo still lived by the movement of the sun. She had never owned a clock or operated her life on a schedule. Life began when the sun came up, and sleep took over when the moon rose in the sky at night. Nothing during the day was plotted, nor was time ever budgeted to work in more activities than one could handle during the sun's time. If work was not completed in one day, it could always wait until the next one. Her life drifted along easily without the stress of watches, calendars or appointments.

Thembekile ached all over from spending the night on the mat and wondered how Gogo had spent her entire life sleeping like that. The rooster heralded the false dawn at 4:30 in the morning. That awakened the dogs, and the morning chorus began. Themby reached for a stool to lean against so she could stand up. She straightened her shoulders and arched her back trying to relieve the stiffness. She was rubbing her sore neck when she heard Gogo laughing at her from across the room.

"So you are awake now, child. I have brewed bush tea for us." Gogo shuffled over to Themby and patted her large body.

"You worry about too much, Themby. I have the answer to your problem, and it is so simple. Why do you modern Swazis always try to make life so complicated?"

Gogo sat back down at the small table and sipped her hot tea. She took a bite of buttered bread and waited to see what Themby would say on her behalf.

"Gogo, life is not simple. That is the problem. It isn't that we make it complicated. The world is a complicated place. I suppose it is hard for you to understand since you live quietly up here in the mountains."

Gogo laughed loudly this time and slapped her hand on the top of the table. Themby jumped back. Sifiso had often slapped his hand on the table when he wanted to emphasize a point. It was a sudden and strange memory.

"You think that life is harder? It is hard, because you make it so. God made the same world for all of us. These plants are the same. Those trees are the same. Do you think the birds make a different sound for you than they did for me at your age? The problem with you, Themby, is that you don't trust the wisdom of the ancestral spirits." Gogo sipped the rest of her tea and sighed. "Your generation doesn't live by the laws of God and Swazi spirits. You all make your life harder, because you try to find all the answers in books. I think the ancestors must be pleased for you now, because you are healthy, and the pregnancy is going well. There is always a reason for a healthy new birth."

She leaned forward so closely that Themby could feel her breath. "Believe me, child." She held Themby's face in her rough hands. "When the spirits are angry, they will let you know." She took her hands away from Themby, and Themby felt frozen for a moment. Gogo leaned away again. Then she pointed her crooked finger in Themby's direction. "Yes, the spirits will definitely make themselves known to you.

So, you should not worry about this anymore. If your baby is in good graces with God and the ancestral spirits, you have nothing to fear from anyone who walks the ground."

Themby left the mountain that afternoon with a new resolve and a sense of comfort. Perhaps her grandmother was right about God and the spirits. It all seemed contrary to anything she had ever learned about science and logic, but it was a benevolent solution to her problem. The conversation was still swirling in her mind when the bus dropped her off near her parents' home.

She noticed little Nathi first. The child, now four years old, came running out of the house towards her mother. Her squeals and cheering brought Nobantu and the rest of the family to the garden.

Thembekile felt their eyes focus on her belly and could sense that the welcoming sounds were diminishing. She forced herself to ignore the stares and kept remembering that if the spirits and God were happy, nobody else mattered.

"Come in, Themby." Sipho took her by the arm while little Nathi tried to lift her suitcase.

Themby swept up little Nathi in her arms. Immediately, she felt relieved and thrilled to be home. She kissed her little daughter all over her face and neck and pushed back her hair to kiss her forehead.

Once they were settled in the house Nobantu brought out cherry cordial, Cokes and sandwiches for teatime. Black tea, Five Roses, was also served on the coffee table.

They all discussed nothing over each other's voices during the tea. Everyone knew the real discussion was yet to come, and it could certainly wait for the right moment. Nathi sat close to her mother wrapping her thin arms around Themby.

Finally, the sandwiches were eaten, and the tea was cold. Nathi was instructed to play outside while Sipho asked Nobantu to take away the remnants of the meal.

Sipho and Mbulelo sat across from Themby. No one spoke for an interminable minute. Themby broke the awkward silence and looked down.

"I know what you are thinking of me, and you are right. I was much too involved with a man in Cape Town. I don't know any other way to tell you."

"Oh, Themby, what are you thinking?" Sipho pleaded with her daughter. "How can you take care of another child? Is this a man that you love? Is he someone you want to marry? Because, honestly daughter, you are limiting your future now."

"Mother, Daddy, I doubt that I will ever see that man again. Yes, he is someone I would have loved for my husband. I thought I could spend my life with him, but he has another lover."

Both her parents let out audible sighs of disgust. "Another married man!" Mbulelo rose from his chair and paced the room. "Where do you get this need to be with men who have wives and are married?"

Themby was still stiff and tired from the trip. Her voice was soft, and she couldn't look up at her parents. She watched the floor, shook her head and continued.

"Oh, Daddy, I said he had another lover. He isn't married to a woman. He is married to a cause, his cause." She gazed at the floor and shrugged her shoulders.

"He can't envision anything in life beyond his political concerns and ambitions. It would be easier to be jealous of a woman. At least I could compete with that."

Sipho and Mbulelo were quiet now. The situation was beyond argument, and what different would it make? This Zulu man was never coming to Manzini to honor the lobola and care for their daughter.

"You have chosen a difficult road in your life, Themby. You have all the education and talent to excel in life, but how will you manage with two children? We love Nathi. You can see that she is very happy living here, but how will you cope with more burden?" Sipho wrung her hands as she spoke while her face grimaced at the thought of Themby's future.

"Well, I guess I will just have to find that out. Gogo says to trust God and the spirits, so that's where I will start."

≡ ≡

The baby girl was born in the same bed that her older sister, Nathi, came into the world. Once again, Sipho and the midwives assisted the birth, and kept praising Themby on the ease of her labor. They related their own tales of childbirth, which didn't please Themby at all. All new life was a dramatic miracle especially the actual birth with the details of the event told over and over for years.

In keeping with tradition, they carried the new child up to Gogo's mountain just as they had done with all the other children born into the family. This would always remain their ancestral homeland. Mbulelo raised his new granddaughter up to the sky and the spirits. He proudly proclaimed that this new life would now be known to the world as Mashama, The Surprise. Little Nathi sang while she danced in a circle with the other women in the family. Themby watched as new life, once again, lengthened their bones.

≡ ≡

It was not difficult for Themby to resume her work at the university. She had been on leave during her year in Cape Town with the security of knowing that her position would be waiting upon her return. Her desk was dusty, but all her books and papers were in order. Nathi was now enrolled in the mission school, and Themby hired a woman to care for Mashama. She hoped that a government house would become vacant soon so that she and her daughters would have their own home. There was always an extensive waiting list, sometimes as long as two years.

⇒ ⇐

A few months after the birth of Mashama the predictable yet unthinkable happened. The chief sent word from the mountain via courier that Gogo had passed over to the spirits during the night. She died the same way she lived. There was no drama, no tears, and no anguish. She was a woman at peace in both worlds.

The rest of the family was not as comforted as Gogo. When she died a piece of Themby's heart went with her to the grave. How could she live without Gogo's beer and counsel? Who could she confide in, and who would solve all her problems? She lay on her bed with her face buried in the pillow and wept bitterly for the person she had loved the most in the world.

Everyone gathered at the homeland for the funeral. It was common knowledge that it would take three days for Gogo to reach the world of the spirits. Only after that would it be safe to lay her to rest with them. It was a solemn affair and orchestrated completely according to Swazi tradition. The procession was lead by the chief who heralded to the ancestors that this good woman was now going to be with them and that they must welcome her and care for her. Mbulelo was one of the men who carried her small, frail body to the burial ground. Behind the men were women carrying special possessions of Gogo so that she would be happy in her new world and wouldn't come back looking for these things. Her wooden drinking cup was one of these. Themby carried it holding it in front of her. She rubbed her fingers all over the cup trying to squeeze some part of Gogo into her own hands. Gogo also had a special woven sisal bowl in which she always kept her beads. Both of these were buried with her. Her body was laid to rest in the burial grounds of the kraal next to her husband, Themby's mkhulu. Together they were now part of the ancestral spirits who would watch over the family. Themby couldn't help but smile knowing that now as one of the spirits Gogo was, indeed, still going to offer her counsel. After the ceremony the entire funeral party washed all signs of death from themselves before they celebrated with dinner. Later Themby walked through Gogo's bare little hut. The scent of Gogo's homebrewed beer lingered in the air, but her voice was now silent.

⇒ ⇐

After waiting for two years Themby was finally awarded a house on the campus of the university. University housing did not have a particularly good reputation, but it was free, and she would be closer to her job. There was a bus that, for a small fee, took Nathi to school every day. The young girls made friends with the children of the other faculty. Except for the fact that the house was practically falling down, Themby decided it was a positive move.

It seemed as though Themby was spending more time trying to get her house fixed than she was teaching her courses. There were so many structural problems with the dwelling that she had to decide which ones took priority when she complained to the housing director.

One night she sat in the living room making a list of needs for the house.

"There must have been a time when these little places were clean and maintained." She thought to herself and shook her head.

On her list were various things such as faulty wiring, a hole in the bathroom door, a leaky toilet, but worse than that a leaky roof. She put her feet up on the stool that sat in front of her overstuffed chair and closed her eyes. Taking care of two children, keeping up with her work schedule and rebuilding the campus house was taking its toll. She wrote numerous letters to the janitors, to the plumbers, and to anyone else she could think of who could help her. No one ever acknowledged her inquiries, and when she ran into a repairman on campus his comment was "I'm thinking about coming over sometime." He never did.

The rains of summer burst through the sky, and Themby knew she was in trouble. One day when she came home she noticed that the house seemed damp. She followed the puddles and discovered that they originated in her daughters' bedroom. The hole in the roof was getting worse and the ceiling was stained with water spots. The whole house took on a musty smell that she attempted to cover with air freshener. She opened the windows in all the rooms to air the place out as well as she could.

Summer was the season of malaria. Those fortunate enough to live in the high altitudes of Mbabane were unconcerned about the deadly disease. The university, however, was in the valley, and the risk there prevailed from November to March. It was hot and humid outside, and Themby's house was still reeking of mold. She left the windows open all night. She was too weary to remember that the anopheles mosquitoes rule the dark. The particularly small malaria bearing mosquitoes are only active from dusk to dawn, but during those hours they strike relentlessly. The female spreads the disease throughout the night carrying the malaria parasite from one infected person to another.

It took about ten days for Mashama to become ill. Nathi noticed it first one morning when she tried to get her little sister to wake up.

"Mommy, come quickly. Mashama isn't moving in her bed. She is hot and isn't moving."

Themby came around the corner and was putting on her necklace when she saw the two girls; Nathi was next to the bed, and Mashama lay listless under the sheet.

"Do something, Mommy. She looks really sick."

"Nathi, call Gogo on the phone. Her number is on the table. Ask her to come here as soon as possible."

Themby felt Mashama's forehead with her lips. The child was burning with fever, and her eyes rolled back into her head at her mother's touch. Her body was limp, and as Themby tried to lift her into her arms she cried out in pain.

"My God, what has happened to you my little one?"

Sipho was just about to leave for her own job when Nathi's call reached her. Instead, she rushed over to the university, to Themby's dilapidated house. She took a brief examination of her granddaughter and looked at Themby.

"Themby, I think she has malaria. We need to get her to a doctor as soon as possible. I am using your father's car today. Let's get her out of here right away."

Sipho drove while Themby held Mashama in her arms. The four-year-old child, wrapped in a light blanket, slept all the way to the clinic in Mbabane.

"This is definitely malaria." The British doctor pronounced. "I will run the customary blood test just to confirm it, but I've seen an awful lot of malaria in my time."

"Doctor, what can I do to make her well?" Themby was shaking with fear. She had never seen such a sick child.

"Quite frankly, there are medications that are very successful in treating malaria, but the problem is her age and size. Little children are susceptible to many complications, and they dehydrate quickly." He walked over to the medicine cabinet and retrieved a bottle of tablets.

"The mosquito is the most dangerous of all the parasite bearing insects. Did you know that 200 million people around the world contract malaria every year? One million of those die, and most of them are African children." He shook his head as he placed the bottle of tablets in Themby's hand.

"We know so much about the disease, but every time we think we have the answer, the insect becomes more clever.

Give her these tablets as directed on the bottle. Keep her quiet and cool and make sure she gets liquids. It will take some time for her to get better."

Themby felt her entire body slump from fatigue and fear. Her voice trembled as she asked the most important question.

"Will she be all right? I know people who have died from malaria, and she's just a small child."

The British doctor patted her on the back. "Give it time. Give her the tablets. She'll rally, you'll see. It just takes good care and medicine and time."

Sipho, Themby, Nathi and Mashama drove back to Sipho's house. Themby couldn't face the musty house at the university, and she needed her family's help. Thembekile laid Mashama gently in her own bed, the bed where the child was born, and she sat on the floor next to her.

Two days passed and Mashama seemed no better. Her breathing was labored. Her face was pale. The nights were the worst. Terrible sweats alternating with pain and high fever plagued the child. By the third night Themby was a fixture at her side, praying endlessly to the God the missionaries and her Christian faith had told her would answer all her prayers and always be in her life. Everyone had told her that He was the hope and the light and whosoever asked him anything would be heard. She chanted prayers throughout the night thanking God for giving her Mashama and begging Him not to take her away to heaven.

She looked into the face of the moaning child and searched for Sifiso's passionate nature hoping that he had blessed his child with that trait. If Mashama were anything like her daddy she would defy all odds and regain her strength. She continued to lie limp and lifeless in her bed.

The morning came and Themby checked Mashama to see if there was any improvement. She had not moved. Themby was terrified. This had gone on too long.

"Nobantu. Please help me." She screamed through the house.

Nobantu was preparing for work, but she came quickly out of her bedroom.

"What is it, sisi? Is there a change? Is Mashama all right?"

"No, she is not all right. Please, I need help. I need a big favor from you. Please, can you stay with her for a while?" Themby was frantic. Before her sister had a chance to respond Themby slipped on her shoes and grabbed her purse.

"Okay, Themby. I'll stay here for you, but where are you going?"

"I'll tell you later." She kissed her sister on the cheek and hugged her tightly. "Thank you, thank you. I have to hurry."

Themby dashed out of the house and ran down the hill. She caught the first bus that came by the main road. The bus trip seemed to take forever. As it approached the stop closest to the path to her grandmother's mountain Themby rose from her seat. She practically flew off the bus as it stopped. She raced breathlessly up the mountain and tore open the door to Gogo's empty hut. She held her chest and panted. Her eyes searched the dark room as she ran to the kagogo in the corner and fell to the floor.

"Gogo, Gogo, please hear me!" She sobbed in loud wails. "How can I please you? What have I done to make the spirits want to take my child? Poor little Mashama, she has done nothing to deserve the anger of the ancestors." Her crying changed to hysterical sobs.

"Gogo, if you could see her. She is lying mostly dead in the same bed where she was born. I don't know what to do anymore."

Themby lifted her head and looked through her swollen eyes at the kagogo. She spread the dust away and tried frantically to rebuild the shrine. "I know what you are thinking. You think I don't honor my ancestors, but I do." She screamed in grief and fell back to the floor crying over and over. "I do. I promise, I do."

After a few minutes she gathered her emotions and stood up in the hut. She walked outside and gathered some flowers that were attempting to grow without Gogo's nurturing. She laid the flowers at the kagogo and pleaded again with the spirits.

"I don't know how to make beer. I know you always wanted me to learn the old ways, and I was too busy." She shook her head and apologized. "I'm sorry, Gogo. I love you so much, and it has been so hard to go on without you. I know you are here. You always told me that 'all spirits must come home.'" She was silent and looked around the small room. There were so many memories of Gogo left behind there. Everything inside the hut remained the same. This was the family ancestral homeland. It was a place to honor, but no one came very often any more. The roof was growing weak, and the mice were invading the space.

"Gogo, if you please help me, I will come more often and clean your house. I will try harder to learn the ways of my ancestors, and I will teach my children. I love you and beg you to help me."

Somehow it was a relief to be so close to her grandmother and a comfort to feel that she had heard Themby's cries. Thembekile collapsed in front of the kagogo, next to the fresh picked flowers and fell asleep.

Late in the afternoon Thembekile finally returned home. The first thing she saw as she walked up the path was the doctor's car.

A bolt of paralyzing fear passed through her body. She had no more strength and could not feel her legs as they pulled her to the house.

Nobantu came to the front door and called out to her.

"Themby, we've been looking for you. Come quickly."

Somehow Themby reached the house. She could hear Nathi's voice coming from the bedroom. As she walked into that room she saw Nathi sitting on the edge of the bed. The doctor was standing in the middle of the room. He had a broad smile of satisfaction on his face as he closed his medical bag. Mashama was sitting up in bed playing hand-clapping games with her older sister.

"Thembekile, I'm glad to see you before I leave." He took off his glasses and cleaned them with a towel. "Didn't I tell you she would be fine?"

He placed his glasses back on his face, patted Themby and said, "I told you it would take time for the tablets to work. You just need to trust the medical profession."

Themby heard herself thank the doctor. Then she seemed to float to the bed where her daughters played. She hugged little Mashama and wept. She looked up at the British doctor and thanked him again. She thanked her Christian God. She thanked her ancestors and her gogo.

Themby would always wonder who really saved Mashama's life.

≫ ≪

Nobantu was getting married. The household was a flurry of excitement. The wedding was to be held at the Anglican Church in Manzini.

Sipho and Mbulelo couldn't have been happier. Nobantu was marrying a man she knew from childhood. They grew up together, went to school together and had much in common. He came from a prosperous family that owned a small shop in town, so he not only was employed, but he would have an inheritance as well.

All of this was important to her family, but what they truly valued were the cows. He gave Nobantu's parents 15 cows, nice fat healthy ones, to show his devotion to their daughter. These cows would surely produce calves and increase in worth.

Thembekile helped her sister dress for the wedding. As she put the veil on Nobantu's head she sighed.

"Themby, what's wrong? Does it look bad on me?"

"No, no, sisi." Themby replied. "I was thinking how beautiful you look. I have two children, and I have never worn a veil."

"Would you like to try it on?"

Themby laughed and replied, "My luck with men is not very good. If I try on your veil my bad luck could rub off on you."

"Who knows?" Nobantu smiled in the mirror. "Maybe my luck could transfer to you."

Themby finished fastening the veil to her sister's head.

"Be happy, sisi. I doubt that I will ever marry. How would it be possible for me to fall in love again?"

Another term began at the university. Themby prepared her notes and lesson plans. Both daughters were in school. Nathi was ten years old, and Mashama, who recovered completely from malaria, was six years old. The university never repaired the house very well, but Themby had fixed it up enough so that it was livable.

She was eating dinner at the German restaurant in Ezulwini with friends when she met Simon Dlamini. He knew some of the people at her table, and they called him over to have a drink. Themby was immediately attracted to him. He was a handsome man, a really handsome man. She had decided long ago that she would never go out with another man as long as she lived, but she couldn't help smiling at him and watching him smile back at her. By the end of the dinner, they were alone at the table.

It was a fast relationship. He came from a family of importance and stature. It seemed that his family owned most of the valley. Simon complimented Themby on her appearance, her brains, and her independent nature. He loved to spend money, and he swept Themby off her feet. She was serious when she vowed never to get involved with another man, but that was before she met Simon.

When she discovered she was pregnant she wanted to die. She thought about ending her life rather than telling her parents that she had been the most foolish woman in Swaziland three times. She didn't want Simon to know anything about a child. He was such a proud man that he would want to marry her, and she didn't love him. Yes, she was terribly complimented and flattered by him, but living with him forever was out of the question.

One night she put Nathi and Mashama to bed. She reached down, patted their heads and kissed them each on the cheek. As she walked out of their room she turned again to watch her beautiful sleeping daughters.

"How can I deny new life into this world? How will my children judge me if I appear to be a woman who doesn't live up to her obligations?" She thought of Gogo so often, and in times of need she felt her grandmother's spirit. Themby undressed and climbed into bed. As she laid her head on the pillow she reminisced about being with Gogo so long ago and imagined that she heard her advice again. "I only want to see tears of joy from you when this little one is born. Always remember, new life lengthens the bones." Themby smiled as she closed her eyes.

"Stay with me, Gogo. Please always stay here with me. I think the length of my bones is getting quite long enough."

⇒ ⇐

"For the loving sake of God! Please marry this man." Mbulelo was furious. Sipho despaired. How could their intelligent daughter behave so stupidly? She was their promise in the family, and didn't seem to have any sense at all.

"This could be your last chance for happiness. You may never find a husband." Sipho tried to speak kindly. She could see her daughter was cowering from Mbulelo's anger.

"If Simon were the last man I could ever be with, I would stay a single independent woman." Themby said defiantly, though she felt otherwise underneath her words.

"Themby, dear, does Simon know about the baby? Has he asked you to marry him?"

"Yes and yes." She said with disgust. The memory of the evening she confessed her situation to Simon raced quickly through her mind. Yes, she did tell him that she was pregnant with his child. He kissed her deeply and hugged her until she couldn't breathe. "Marry me, Themby. I can make you happy. You won't have to work, and I will take care of everything."

"But Simon," She responded. "I love my work. I went to college for many years to do what I do. I sacrificed a lot to get an education. I don't want to quit work and sit at home. I'm sorry, Simon, I just can't marry you." She caressed his cheek and smiled. He was a decent man, but she didn't love him, not enough to give up her own life and freedom for marriage.

He was stunned. No one had ever told him 'no' before in his life. He was raised with plenty of everything, and he was the first son of a first son in a prosperous family with an ancestry of royal blood. No one ever said no, especially a woman. He begged her and pleaded his case, but she never changed her mind.

Her parents were speechless. "So, what you are saying, daughter, is that this man, a rich man, who loves you wants to marry you. He doesn't care that you have two daughters, and yet you aren't interested." Mbulelo threw up his hands and stormed out of the room.

Several days later Simon came to the house. He tried to convince Mbulelo of the necessity of a wedding, and when he got to the lobola he could see that Mbulelo was impressed.

When Themby heard about his visit she was the one to be furious.

"You are not to arrange my life, Father. I have no interest in marrying him if he were to give me the king's cattle. The fact that he has come here against my will to deal with you behind my back confirms that I am right. Can't you see that he is driven by his ego and pride, not his love for me?"

Mbulelo glared at Sipho. "You realize wife, that this is your fault. You have raised a willful daughter. She thinks she is equal to a man. She thinks she can act like a woman and be taken seriously like a man."

⇒ ⇐

This time Thembekile delivered a son. Nathi and Mashama were thrilled. Even Mbulelo had to admit that he was impressed. Finally, Themby had done something right. They took the trek up to the mountain, and Simon came along. He had the right to name his son, and he accepted it with pride. Themby's heart was full as she honored her ancestors with new life.

Simon kissed his son and held him up to the sky and the ancestors. The mountains echoed his voice as he called out the spirits to love and protect his son, little Ndumiso, the one whom praise will follow.

As they were feasting on chicken and curries Sipho couldn't help herself. She whispered into Themby's ear "I think you misjudge Simon. He is a good man."

Nobantu, who was five months pregnant, came over to Themby. "Sisi, what did Mother say?"

Themby laughed. "I think she said something like 'think of the lobola he could have given daddy and me.' "

⇒ ⇐

Thembekile stayed at the university. It was nearly impossible for her to support three children, and she was forced to teach additional courses in Mbabane at the Swaziland Government Institute to supplement her income. There were times that she grew depressed from all the responsibilities that she was faced with in her life. It had always been her dream to further her education and obtain a Ph.D. When she was younger she had planned to go to the United States for graduate school. Any idea of that nature was certainly out of the question now. There would be no more travel, no more education, and no more adventures away from Swaziland.

Ndumiso was five years old and adored by the family. Themby gave him the Christian name of Simon, after his father, in the hopes that the man would bond with his son and not forget his paternal responsibilities. Even at that, support was sporadic, and Themby found it difficult to make ends meet. Occasionally, Simon would come by with a support check and use it in an attempt to manipulate Themby into marrying him.

"Come on, Themby. I am the father of your only son, your youngest child. Do you want to be an old woman with no one to love?" He would look sincere and wave the check in front of her. "If you marry me, you have no money worries."

Themby would shake her head and reply with the same degree of disgust at every encounter. "Simon, thank you for the check, which you owe me, anyway." She would take the check out of his hand. "If I married you, no one would be happy. If you really love me you will honor Simon's support regularly without letting me suffer and worry."

Themby's parents were equally concerned about her decision to remain single. Sipho couldn't help but remark that a boy should be raised with a father, and after all, his father had a very nice bank account and a royal name.

On the rare occasion that Themby allowed herself to think about men and love she always reminisced about Sifiso. He was the man she had truly loved, and that relationship had left her distrusting men in general.

One day she walked into the Swaziland Government Institute with an armful of roses. She passed Busisiwe's office in the entry hall.

"Ooh, sisi, those flowers are gorgeous!" Busi remarked. "Where did you get them?"

"Would you like some?" Themby asked. She stopped walking and opened the paper that held the bouquet. She divided the flowers and said "There is a woman near Manzini who grows these. Her name is Anna. If you ever get down to the valley, you should find her. I have never seen so much love in a flower." Themby was happy to share her roses with Busi. She knew that Busi was having a difficult adjustment. She had recently returned to Mbabane after spending six years in Washington DC. "Busi, I keep telling you that you should go to Manzini sometime and shop. I know it's not America, but it is still more fun than sitting at home with your mother and your nieces."

Themby thought, "If I had a chance to go to the United States I'm not sure that I would ever come back."

"How are your children?" Busi inquired. "You are so lucky to have three children. I would feel blessed from God to have a child of my own."

"Well, that might be a matter of opinion." Themby laughed. She threw away some of the paper that held the flowers. "You should see my eldest daughter, Nathi. She's a teenager and challenges my authority every day. Then there is Mashama. She just wants to be like her big sister. Of course, you know my little Simon. I must be very careful that he doesn't become too spoiled."

"If I had a beautiful son I would spoil him with love." Busi sighed.

"You should see my parents with that boy. They never had a son of their own, so he is the special one in the family. They still beg me to marry his father." Themby shook her head and leaned over the reception desk toward Busi. "I think that when my sister got married they became spoiled with the lobola. They just imagine all the cows they could have, but they don't seem to appreciate my feelings. Even now, I am having trouble getting his daddy to pay money for his school fees." Themby leaned in again and, with a gleam in her eyes, smiled.

"But do you want to know something? I have a plan. If he doesn't pay money I'm going to tell him that Simon is not his son after all."

Busi and Themby laughed with delight at this deception.

"Themby, you are so clever." Busi was still laughing. "Did you know that in the United States they have chat shows on television where couples argue, because the man will not admit he is the father of a child? Can you imagine any man denying his virility and parenthood like that?"

Themby plotted her meeting with Simon on the bus ride back to Manzini that afternoon. Simon was very proud of being Ndumiso's father. He was especially impressed that Themby gave him his own Christian name.

Themby arrived at home tired and hot. The bus stopped at the gate of the university, and she had to walk almost a mile after that to reach the faculty housing campus. Nathi rushed to greet her.

"Mommy, you have to call mkhulu. Grandpa needs to talk to you right away. Gogo is sick. She is so sick that he has taken her to the hospital."

Themby was stunned. Sipho had developed diabetes over the last couple of years, but she had controlled it with a strict diet.

"What's wrong, Nathi? Did Grandpa tell you what's wrong with her?"

"It's something about her foot. It didn't make any sense to me. Just call him right away."

Themby tried to find Mbulelo, but he wasn't home. She called her sister, Nobantu, and she was out, too. "They must be at the hospital." She reasoned.

She tried to call the Mbabane Government hospital, but the lines were full. After several attempts someone did answer, but the call was quickly disconnected.

Themby slammed down the phone. "These phones are worthless. Nathi, you must take care of your sister and brother. I have to get to Mbabane to see Gogo."

She ran out the door and rushed down the street. It reminded her of the time she ran up the mountain to save Mashama's life. She tried to drive the memory out of her mind. As she was running she heard a car honking behind her.

"Thembekile. Are you all right?" A colleague at the university was driving out of the gate.

"I can't talk right now, Robert." She gasped for air as she kept running.

He leaned his head out of the window and continued, "Is there some place I can take you?"

She stopped running and stood staring at him for a minute. "It's my mother. She is at the Mbabane hospital. It must be awfully bad, because she would never go to that place unless she was terribly sick." Themby was breathing heavily.

"Get in the car. I live in Mbabane. I'll drive you up there."

Themby was so confused and concerned she accepted the ride without protest. When she arrived at her mother's hospital room Mbulelo was sitting in a chair by Sipho's bedside. It startled Themby to see her mother so weak. That vision was diminished by the conditions she noticed around her.

The large government hospital was understaffed and filthy. The patients were lined up on small dirty cots. Some patients didn't even have a sheet or blanket. The wards were so full that people were sleeping on the floor and under the beds. There was moaning from patients who could not get medication to relieve their pain.

"My God, Daddy." Themby whispered to him. "What is going on in this place? I always knew that this hospital had problems, but I never realized it was this bad."

Mbulelo rose from his chair, kissed his wife's forehead and took Themby out to the hallway. "It is the AIDS." He said quietly. "There are too many sick and dying people in this country, and there isn't enough money or medicine to help them."

"Daddy, we have to get Mother out of here. The smell, the noise, the people, it makes me sick just standing here. Let's get her home."

"Themby, Sipho has a bad infection in her foot. She is in terrible pain. The diabetes is keeping her from healing." Mbulelo looked sick and said, "The doctors say that they might have to amputate her foot."

Themby covered her mouth and gasped. "We have got to get her to South Africa. She can't get the care here that she deserves."

"I've talked to the doctors, and they say that she is too ill to travel. The infection is all over her body and in her blood now."

Themby turned away and started to cry. She noticed Robert out of the corner of her eye. He had not left the ward.

"Oh, Robert, I'm so sorry you're still here. Please, you don't have to get involved with all this. I appreciate the ride. Thank you so much."

He didn't move. He just smiled and asked, "Do you need a ride back to the university?"

"Oh no, no, it's a half hour trip. My father will take me back. Thank you so much."

She didn't know Robert very well at all. Several times during the academic term he had come by her office and tried to strike up a conversation. There were days he had offered to take her to tea, but she had always declined. The last thing she wanted in her life was another disastrous relationship. She did know that he was from Zimbabwe, and he had a Ph.D in economics. He appeared to be in his forties, and he was popular with the students.

"If you are sure that you can manage. I am not trying to interfere in your personal affairs."

Themby was flustered. She quickly introduced him to her father and then took Robert's hand.

"Thank you again. We'll be fine. I'll see you at the university. Thank you."

Robert left, and Mbulelo raised his eyebrows at his daughter.

"Don't even give me that look. I'm not interested in him or any other man for that matter. We must concentrate on Mama now."

The Mbabane Government Hospital was not unlike other African public hospitals. It boasted state of the art equipment donated by well meaning international organizations. The United States had donated cutting edge AIDS testing devices. The European Union had outdone that by giving the hospital elaborate x-ray diagnostic equipment. The Chinese government, too, was well represented in the list of donors. These miracle machines sat idle gathering dust. The super powers of the world gave generously, but they believed that if they gave the equipment the recipient government would find the funds necessary to train people to operate it and repair it. They were mistaken. The machines were rarely used, or were improperly used, and when they were broken there was no one capable of repairing them.

Themby thought those problems were the least of her worries now. The hospital could not even provide linens, towels or food. Any patient who did not have a relative as an advocate or caregiver could starve right in the hospital.

"Daddy, Nobantu and I will take turns coming in the mornings to give Mama food and clean linens. You look so weary. Go home and rest. We will work out a schedule so someone will always be here for her." She looked back into the ward and saw her mother sleeping quietly.

Sipho would never complain about pain or discomfort. Themby kissed her father's cheek and felt the wet of his tears on her face.

⟹ ⟸

For several days Themby came to work late at the Swazi Government Institute in Mbabane. Every morning she awakened two hours early so that she could get her children ready for school, prepare food for Sipho, and pack clean towels and sheets. She took the bus up to Mbabane at daybreak so that she could bring a hot breakfast to the hospital. Every morning Sipho smiled weakly and told her daughter that she was feeling better, but Themby was skeptical. Sipho's wound produced a sickening acrid odor as the pus and infection seeped through the bandages.

One morning Themby was so exhausted from worry she put her head down on her desk and closed her eyes.

"I know there is more that I can do to help you. Why are you avoiding me?" She remembered Sifiso asking her that once years ago, and it startled her. She quickly raised her head to see Robert standing by her desk.

"Oh, I'm sorry. I just put my head down for a minute. I'm fine now." She was embarrassed and felt her face grow hot. How silly to think of Sifiso at a time like this.

"Don't be sorry. Please, Thembekile, let me do something for you. You have so much burden right now." He pulled up a chair and almost placed his hand on her back, but he drew away feeling that it would appear too forward.

Themby couldn't help but smile at him. Why would anyone be interested in her at this age? She was a single woman with three children and too much responsibility.

"You know, there is something that I would like to do tomorrow if you aren't busy and don't mind a long drive."

"Tomorrow is Saturday; I have no plans. Tell me where you want to go."

"I need to see my gogo in the mountains. She died several years ago, and I need to be with her for awhile." She looked at Robert to check his expression, but he sat passively waiting for her to finish.

"You see, her spirit helps me, and I feel it there. This all sounds stupid to you, doesn't it? You are so educated. All this ancestral talk sounds like nonsense to you, but it is part of my culture."

Robert leaned forward and placed his hand on her back. "Don't you think that I have loved ones who are with the ancestors? Do you think that in Zimbabwe we have no respect for our spirits? Let me take you to the mountain."

=== ===

Nobantu took her turn to care for Sipho on the weekend. Themby awakened Saturday morning and chided herself. She felt guilty for feeling a little excited that Robert was coming to pick her up for her pilgrimage to Gogo's homeland.

"You fool, this isn't a date to Gogo's house." She said to herself in the mirror. She picked up her perfume, but she placed it back on the vanity without using it. "Stop it, you crazy woman." She yelled at herself. "Look here. You have three children. Your mother is terribly sick. You don't know this man very well. He isn't even Swazi."

They drove the trip up the mountain. Along the way he listened to Themby's stories of Gogo. She told him about Gogo's shrine, her kagogo to the ancestors. She laughed when she related Gogo's interpretation of Swazi history. Robert told her about his own grandmother who was the matriarch of his family.

"My grandmother lived to be almost 80 years old. In our village people believed that she was a seer, someone who could predict the future." He smiled and glimpsed at Thembekile as he steered up the steep dirt road. "My grandmother always thought that was humorous. She told me that she only appeared to know the future, because she knew so much about the past."

They arrived at Gogo's house, and Themby felt the past overcome her. The smell of wood fires burning in the village brought back memories of Gogo sitting outside the hut with her chickens and dogs around her. She closed her eyes as the breeze from the flame tree enveloped her senses.

"I feel such peace here." She turned to Robert and sighed. "Every time I come here I tell Gogo that I will bring the children with me next time, but I always get too busy." She brushed her hair away from her face. "You know, Robert, sometimes life gets in the way of living."

They walked into the hut and Themby kneeled down at the kagogo. She told the ancestors all the news of the family. She explained poor Sipho's health. She asked for their guidance and help. Before she left she placed fresh flowers by the kagogo. Then she shut the door behind her.

"Thank you, Robert. You're such a good friend to help me."

Robert smiled, but he was disturbed. He had tried to get closer to her for a long time. Being friends was certainly not the relationship he aspired to have with her.

⇒ ⇐

Sipho languished in the hospital for weeks. Themby and her sister never stopped their vigilant care, but it was proving to be little help in curing the infection. Finally, one day the doctors came to Themby as she was sitting by her mother's bedside.

"Thembekile, can we talk to you out in the hall?" One of them inquired. He was the senior doctor, all dressed in a sparkling white coat. It was the cleanest thing she had seen in the hospital.

"Your mother's foot is not healing, and we are afraid that the infection is taking more than her foot. She has had a fever that is unrelenting. We believe that the sooner we take her foot the better it will be for her health. Without amputation she could die."

"Please," Themby insisted. "You will have to talk to my father about this. It's not a decision that I can make."

"We spoke to Mbulelo last night when he was here, and he agreed. We are planning to operate in the morning." The doctors looked at each other with resigned satisfaction.

"I suppose you have done everything you could. I'll call my sister, and we will both be here early in the morning."

Themby went back into her mother's room. Sipho opened her eyes and smiled weakly at her daughter.

"Don't worry, little one." She said quietly. "This is God's plan for me. I know what we have to do."

Themby told her mother about Robert and her trip to the kagogo. Sipho enjoyed hearing about Themby's life. Themby told her what the children were doing lately, and she told her mother how Robert had taken them all out to eat at the local Chinese restaurant. They both laughed when she recounted his lessons on using chopsticks.

"Do you hear yourself?" Sipho asked. "Every sentence you tell me something about Robert. I think you like him more than a friend."

"Don't be ridiculous." Themby laughed. "I have to admit that he is a great comfort, but he wouldn't be interested in a relationship with me."

"You underestimate yourself, my child. You are a beautiful and intelligent woman. Don't throw yourself away. You must continue to live and be happy. Love is part of life. You are alive, so act like it." Sipho's words sounded like Gogo to Themby.

Themby spent the night at the hospital. She tried to sleep in the chair that was provided for her. The sounds, smells and general atmosphere in the ward were disturbing.

The sun rose, and the doctors came nervously into the hospital ward. Thembekile looked up sleepily and heard bits of their conversation.

"What are you saying?" She blinked her eyes to look at them directly. "Did I just hear you say that the operating theater is not functioning this morning?"

The doctor looked embarrassed. "It seems that the anesthesia required for surgery has been delayed in South Africa." He took off his glasses and cleaned them on his sleeve. His voice was edgy as he continued. "I'm so sorry for the delay, but we cannot operate until the anesthesia is shipped here."

Sipho had a look of relief on her face. Themby was relieved but furious as well.

"Look what you have put my mother through. She has been in your care, and she is still in this condition. She has been so scared and nervous. You have told her terribly frightening things, and just as she resigns herself to your prognosis, you can't do your job. That does it. We're through with this place!" Themby rose out of her chair like a bullet from a gun. "This was a blessing and a sign from God and the spirits. Gentlemen, you will not operate on my mother today or any other day. I am taking her out of here."

"You can't do that." The doctors were incredulous. "She is too ill. She can't even walk down the hall."

"That's my problem. I will not have my mother die in this horrible smelly place, and she certainly will not die at the hands of you butchering idiots!" Thembekile started tossing her mother's belongings in a bag. "Now, please, doctors, leave us alone."

The bewildered doctors were leaving the ward just as Robert came through the door. "What is happening here, Thembekile?"

"We are taking my mother home. I knew it. I knew it. The failed surgery was a sign from God and Gogo. She must get out of this disgusting place."

⟹ ⟸

Six months later Sipho's foot was healing nicely. She was cared for and nurtured by the family and the British doctor who had helped save Mashama's life. She would live a long life and would never require the amputation they had all feared.

Robert loved Thembekile and finally got the courage to ask for her hand in marriage. Sipho and Mbulelo were relieved and pleased. He offered love and devotion to their daughter, and he gave them a healthy lobola. Robert gave them the equivalent of 30 cows. Fifteen were nice fat sturdy cows. The rest was the worth of 15 cows in thousands of emalengenis.

Thembekile would bear no more children. Lengthening the bones would be left to the next generation.

Just before the wedding Simon came back to plead with Thembekile to change her mind and marry him.

"Themby, what do you find in that man that you don't see in me?"
He sat in her office at the university and tried to hold her hand. "He
isn't the father of any of your children. For God's sake, the man's not
even a Swazi. What will he understand of our culture?"

Themby drew back her hand and laughed. "What do I see? I see
a man who loves me, ME!" She threw her hand against her breast. "I
see a man who doesn't think of himself first, or his cause first, or his
needs first. I see a man who puts my needs and those of my children
above all else. He is a man who loves me more than anything in the
world. He loves all of my children. He makes me happy. He makes
me laugh, and when I am hurt or sad he comforts me. Robert loves
me and respects me, and so dear Simon, I will marry that man." She
sat back and reflected on all the attributes she had just related. Simon
sat quietly.

"You see, Simon. I think Gogo told me many years ago to wait for
that man."

⇒ ⇐

Thembekile and Robert drove up the dirt mountain road to pay their
respects to Gogo and the spirits. They had only been married a
few days, but Themby felt it was critical to make the pilgrimage.
Evening was approaching as she put fresh roses on the kagogo. She
left the hut and looked at the sky above her. The winter air was bitter
cold. She could see her breath in the night, and she wrapped her
shawl tightly around her. The winter fires burned in streaks up the
sides of the mountain as they had burned every winter for centuries.
There was comfort in that. Tradition and culture were constants

that would always be waiting for her. She and Robert walked hand in hand to the car and drove back down the mountain.

Epilogue

Thembekile drove Robert's car up Malagwane Hill to Mbabane. She was happier than she had ever been in her life. The girl sitting next to her seemed nervous, and Themby reached over to pat her hand.

For a long time Themby had been curious about the woman in Manzini who grew the beautiful roses in her garden in the hills. After Themby was married she decided to learn more about Anna.

She drove through Mbabane traffic with ease, and came to the edge of the city. Turning right she took the steep rocky road that led to Panorama Drive. She and Robert had just bought land on the edge of the mountain and were planning to build a beautiful home there. The mountains were varying shades of purple against the morning sun. It was be impossible for anyone to capture the beauty of Swaziland on canvas or in photographs. One had to be there to drink in the breathtaking depths and colors and dimensions of the landscape of the kingdom. She pulled the car over for a moment and reflected on her life and on the life of the woman she had just learned about from the villagers.

"Are you ready?" She asked her passenger.

The girl said nothing; she simply nodded and smiled.

They approached the large wooden gate with the carved buffalo head on it. Themby honked the horn and a guard came running. He opened the gates and saluted to her. She parked the car, turned off the engine and sighed.

"Let's go." She said cheerfully.

They walked to the front door, and Themby rang the bell.

A heavy middle-aged Swazi woman answered it. She was dressed in a white uniform, had a scarf wrapped around her head, and was still carrying her dust cloth.

"Sawubona, unjani." Themby said. She couldn't stop her smile. She gently nudged the young teenage girl who came with her.

The girl looked wide-eyed at the maid and said "Are you my gogo? My name is Anna."

The maid was shocked and screamed in amazement. "Yebo, my baby! I am Anna, too, oh my baby, my baby. I never dreamed I would see my grandchildren. This must be a dream. God granted my prayers, and He made my greatest dream come true."

She swept up the girl in her arms and laughed and wept until she was breathless. Anna couldn't contain her happiness and gratitude. She pulled away from the child and looked at her face. Then she embraced her strongly in her heavy arms.

The girl wept, and Thembekile was overcome with emotion. She quietly tried to back out of the foyer so they could be alone, but Anna pulled her into the embrace. Anna's face was soaked with tears that found a home in the lines of her smile.

"Siyabonga, siyabonga, sisi. How did you know to bring this child to me? I can never thank you or repay you for this greatest gift."

"But you have repaid me many times." Thembekile said softly. "Every time I bought your beautiful roses in the market my day was brighter. You have touched more lives than you will ever know."

She hugged Anna, left them together, and walked alone to her car.

"Yebo, Gogo," She spoke aloud as if her gogo's spirit was in the car with her. "It is as you have always said. A tear is a tear no matter who you are, and a smile is the same all over the world. We are not that different from one another, are we?"

Acknowledgements

My husband, John, and I spent ten months in the Kingdom of Swaziland during the 1998-99 academic school year. He served as the Fulbright Senior Scholar to that country. It was a year marked by highs and lows, homesickness and adventure. Swaziland is a beautiful mountain kingdom, but deep poverty and a rigid culture often mar its progress compared to that of its neighbor, South Africa.

Our research and love of Swaziland have drawn us back to the Kingdom every year since the first Fulbright experience. In 2005-2006 we spent another year living in Swaziland when my husband was awarded a second Fulbright grant. We lived on the campus of the University of Swaziland (UNISWA) where he taught Public Administration.

In the course of these travels we have been blessed to meet and become close friends with some very remarkable people. There is no possible way I can thank fully our dear friends Joyce Barrett and Bill Marjenhoff. Their kindness, assistance, humor and encouragement made our first year a success in more ways than I can enumerate. Willy and Gil Holleweg also provided us with an endearing and enduring friendship. Our friends Rajan and Gigi Mathew of India were incredibly supportive and caring neighbors at the University of Swaziland. Marjorie and Luchi Balarin have been wonderful and steadfast friends.

I am also grateful to lifelong friends in the United States who encouraged me to write this book. Particularly, warmest thanks go to Mike and Sheila Morone, Mike and Julie McAninch, Mike and Karen Kuehn, Dr. Buster and Susan Dunsmore, and Dr. Emmett Doerr and Dr. Bridget Doerr.

None of my experiences in Africa would have been possible without the adventuresome spirits of my parents: my mother, Beverly Liebenow, and my late father, J. Gus Liebenow, Ph.D. They inspired my sister, Diane, my brothers, Jay and John, and me, to examine closely the world around us and never be content with the status quo of life. My family shaped my positive belief in the timeless perseverance and optimism of human kind all over the world. These qualities in people of all faiths, ethnicities and races continue to inspire me.

I want to thank my wonderful children, Beverly and John. They respect and appreciate our need to continue our research in Africa and endure our absences with great sacrifice. Our grandchildren, Abigail and Tyler enrich us all every day and remind me that new life does, in fact, lengthen our bones.

Finally, my love and my heart go to my husband, John. He is my traveling companion, greatest support, and soul mate. It is to him that I dedicate this book.

References

Center for Disease Control (CDC), "Schistomiasis," Internet Site http://www.cdc.gov/ncidod/dpd/parasites/schistosomiasis/factsht_schistosomiasis.htm.

Enchanted Learning, "Anopheles Mosquito," Internet Site http://www.enchantedlearning.com/subjects/insects/mosquito/Mosquito.shtml

Geocities, "Life in Mandela's South Africa:Glossary of South African Terms," Internet Site http://www.geocities.com/CapitolHill/Senate/6367/glossary.htm.

Kasenene, Peter, Swazi Traditional Religion and Society, Mbabane, Swaziland:Websters Mbabane, April 1993.

Liebenow, J. Gus, African Politics:Crises and Challenges, First Edition, Bloomington, Indiana:Indiana University Press, 1986.

Matsebula, J.S.M, A History of Swaziland, Third Edition, Cape Town, South Africa:Longman Penguin Southern Africa (Pty) Ltd., 1988.

Rational Medicine, "Anopheles mosquito," Internet site http://www.rationalmedicine.org/malaria/AnophelesMosquito.htm .

Smith, Charlene, Baby Names for South African Babies, First Edition, Rivonia, South Africa:Zebra Press, 1999.

Sibiya, Terence, "Choosing the King of Swaziland," Internet Site http://www.swazi.com/sibiya/inkhosi.html.

UNICEF, "Malaria," Internet Site http://www.childinfo.org/eddb/Malaria.

World Health Organization (WHO), "Schistosomiasis," Internet Site http://www.who.int/ctd/schisto/disease.htm.

Yahoo! Health, "Malaria," Internet Site http://health.yahoo.com/health/ dc/000621/0.html.

Biography of Author

Debra Liebenow Daly was raised in Bloomington, Indiana where her father was a distinguished professor of African political science at Indiana University. During her childhood she lived in both West and East Africa and traveled extensively throughout the continent. Recently, she returned to southern Africa. She has spent two years living in Swaziland, and has continued her travels to southern Africa for over ten years.

She holds a degree in English Literature from Indiana University and has published a book of children's poetry entitled <u>A Child's World</u>. Debra and her husband, John, live in Lutz, Florida.